TENTACLES & TRIATHLONS

Ashley Bennett is a small-town paranormal and monster romance author from Baltimore, Maryland. She writes stories that are equal parts spice and swoon. When she's not writing, you can find her reading webtoons, playing cosy video games, and taking care of her houseful of rescue animals.

Also by Ashley Bennett
Muscles and Monsters

LEVIATHAN FITNESS #2

TENTACLES & TRIATHLONS

ASHLEY BENNETT

ZAFFRE

Originally self-published, in different form, in 2022
This revised and expanded edition first published in the
United States of America in 2026 by
Berkley, an imprint of Penguin Random House LLC

First published in the UK in 2026 by
ZAFFRE
An imprint of Bonnier Books UK
5th Floor, HYLO, 105 Bunhill Row,
London, EC1Y 8LZ

A CIP catalogue record for this book is available from the British Library.

ISBN: 978-1-78512-779-3

Also available as an ebook

1 3 5 7 9 10 8 6 4 2

Typeset by IDSUK (Data Connection) Ltd
Printed and bound in Great Britain by CPI (UK) Ltd, Croydon CR0 4YY

The authorised representative in the EEA is Bonnier Books
UK (Ireland) Limited.
Registered office address: Block B, The Crescent Building,
Northwood, Santry, Dublin 9, D09 C6X8, Ireland
compliance@bonnierbooks.ie
www.bonnierbooks.co.uk

To anyone who wants to be fucked by tentacles . . .

AUTHOR'S NOTE

Tentacles & Triathlons is a slice-of-life monster romance; however, it also contains the following: death of a parent (past mentioned), verbal abuse (past, from a parent, recounted), struggles with mental health (depression, mentioned), near drowning (brief), sex (including breath play, restraints, light degradation), and adult language. For an exhaustive list of content and trigger warnings, please refer to the author's website, AshleyBennettAuthor.com.

TENTACLES & TRIATHLONS PLAYLIST

"DON'T TELL THE BOYS" by Petey
"DRAG" by Day Wave
"UNDERWATER BOI" by Turnstile
"FUCK JUNE" by Sipper
"DEAR TO ME" by Electric Guest
"BOYS DON'T CRY" by The Cure
"AGE OF CONSENT" by New Order
"THIS CHARMING MAN" by The Smiths
"LOVE WILL TEAR US APART" by Joy Division
"CLOSE TO ME" by The Cure

Prologue

REECE

Age 10

"DAMMIT," MY FATHER GRUMBLED, HIS EYES FOCUSED ON THE smoldering embers in front of us. "We're getting low on firewood."

We were on our monthly father-son camping trip at the campground that sat on the edge of Briar Glenn.

The monthly camping trip I dreaded because it meant alone time with my father.

Every time we were out here, it was the same thing.

He'd sit on a tree stump next to the fire and pound beers while he told me about his glory days playing football for Briar Glenn High. Until my mom's surprise pregnancy, the one that locked him down and stole his dreams. The one that brought me into the world.

"I can grab some from the storehouse in the morning," I offered.

The thought of walking through the woods alone sent a shiver down my spine. As familiar as I was with the campground, there were still urban legends about things lurking in the woods.

The Moth Madame of Briar Glenn was one of them.

According to the legend, she was an old crone of a monster, grumpy and coldhearted, with tattered wings and glowing red eyes. It was rumored that she lived in the dilapidated old mansion on the edge of the campground. On dark nights, she wandered the woods looking for lost children to torment.

My dad said it was horseshit, but that was his opinion on most things.

"If you want breakfast in the morning, you're gonna go get us a bundle right now. Take the flashlight and go." He dug through the duffle bag at his feet and tossed me the flashlight.

I flicked it on and a pale stream of yellow light illuminated the ground in front of me.

"Do I really have to go now?" I asked.

My father scrubbed a hand over his face and sighed. "It's not far. Just follow the trail to the storehouse and get the damn firewood."

"Will you go with me?" I gave him a pleading look, but I already knew the answer.

By now, he was probably so drunk, he couldn't walk a straight line.

"Reece Michael," he snapped. "You have been coming to this campground for years. You're a big boy. Now go on."

Wordlessly, I rose from the stump I was sitting on and turned my back on my father.

My lip quivered and I clenched my fists, willing the tears away. There was no way I was gonna let my old man see me cry.

Gods, I hated him. No matter what I did, it was never good enough for him.

I pointed the flashlight in front of me and set off through the woods.

Leaves crunched under my feet, the pitch black of the forest making me grow more and more uneasy with each step. For a spring evening, it was eerily quiet.

There were no crickets or frog songs, just the soft rustle of leaves as a breeze passed through the trees.

I kept following the tiny dirt path etched into the ground, hoping I didn't lose it.

The walk seemed much longer than I remembered.

A twig snapped nearby and I whipped around, scanning the darkness for the source. Except there was nothing there.

I peered through the trees, looking for the warm glow of the campfire.

But that wasn't there, either.

I was lost.

Panic gripped my chest, making my heart pound in my ears.

There was no way I was going to call out to my father for help. He'd never let me live it down.

Another twig snapped, closer this time, the sound breaking the quiet like a shot.

"H-hello," I stammered, waving the flashlight through the darkness. "I-is anyone out there?" My voice wavered. I was on the verge of tears.

My question was met with silence.

I forced myself to keep moving, to find the storehouse or my father—*anything* to make me feel more at ease.

The sound of the leaves crunching under my feet echoed as I picked up the pace.

Was it an echo?

Or was there someone out here with me?

I started to run, racing through the woods like my life depended on it—because for all I knew, it did.

The sound was at my back now, loud enough and close enough that I could hear it over my panting breaths.

I didn't dare turn around. I just kept running, scrabbling over twigs and rocks until the glow of the campfire came into view.

I had never been so happy to see my father.

"What the fuck, son?" he bellowed as I collapsed at his feet, my chest heaving.

"There was something in the woods," I sobbed. "The Moth Madame is out there."

My father tsked. "That's just a story, Reece. There's no Moth Madame. Now, get your ass off the ground. I'm guessing you didn't get the firewood."

Still crying, I shook my head no.

"Dammit. I ask you to do one fucking thing and you come back crying. You're too old for this shit. Get in the tent and go to bed. I can't even look at you right now."

I used my sleeve to wipe the snot dripping from my nose and crawled inside the tent.

"Worthless kid," I heard my father mumble under his breath.

The tears continued as I settled inside my sleeping bag. He could think whatever he wanted, but something was out there.

It was awful—and scary.

And as much as I hated being afraid, I hated my father more.

One

CYRUS

I BLINKED AT THE BRIGHT WHITE CANVAS IN FRONT OF ME, willing something, *anything*, to inspire me to paint.

My art dealer, Eduardo, had been ringing me nonstop about new pieces, but over the last few months, I'd been at a creative standstill. Everything in my life had become boring. Repetitive. Bland, even.

Being one of the oldest monsters around, and potentially the last of your kind, could do that to you.

My tentacle clenched the paintbrush tighter, almost as if commanding it to move, but it was no use.

"Bollocks," I cursed, and whipped the brush at the canvas, coating it with a splatter of yellow paint.

The door to the studio cracked open, and my roommate, Fallon, peeked his head inside. "Everything okay in here?"

"Fine," I huffed and collected the brush from the floor.

Fallon's beady eyes followed my movements before focusing on the smeared canvas. "Still nothing?"

"Not a damn thing."

He stepped through the doorway, padded across the wood floor on his paws, and gave me a sympathetic look. Well, as sympathetic as someone with a beak and a feathered face could look.

"Cyrus, are you going to be able to handle tonight? I can find another ride and we can always say—"

"I'll be fine," I said in a clipped tone. "This is important to Atlas and Tegan. As one of his oldest friends, I should be there to show my support."

Atlas had always been there for me when I needed him. Through my most recent college experience, my move to Briar Glenn, and now in my current existential crisis. After everything he went through with Jade, he deserved happiness, and tonight I'd be there to celebrate his and Tegan's engagement.

Fallon dipped his head in a slow nod, his tail flicking back and forth behind him. I could tell there was more he wanted to say, but for once he didn't press the issue. "Okay, then. Well, I should probably start getting ready."

With that, he headed down the hall to his room, leaving me alone in my studio.

I tilted my head from side to side, rolled my shoulders, and let out a deep breath. My frustration and anxiety were getting the better of me, leaving my body feeling sluggish and drained.

There wouldn't be enough time to make it to the gym for a swim, so a soak in the tub would have to suffice.

I shuffled across the hall to my bedroom and into the adjoining en suite. Popping sounds filled the space as the suction cups of my tentacles stuck to the tile floor with my movements. The sticky buggers could be a nuisance, but they had their advantages. I never had to worry about slipping in the shower.

While the tub filled, I stared at myself in the mirror, the fluorescent lighting reflecting off my skin. I admired the perfect turquoise shade, decorated with deep blue-green stripes and splotches that allowed me to blend into the water. In terms of my appearance, they were probably my favorite attribute.

Unlike humans, I didn't wear clothes. My muscular chest was always uncovered, tapering down into a narrow waist that flared to my tentacles. I had eight in total, but preferred to use six of them for movement, keeping the other two—my mating tentacles—wrapped around my arms. They were quite helpful, serving as extra hands for painting or cooking or whatever task I was undertaking.

Some days I truly enjoyed being a kraken, but others, I felt like a total abomination. Even by monster standards, I was quite odd.

I shut off the tap and used my tentacle to open the jar of raw sea salt I kept on the edge of the tub. I sprinkled a generous amount into the bath and used the strength of my tentacles to agitate the water, dissolving the crystals.

"Mmm," I hummed and slid into the warm salty water.

My tentacles fanned out around my waist, slithering and sliding with delight. It often felt like we were two separate entities. There was me, and then there were the tentacles acting of their own accord.

While they soaked, I grabbed my phone from the ledge of the tub and scrolled through my social media accounts.

A series of engagement photos of Atlas and Tegan popped up on my feed.

His snout was scrunched into a happy smile as he stared down lovingly at his human mate.

Simply put, the two of them were adorable.

I was happy for them.

Truly I was.

But if I was being honest with myself, I was also quite jealous of my friend and the love he'd found.

Being one of the last kraken, the majority of my seven-hundred-year life had been quite lonely. Sure, I'd partners. Trysts with monsters and with humans who found a certain appeal to my tentacles. But in comparison to mine, their lifespans were rather short. There was no point in embarking on a long-term relationship with someone unless they were my fated mate.

For krakens, our mating bond clicked into place the moment our mating tentacle made contact with our mate. An innocent touch that often culminated in an orgasm. There was no mating bite, no claiming. Just a deep connection krakens formed with their partner, one that tied their lifespans together.

At this point, it was unlikely that I'd find a mate. And even if I did, would they want to be with me? Rejection would be more than I could handle.

I dug the sharp tips of my teeth into my thin lower lip, willing myself not to cry. I was supposed to be replenishing my saltwater stores, not depleting them.

With a sigh, I set my phone aside and submerged myself under the water, allowing the warmth to wrap around my body.

As I floated, weightless, my thoughts drifted back to the photos of Atlas and Tegan.

Would I ever be worthy?

Would I ever find that type of love?

Two

REECE

SWEAT TRICKLED DOWN MY FOREHEAD AND STUNG MY EYES.
It was still early in the morning, but the July sun was out in full
force today.

July.

That meant I had a little over two months left before the Briar
Glenn Triathlon.

I closed in on the final stretch of my run, my feet pounding
against the ground as they pushed me up the hill. My calves and
quads were screaming, but I glanced down at my watch, the fact
that I was so close to a personal best motivating me to really dig
deep.

"Yes!" I whooped as I reached the top of the hill. My lungs
burned with each gulp of air I desperately sucked down. I smiled
at the time on my watch before throwing my arms up over my
head and walking in slow circles.

Every Saturday, I went for a run at the park to train for the
triathlon, and this was my best time yet. At this rate, I'd have no
problem with the 5K run and 20K bike portions of the race.

That 750-meter swim, though? That was a different story.

Due to my muscle mass and poor form, my swimming prowess resembled that of a manatee. I had no speed or stamina whatsoever.

I either had to take my training to the next level or let go of this pipe dream.

And I wasn't a quitter.

"Struggling a bit there, huh, Rollins?" Jimenez said with a sly smile as he slowed to a stop beside me. The asshole had barely broken a sweat, and that would explain why he finished so far behind me.

"Go fuck yourself, Jimenez," I said with a laugh.

My eyes focused on the round globes of his ass in his tight athletic shorts as he trotted off toward the tennis courts to do his usual cooldown routine.

Javier Jimenez was the most attractive guy in Briar Glenn, and he just so happened to be my subordinate at the Parks Department. More recently, he'd become one of my closest friends. To my dismay, that put him strictly off limits.

I needed to get laid. *Bad.*

Since I started training for the triathlon, I hadn't had time for hookups or dating apps. That dry spell was finally starting to take its toll. A guy could only jerk off and play with toys so much before he craved the real thing.

As I fought to get my libido under control, my phone vibrated in my pocket.

My mother.

"Ay, Ma. What's up?" I said as I plopped down on a park bench and tugged my sweaty tank top away from my skin.

"I wanted to make sure you're coming over to Tegan's later." She used that authoritative tone that all moms seemed to take with their children—even the adult ones. "This is important to her, Reece."

I tsked and ran a hand through my sweat-soaked hair, brushing the light red strands out of my eyes. Tonight was my sister Tegan's engagement party. I'd met her fiancé once, at the mayor's daughter's wedding, where I caught him hanging out with her in the garden. That night somehow led to them dating, then mating not long after that. In my mind, the entire thing had moved too fast. Fated mates or not, she didn't really know the guy. Everything came to a head when I told my sister as much.

Since that shouting match in her driveway, we hadn't spoken or seen each other. Our mom was working as a mediator of sorts, pushing Tegan and me to work through our issues. By showing up tonight to celebrate her and Atlas, I was hoping it would start us on the path to making amends.

I wanted my sister to be happy, and I was sure Atlas was great. I just hated the way everything went down.

My awkward silence was a dead giveaway of how I felt about the situation.

"*Reece.*" My mother's voice was laced with tension.

"C'mon, Mom. I didn't forget. I'll be there."

"You better be on your best behavior, Reece Michael. Atlas is wonderful and we want him to feel comfortable around our family."

"I promise I'll behave."

It was the truth, too. I wanted to like my sister's mate, and more importantly, I wanted to improve my strained relationship with her.

Things between Tegan and me had soured since our dad died. As much as I tried to move past it, I was still carrying some of the resentment I'd felt toward her since childhood. I wanted the best for her, to protect her, but at the same time, I was insanely jealous of the favoritism our father extended to her and not to me. Now that he was gone, I really had no way of reconciling those issues. Not with him, and would it even be worth it to bring it up to Tegan?

"Were you listening to a single thing I said?" my mother asked.

"Sorry, I spaced out for a second. I just finished my run."

"Please try to be open-minded. And you never know, maybe there will be some nice guys there for you to meet."

I exhaled a deep breath and rubbed my sweat-streaked temples. "I don't need you, Tegan, and her mate playing matchmaker, Ma. I'm happy being single."

It was the truth.

I liked hooking up, but at the first hint of someone catching feelings for me? Wanting more? That just wasn't something I could give them.

"Whatever you say, honey. Love you, see ya later. And, Reece, don't forget the veggie tray."

"I won't. Love you, too."

I ended the call right as Jimenez sat down next to me on the park bench. Sweat trickled down his temples and slid along the bronze column of his neck.

Fuck.

"How was your time?" he asked as he lifted his tank top to wipe the sweat from his brow, revealing a sculpted six-pack underneath.

I puffed out a breath and quickly averted my gaze, focusing on a centaur couple playing Frisbee in the field across from us. "My best yet."

He gave me that winning smile of his, all straight white teeth and full lips, and shook his head. "Wasn't your bike time the other day your best, too?"

"Mm-hmm." I leaned against the back of the bench, cradling my head in my hands before tilting my freckled face up toward the sun.

"And swimming?"

"Damn, dude," I scoffed. "Way to kill my runner's high."

One corner of his mouth tilted downward. Even when he was frowning, he was still hot as fuck. I needed to get a grip.

"Still struggling?" Jimenez asked.

"It's improving—slowly. I need more time to practice, but it's hard to get down to the lake with our work schedule."

Thanks to the mayor's rejuvenation initiative, Briar Glenn was thriving. More people were moving here and opening businesses, and with that, we'd seen a serious surge in tourism. As the lone employees of the Briar Glenn Parks Department, we were responsible for maintaining the town's public parks and hiking trails—the amenities that tourists came here to enjoy. Our department was the busiest I'd ever seen it—almost too much for me and Javier to manage on our own.

"I feel that, man. You need to join a gym with a pool." He put his arms along the back of the bench and stared at me.

"No way. No fucking way." There was only one gym in town, and it just so happened to be the gym that my sister's mate owned. After the way things started out, there was no way I could just walk in there and sign up for a membership. Not yet at least.

"Look, Reece. You're going to have to get over this at some point. Atlas is your sister's mate. He owns a gym with a pool. Might as well make the most of it."

"Yeah, I guess," I sighed. "You and Selene are coming to the party, right?" I asked, hoping I'd have someone there to talk to.

"I'll be there, but Selene's still in Puerto Rico taking care of our abuela."

Javier's little sister, Selene, worked at my sister's bakery, and the two of them had gotten close. Tegan was probably bummed out that one of her best friends wouldn't be there, but taking care of your elderly grandmother abroad was a valid reason to miss a party.

"How would you feel if Selene jumped right into a commitment like that?" I asked. "You wouldn't be concerned?" I knew that Jimenez was just as protective of Selene as I was of Tegan.

"Nah, man. If they treated her right and made her happy, that would be enough for me—regardless of the timeline."

Maybe Jimenez was onto something.

Atlas had been nothing but a gentleman to my sister.

She was happy with him. She was cared for.

That would have to be good enough for me.

TEGAN'S HOUSE WAS JUST OUTSIDE OF TOWN, A TINY COT-tage tucked back into the woods. I turned onto the long gravel driveway, and the memory of the last time I was here flashed through my mind, a tight knot of regret settling in the pit of my stomach.

I couldn't remember exactly what I'd said, but I did remember the look on my sister's face. The anger. The pain.

Instead of having an honest conversation like an adult, I'd ambushed her.

Why did I have to be such an asshole?

Cars were parked bumper to bumper on both sides of the driveway.

Did they invite the entire town of Briar Glenn? This was ridiculous.

I finally found a spot and parked my car. As I walked closer to the house, that's when I saw him.

Atlas.

My baby sister's mate.

He was a towering wall of dark gray fur that deepened to black at the tips of his ears, paws, and tail. Speaking of which, that fluffy tail wagged as he leaned over and gave my sister a kiss. Atlas's ears twitched as I approached and he turned to face me, his bright yellow eyes catching me off guard.

"Uh, hey!" he said in a deep, gruff voice as he waved a massive claw-tipped hand in my direction.

Tegan turned and gave me a tight smile. "Hey, Reece. Glad you could make it." She gave me one of those awkward side hugs and cleared her throat. "Reece, this is Atlas. *My mate.*" She emphasized the last part like I needed the reminder.

Atlas gave me a toothy smile, and the sharp white points of his teeth gleamed in the late-afternoon sunlight. "Nice to meet you, bud." He extended a furry hand out to me.

I hesitated, not being into casual touch, before taking his hand in mine and shaking. For being a massive muscle bro, he was surprisingly gentle. "Nice to meet you, too. Our mom has told me a lot about you."

Tegan glared at me, throwing her hands on her hips.

"And, uh, we're happy to have you as part of the family," I added.

Atlas smiled even wider. "That means a lot to me."

I nodded and extended the veggie tray out to him like it was some sort of peace offering. "I brought the veggie tray."

"Come on, we'll get this on ice and I'll introduce you to some people," Atlas said.

He grabbed my sister's hand and I followed them inside the cottage. It had been our nana's house, and after she passed, she left it to my father. When I moved out, I had to find my own place to live, but when Tegan was old enough to move out? The cottage was ready and waiting for her—even if it was outdated.

That didn't seem to be the case these days.

The wall separating the living room from the kitchen had been removed, making the space bright and open. There were new cabinets, appliances, and countertops, but it still had that rustic cottage appeal in the fixtures and finishes.

Very on-brand for my sister.

"House looks nice," I told them.

"Doesn't it?" Tegan said, beaming at her mate. "Atlas has been doing some renovations."

"Just a few things here and there when I have time on the weekends," Atlas said, obviously trying to downplay things. "The en suite was the first big project, and the kitchen was the second. I had to rush to get everything finished up for the engagement party."

Shit. All the times my sister and mother had asked for my help with projects, and I'd shrugged them off. Now this guy was stepping in to fill in all the gaps.

It stung a little bit.

"Uh, you did a great job," I admitted. It was a hell of a lot better than anything I could have done. Maybe it was for the best that they didn't leave it to me.

"Thanks," Atlas said, his muzzle wrinkling with another wide grin. "My parents own a hardware store, so I grew up doing a lot of home improvements."

Well, that was unexpected. Given his meathead looks, golden retriever personality, and the fact that he used to own a mansion in Briar Glenn's most affluent neighborhood, I figured he came from money.

The three of us stood there for a second just staring at one another, obviously unsure of where to take the conversation next. Social cues weren't really my thing, and I wasn't sure if I should apologize or if I should just carry on like everything was cool.

"Uh, where can I find a drink?" I asked when I couldn't handle the awkward silence anymore.

"Oh! The cooler's on the deck," Atlas said.

"Thanks." I tipped my head and exited through the slider that led to the back deck.

A giant tent was set up in the backyard, and lawn games were spread out over the grass. With the summer heat, it seemed that most of the guests were trying to keep cool in the shade. From a distance, I could make out a few familiar faces. The mayor and his wife were talking with Tegan's centaur neighbors, and the local mechanic was playing lawn darts with one of the girls who worked at the diner. It might have been a hot day, but the town had really shown up to support Atlas and Tegan.

I bent over to dig around in one of the coolers when a voice chimed in from behind me.

"Are my eyes deceiving me or is that Reece Rollins's fine ass gracing our presence?"

Fuck.

I'd been here a whole two minutes, and he'd already found me.

I plucked a bottle of water from the cooler and turned around to face my sister's other best friend, Declan. He was the owner of Dale's Diner, one of the only restaurants in Briar Glenn. Usually, he was dressed in mismatched clothes splattered with grease, but today he'd made himself presentable.

I shook the water bottle in his direction, sprinkling him with little drops of condensation. "What did I say about talking about my ass like that? I've known you since we were kids. It's weird."

Declan shrugged. "It's only weird if you make it weird. I didn't know you were going to grow up to be hot."

I leaned against the railing and puffed out a breath. "Is Javi here yet?" When we weren't at work, I tried to call Jimenez by his first name.

"He is. I think he's chatting with your mom under the tent."

I hummed and took a sip of my water.

"Honestly, I'm surprised you showed up," Dec continued. "After all the shit you've been pulling."

"Fuck, Dec. I don't need a lecture from you."

He put his hands on his hips and stared me down. It reminded me of how his dad would scold us when we were kids. "Apparently you do. This has really been bothering Tegan."

"I know," I said quietly. "It's really been bothering me, too."

"So quit your shit, then," Dec huffed. He wiped a bead of sweat off his temple. "I have got to get out of this sun. Enjoy the party." He gave me a little wave and walked off toward the tent.

I was about to follow Declan when the sliding door opened and Atlas joined me on the deck.

"Find something to drink?" he asked.

"Yep." I held up my water bottle.

"Javier told me you're training for a triathlon. How's that going?"

Fucking Jimenez and his big mouth. I knew he was trying to be helpful, but I could figure out how to improve my swim time on my own.

"I'm having a hard time with the swimming portion."

"You should come to the gym and train in the pool," Atlas offered.

"I couldn't do that."

"Well, the offer's there if you change your mind. Why don't

you come with me, and I'll introduce you to some of my friends?" he suggested.

I had to give it to him. He was really making an effort to break the ice between us, and if I could get in with him, working things out with Tegan would be much easier.

"Uh, sure," I said, and followed him out into the yard.

Three

CYRUS

THE BEANBAG FLEW OUT OF MY WEBBED HAND AND CA-
reened toward a cornhole board emblazoned with the Leviathan
Fitness logo. With a loud thud, the neon green bag dropped into
the hole, giving me another three points.

"You've got to be kidding me!" Fallon groaned from the other
end of the yard where the cornhole boards were set up. "When
you said you'd never played before, I didn't expect you to be this
good."

I blinked my wide eyes, giving the griffin an innocent smile.
Although I'd never played, my kind took to new games easily.
You'd think Fallon would know this after fourteen years of friend-
ship. There was a reason I wasn't allowed to join in on game night.

"Hmm, maybe it's the tentacles or something," I said with a
shrug. My grin widened as one of the thick tendrils in question
uncoiled from where it was wrapped around my forearm and gave
Fallon a playful wave.

He shook his head and trotted over to me. "I've had enough
getting my ass kicked for one day. Let's grab a drink and mingle."

Initially, I'd been hesitant to attend the party, but Atlas and Fallon were both adamant that I should be present.

I knew my appearance could be unsettling to humans, and I hated the thought of any of Atlas and Tegan's guests feeling uncomfortable. It wasn't every day that you saw an ancient blue-green sea creature shuffling around on six tentacles. I resembled something you'd see in a Guillermo del Toro film, not a guest at a backyard barbecue.

Fallon led the way to the cooler and I scuttled close behind him, my tentacles rolling and writhing over the grass to propel me along.

"Water for you, Cy?" he asked, digging through the cooler with his scaled talons.

"Please," I said, scanning the crowd around us. It was a mix of humans and monsters, locals and small business owners engaging in companionable conversation.

Fallon used his talon to pop the cap off his beer, and just as he was about to speak, Atlas called out to us.

"Hey, guys. Come here for a second. I want you to meet someone." The wolven shifted his giant body, and that's when I caught my first glimpse of *him*.

The rays from the sun caught his hair, illuminating the light red strands in a fiery blaze of color. His face was handsome—chiseled and masculine—with a thick mustache above his lip and a beard covering his jaw. A light dusting of freckles coated the bridge of his nose and cheeks. Forest green eyes accented with tiny flecks of gold assessed me, watching my every move as Fallon and I neared the small group.

"This is Tegan's brother, Reece," Atlas said, his body swaying slightly. "He's the head of the Parks Department here in Briar Glenn."

I'd heard all about Tegan's brother from Atlas. His bravado

and alpha male posturing when it came to his sister's relationship. What Atlas didn't tell me was how ridiculously hot he was.

Fallon waved a talon in Reece's direction and ruffled his feathers. "Fallon. Nice to meet you, bud."

Reece paid him no attention and instead kept his vibrant green eyes focused on me.

This was exactly what I was afraid of.

I was a tentacled creature of the sea making the brother of my best friend's mate uncomfortable.

"Hello," I muttered. "I'm Cyrus. Cyrus Jennings." I extended a hand to Reece, my tentacle gripping my arm tightly, almost cutting off my circulation.

Reece stared at my outstretched palm for a moment, his handsome face set in a wary scowl.

It was like he was judging it.

Judging me.

Right when I was about to pull away and die from embarrassment, Reece placed his hand in mine.

His skin was soft and warm, and as we shook, he locked eyes with me. "Pleasure," he said in a rich baritone voice, which sent warmth spreading through my body.

As we stood there, it felt as if everything in the background became muted and faded away. But him—I could see him bright and vivid. Like I was seeing color for the very first time.

For a moment that seemed to stretch on forever, it was Reece and I shaking hands, staring into each other's eyes.

But then it was over.

Reece cleared his throat before pulling his hand away and wiping it on the fabric of his khaki shorts.

His reaction surprised me. I wasn't wet and slimy like an octopus. My skin and tentacles were smooth and cool to the touch, but they didn't leave behind any residue whatsoever.

Maybe his palm was sweaty?

A small frown tugged at the corners of my lips.

Atlas must have noticed and attempted to break some of the tension. "Reece is training for the Briar Glenn triathlon. He needs to work on his swim time, so we'll be seeing him at the gym." Atlas clapped Reece on the back and he had to brace himself to avoid stumbling forward, obviously caught off guard.

"Yeah, about that . . ." Reece started to say before Atlas cut him off.

"None of that," Atlas said. "We're family now. The pool is there, use it. You'll probably see Cyrus there from time to time, too."

I loved Atlas like a brother, but he could be oblivious at times. I was sure that the last thing Reece wanted to do was spend time with his sister's mate and his friends.

"Uh, yeah. I use the pool quite a bit." My tentacles clenched tighter around my forearms with each word that came out of my mouth. One conversation with an attractive man and I was a ball of nerves.

"Hey, Atlas!" Tegan yelled from across the yard. A raging inferno was coming from the grill in front of her. "Can you and Fallon give me a hand with this?"

"Holy shit," Fallon chirped. He and Atlas bolted to help her, leaving Reece and me standing alone.

Reece bit his lip, scowling at the scene unfolding in front of us.

"That got out of control rather quickly," I commented.

He chuckled awkwardly as we watched them trying to get the fire under control. "My sister was never much of a cook. Apparently, all her food-related skills went to baking. I hope Atlas knows his way around the kitchen or he'll be eating out five nights a week."

My mouth hung open in disbelief. "Five nights a week? Really?"

Again, he laughed, but this time it was warmer, more genuine—like he was finally starting to relax in my presence. "Oh yeah, like a fucking college kid. Freaking college kid—sorry." He scrubbed a hand through that gorgeous red hair before turning away.

"No need to be sorry. There are actually studies that show people who swear are more intelligent." I gave him a thoughtful smile, admiring the way his expression brightened over my words.

"No shit?" he said with a laugh.

I chuckled, the soft fins along my neck fluttering as my body vibrated.

They caught Reece's attention and he cleared his throat, the jovial nature of our conversation ending right then and there.

My tentacles shuffled beneath me. I needed to think of something to fill the uncomfortable lull in conversation.

"So, uh, you work for the Parks Department?" *Stick to your guns, Cyrus. Go with what you know.*

"Yup," Reece said, his full lower lip popping the *P*.

"That must be an interesting job."

He shrugged, his muscular shoulders straining against the fabric of his shirt. "It's all right. We maintain the baseball fields and keep the parks clean. I get to spend most of my time outside, so I can't complain. What about you?"

"Oh, I'm an artist. Oil paintings mostly but—"

He cut me off and stepped closer. "You make a living off of that?"

I tried not to be offended. That was the usual response I received when I told someone I was an artist.

"Well, it's sustained my lifestyle for the last six hundred years, so I would say so." I restrained myself, but it still came out quite snarky. What I really wanted to say was that most of my pieces sold for well over six figures and my bank account was flush with cash.

All the color seemed to drain from his face, and his thick mustache pursed down over his lip. "Shit. I'm sorry. I fucking knew that was a stupid question."

As if of its own accord, one of my tentacles unraveled and snaked around his forearm. It was one of my breeding tentacles, my hectocotylus, and the moment it made contact with his skin, a little electric jolt ran up my tentacle and—I almost came.

Oh gods, no!

That was a male kraken's mate bond response.

There was no way that this was happening.

The three hearts inside my chest thumped rapidly, and I fought to get my words out, to do anything to hide the fact that Reece Rollins and I were mates.

I tried to play it cool but blurted out the words in one breath. "I-it's fine. Really."

Reece looked down at where we were attached before wrenching his arm away. He stared at where the frond had gripped him with a panicked expression.

"I gotta get going," he mumbled under his breath before stalking off, presumably to talk to anyone other than me.

As I watched him walk away from me, it felt as if I'd been punched in the gut. Of course a man like him would find a monster like me repulsive. And of course out of all the beings I'd met in my long life, that man was my mate.

Four

REECE

"MOTHERFUCKER!" I YELLED THE MINUTE I SLAMMED MY FRONT door shut.

What in the ever-loving fuck is wrong with me?

Since my abrupt exit from Atlas and Tegan's engagement party, I'd been in an absolute state of panic. For the most part, I'd managed to keep my cool, but my interaction with Cyrus had me rattled.

When he reached out and touched me with his tentacle, it felt like little bolts of lightning lit me up from the inside out. I couldn't help but pull away. It was hard enough for me to accept a casual touch from people I was close to, but someone I just met?

Hard no.

I really hoped he wouldn't tell Atlas or Tegan what happened. Until that moment, everything had gone so well. We were getting along and then I had to go and do something to fuck it up.

Why did he have to touch me?

And why the fuck did I have to react that way?

"Shit," I huffed under my breath and threw myself down onto the couch.

My head whirled with thoughts of the party, and I replayed the interaction between Cyrus and me on a loop.

Gods, I needed to expend some energy and clear my thoughts. There wasn't a better way to do that than a bike ride.

I got all my gear on, rolled my bike out of the garage, and pedaled off toward the perfect place to clear my head: the lake. The sun was starting to set as I rode down the winding back roads, lowering the temperature. Trees whizzed by on either side of me, and the evening breeze felt cool against my skin as it rushed by.

My heart rate soared, but my thoughts slowed to a crawl, giving me the time I needed to process things.

There was one thing I kept coming back to, though—the fact that I was a fucking idiot.

Was it true what Cyrus said? About people who curse being more intelligent. I mean, I wasn't a rocket scientist, but I'd always done well in school. I excelled at pretty much anything I put my mind to.

Since childhood, my father had drilled it into my head that I had to be the best. I was pushed to be the fastest and the strongest. If I was anything less, I was worthless to him. A disappointment. Maybe that's why the whole slow swimmer thing was throwing me for a loop. It's the first time I wasn't good at something right away.

For a kraken like Cyrus, though, swimming was second nature. If I had tentacles to propel me along and a streamlined body that cut through the water, I'd be golden.

Krakens.

Why weren't there more of his kind?

I could have asked if I hadn't completely offended him.

What in the actual fuck was that?

Why couldn't I be normal about a little friendly gesture?

Sweat dripped down my face as I pulled my bike to a stop in front of the lake.

The sun was setting, its bright red rays reflecting off the lake's surface, almost like it was on fire.

In a few short months, I'd be jumping into that cold water and swimming like my life depended on it, and I was wildly unprepared.

I needed to get my ass in gear and get in the pool.

Atlas wouldn't have offered to let me train at Leviathan if he didn't mean it. It wasn't like my sister put him up to that shit.

But swimming at Leviathan meant I'd run into Cyrus at some point.

And when I did, I'd have to apologize for my behavior at the party.

I saw the hurt flash over his face at my reaction, but in the moment, I was too much of a prick to care.

I unhooked my phone from where I had it clipped to my handlebars and typed out a text to my baby sister.

Reece: Hey, Teg. Had a great time at the party. Can you ask Atlas when I should stop by Leviathan and see him about swimming there?

I puffed out a breath and hit send. My sister would probably see this as me being selfish and taking advantage of her mate—and in a way it was—but it would also give me an opportunity to chat with Atlas some more. And even Fallon, although the griffin gave off major gym-bro vibes.

They were important to her, though. Therefore, they had to be important to me.

My phone buzzed with a notification.

Tegan: We were really glad you came,
and I know Mom was too. Atlas said
to stop by next Wednesday and he'll
get you signed up. Have a good
night, Reecie!

Reecie.

That was what Tegan called me when we were kids. Shit, it had been years since she'd referred to me as Reecie.

It was my fault that things were like this between us. I'd been such a stubborn, insufferable ass since Dad died—about Atlas, about a lot of things, really.

I was so tired of letting the past dictate my life.

It was time for me to work on moving forward.

Five

CYRUS

"SOMEFIN' IS BOVERIN' YOU," FALLON SLURRED FROM WHERE
he was sprawled out in the back seat of my SUV. It was preplanned
that I would be his designated driver, but I hadn't anticipated him
drinking quite this much at the engagement party.

"Nothing is bothering me," I said flatly.

I kept my eyes on the road and tightened my grip on the steering wheel. I really didn't need him blabbing to Atlas about what
happened. Tegan would inevitably find out and it would get back
to Reece that I'd said something . . . And the mating bond? There
was no way I was even remotely ready to talk about that. I was still
processing it myself.

Fallon sat up and leaned in close. "I know you, Cyyyy . . . Did
somefin' happen with Reece?"

Gods. We'd been friends for too long. He knew something
was up. Just like he always did.

I took a deep breath, and the tentacles wrapped around my
arms relaxed slightly. "I—I think I made Tegan's brother uncomfortable. He made a comment about me being an artist—"

Fallon gasped. "No. What did he say?"

"Just the usual criticism, but when I corrected him, he was worried he'd offended me. Then my tentacle reached out and grabbed his arm. Like it was trying to reassure him it was fine."

"Tha' doesn't sound too bad. Your tentacles are jus' touchy-feely."

I sighed and rubbed the fin on the side of my head with one of my tentacles. Fallon could be exhausting, especially when he was drunk.

"He pulled his arm away so fast." I lowered my voice, my throat feeling tight at the memory. "Like he thought I was disgusting."

Fallon gasped again, this time so loud I nearly swerved the car into oncoming traffic.

"Fallon!" I yelled, but he was completely unaffected.

He simply leaned closer and nuzzled his beak against my shoulder. "Don't you ever say tha', Cy. You're beautiful. Tha' guy is an asshole."

I tried to fight off a smile. Even if he was annoying and drunk, Fallon was a good friend. And he was right; Reece was an asshole. A handsome asshole, but still an asshole.

"Thanks, Fal." I ran a tentacle through the downy feathers along his neck.

"Do you thin' we can stop at Tito's Tacos on the way home? I'm starving."

Tito's Tacos was a Tex-Mex fast-food establishment that was outside of Briar Glenn, right off the interstate. The drive there and back was at least forty minutes. But it wasn't like I had anything better to do besides lie in bed and sulk.

I sighed again. "Sure."

"Yaaay," Fallon drawled as I pulled onto the highway.

After a few miles of silence, I glanced in the rearview and noticed Fallon slumped over in the seat.

"Did you have a nice time at the party?" I asked. I already knew the answer was a resounding yes, but I wanted to keep him talking. If I was driving out of my way to get him food, he was going to stay awake and keep me company.

"Yeah," Fallon murmured. "It was good."

"It seemed like you got along well with that one guy. What was his name?" Tegan had introduced us, but for the life of me, I couldn't remember his name. Just that he was incredibly attractive.

Not as attractive as Reece, though.

"Javier!" Fallon screeched. "He's a li'l sweetie pie."

"Ah, yes. That's him. The type of sweetie pie who forces you to take shots with him."

"Mm-hmm," he hummed. "My fav'rite."

"Don't you think you're getting a little too old for shots?"

He shushed me. Or tried to at least. Because of his beak, it didn't quite have the same effect. "Your friend only gets engaged once."

I laughed. "Atlas has been engaged twice, Fal."

"Pshhh. The first one didn't count."

No. No, it did not. Prior to meeting Tegan, Atlas was in a fourteen-year relationship with his girlfriend from college. Fallon and I hated her just as much as she hated us, and when Atlas called off their relationship, we let out a collective sigh of relief. Our friend deserved someone who loved him for who he was, not for what he could give them, and he'd found that in Tegan.

"What would you like?" I asked Fallon as I pulled into the drive-through of Tito's Tacos. "Your usual?"

He leaned over my shoulder, his beady eyes scanning the flickering menu board for a moment before he finally said, "Yeah. The usual."

I should have known.

I rolled my eyes, gave the lovely person working the drive-through our order, and pulled up to the pickup window.

"Any sauces?" the very unamused-looking naga working the drive-through asked.

"Ghost pepper!" Fallon shouted from the back seat.

The drive-through window snapped shut, and a moment later, the girl returned, thrusting a grease-stained paper bag and what appeared to be a gallon of soda in my direction.

"Thank you," I said, but she was already closing the window and slithering away.

I passed Fallon his drink and the heavy bag of food. "Fal, I swear, if you throw up in my car, I will—"

"Cy," he slurred, "you know I have an iron stomach."

"Bullshit, you do," I said with a laugh.

"Don't tell Javier about that." Between his state of intoxication and beakful of tacos, I could just barely make out what he was saying. "He won' wanna hang out with me."

"Oh? You're already making plans to see each other again?" I asked with a smile.

"Yeah. I got his number an' everything."

"A new love connection?" I teased.

Fallon chuckled. "No way. But I'm gonna pick up so many girls wif him around."

"I hope that doesn't backfire on you."

He ignored me, happily eating his tacos and slurping away on his soda.

By some stroke of luck, I managed to keep Fallon awake for the drive back to our apartment building. Now I just had to get him inside and up to our apartment.

"Come on," I said, opening the back door of the SUV for Fallon. "Let's get you to bed."

He tried to climb out of the back seat, but his massive wings got stuck on the doorframe. "Shit," he giggled, making me laugh. I was past the point of annoyance and found his drunken antics amusing.

When he finally worked his wings free, he stumbled, nearly falling face-first onto the pavement.

"Whoa there." I reached out with my tentacles, scooping him up under his armpits. At six foot three, with the muscular upper body of a bird and the lower body of a lion, Fallon was by no means a small monster. I was just that strong.

"Thanks, buddy," he mumbled as we made our way inside the building.

"It's no problem." I held him steady in front of the elevator while I pushed the button for our floor.

While we waited for the doors to open, he leaned into me, rubbing his soft feathers against my shoulder. "I'm so lucky to have you, Cy."

I patted his head affectionately. "I'm lucky to have you, Fal." It was the honest truth. He could be a pain in the ass, but he was a good friend.

We rode the elevator up to our floor, and I led Fallon inside our penthouse.

"Bathroom," he shrieked, bringing his arm up to his mouth. "I need to go to the bathroom."

"Oh, fuck me," I hissed, dragging him into the hall bathroom. I knew drunken tacos were a bad idea, but I'd humored him anyway.

Fallon heaved into the toilet a few times, and when I was sure he was no longer at risk of choking on his own vomit, I got him into bed and retired to my room.

"Fuck," I groaned, collapsing onto my mattress.

Moonlight drifted into the room from the skylight above my bed, the stars twinkling against a backdrop of black velvet. It was late and I was exhausted, but every time I closed my eyes and tried to drift off to sleep, the same memory clouded my brain: Reece Rollins.

Pleasure.

The first word he ever spoke to me in that deep voice. It was like a caress against my soul, and exactly what I wanted to bring him. When I made him laugh, a warm, genuine, full-body laugh, it felt like I'd won the lottery.

As Fallon and I had already established, the guy was an asshole. But he was hot. Vivid green eyes, silky red hair, and I was sure I'd find a perfectly sculpted body underneath his clothes.

My mate called to the creative part of my brain like a siren drawing me in.

For the first time in months, I felt inspired.

I had to paint him.

The apartment was fairly quiet as I shuffled across the hall to my studio. Light snores came from Fallon's room, but he wouldn't be waking anytime soon. Even if he did, he was used to my odd hours. He'd probably feel relieved that I was painting again.

My tentacle flicked the light switch, illuminating the open space with warm white light. For me, this room was the major draw of the apartment.

One wall was composed entirely of windows, allowing an abundance of natural light to fill the studio during the day, and the black of the starlit sky to shroud the space at night.

The opposite wall was lined with canvases. Some were finished pieces awaiting gallery display, and others were pristine white backdrops, ready for inspiration to strike.

And tonight it had in the form of a fiery-haired god.

I queued up The Cure on my phone, and Robert Smith's crooning voice flowed out of the studio's surround sound, allowing me to get lost in the music while I set to work sketching out the scene.

For several hours I painted, applying layer after layer of color to the canvas until the sun began to rise.

I hummed the notes in unison with the guitar, my head bobbing to the beat of the music with each stroke of my brush against the canvas.

My tentacle stilled as the last few notes drifted out of the speakers, and I shuffled back to get a better look at the piece I was working on.

I'd covered the canvas in a dusky sea blue. In the center, I'd painted a merman and a human man tangled together in a romantic embrace. Sunlight filtered down into the water and illuminated the bright red strands of the human's hair—almost like a halo.

The merman's handsome face was solemn as he clung to his lover beneath the surface. He knew their time together was waning. Two worlds separated by vast differences.

It was wishful thinking.

All the things I'd dreamt of laid out on canvas.

Would my mate ever look at me that way?

I'd never be a handsome merman.

With a deep sigh, I rinsed my brushes, shut off the lights, and closed the door to the studio.

Six

REECE

THE SOLES OF MY SLIDES SLAPPED ALONG THE PAVEMENT AS I walked down the street and up to the front door of Leviathan Fitness. I wiped my clammy hands on my shorts before reaching for the door handle.

Why the fuck was I so nervous?

Oh, right. Because I was taking my sister's mate up on his offer after being a total dick to him *and* his friend.

"Damn," I murmured under my breath when I stepped inside. My eyes scanned the space, taking it all in.

It was nothing like the rec center of my childhood.

Sure, I could tell from the brick walls and open space that we were in what used to be the basketball court, but for the most part, it was unrecognizable.

Weightlifting machines, free weights, and racks were set up on the first floor, positioned in front of tall mirrors so you could watch your form while lifting. The scuffed wood of the basketball court had been replaced with springy rubber flooring, perfect for rebounding dropped weights.

Because the ceilings were so high, Atlas had added an open second story. Cardio machines like treadmills, bikes, and Stair-Masters now overlooked the first floor.

It was nice. Modern. Clean. Well lit.

And to think I could have been working out here instead of in my garage this entire time.

Atlas stood behind the front desk, his ears perking up when he noticed me. His body started to sway, that massive puppy dog tail wagging behind him.

I had to give it to my sister. The tail-wagging was pretty damn cute.

"Hey, man! How are you this morning?" He smiled, the sharp tips of his teeth showing.

"I'm good," I lied. Certainly not anxious about being here. Not one bit.

"Come on over and we'll get you all set up. Tegan is super excited you decided to join."

Was she? Or was he just saying that to make me feel better?

"I, uh, I appreciate you doing this for me," I said. "I really need to work on my swim time."

Atlas slid some papers and a pen across the counter to me. "It's no problem at all. We're family."

I gave him a sincere smile.

What could I say? He was growing on me.

I scribbled my signature on the forms and handed them back to Atlas.

"Welcome to Leviathan Fitness!" He grinned before turning around to dig through a cabinet. "What size shirt do you wear?"

"Uh, extra large, please."

He passed me a black T-shirt with the Leviathan Fitness logo in the corner.

The tentacle and the weight.

It all made sense now.

Cyrus was the inspiration behind the gym's logo.

The two of them had to be close.

Knowing that I'd upset one of Atlas's best friends made me feel like even more of an asshole.

Atlas was acting normal and I hadn't received any angry text messages from my sister, so I guess Cyrus had kept our awkward interaction on the down-low.

For the time being, I was in the clear.

Now, if I could avoid running into him.

"Let me show you to the pool," Atlas said as he walked around the counter.

I slung the T-shirt over my shoulder and followed behind him, doing my best to keep up.

Gods, he was massive.

If his equipment matched the rest of him, how did he and my sister even work?

My face scrunched up at the thought.

Don't think about your sibling doing the deed. Fucking gross.

"Here we are!" Atlas said as he pushed open a door labeled POOL.

It opened to reveal a bright room with glass panels covering the ceiling and a shimmering Olympic swimming pool smack dab in the center.

"Shit," I mumbled under my breath. "This is really nice."

The pool had been completely refinished with shiny white tiles, and dark blue tiles marked the swimming lanes.

Atlas let out a deep, rumbling laugh, which roared through the open space. "Thank you. It's salt water, too. None of the smell or sting of chlorine. I wanted the gym to be state of the art."

He pointed a clawed finger to an area labeled LOCKER ROOM. "You'll find the showers in there." He looked down at his watch.

"I have to get back to the desk, but after your swim, I'll give you the full tour. How's that sound?"

Movement in the water on the opposite end of the pool caught my attention.

Shit.

"Oh yeah. Cyrus is here for a swim," Atlas added. "If you have any questions about the facility, he should be able to help." Atlas gripped my shoulder affectionately, and I had to force myself not to shy away from his touch.

"Uh, sounds good. I'll catch up with you later about that tour," I said quietly, watching the blue-green kraken glide through the water.

Atlas gave me a nod and headed back through the door.

I puffed out a breath and ran my fingers through my hair.

This was just my luck.

My first day using the pool, and of course Cyrus was here, because why wouldn't he be?

Stepping into the locker room, I sat down on the bench in the middle of the aisle and rubbed my hand along my beard.

It wasn't like I could leave. I just got here. Atlas would think something was up. And I really did need to work on my swim time.

I mean, we'd be in the water. We'd both be focused on swimming.

It wasn't like there'd be a ton of time for idle chitchat. If I stayed in my own swim lane, maybe he wouldn't even know I was there.

"Motherfucker," I grumbled as I pulled my T-shirt over my head and threw my shit in a locker.

Deep breaths, Reece. Deep breaths.

I strolled out to the pool and stood by the ladder for a moment, my eyes scanning the water, looking for Cyrus.

He was near the bottom of the pool, his tentacles undulating and propelling his body through the water with ease. He seemed to glide along fluidly, becoming one with the water around him. I was mesmerized, and for several minutes I stood there and watched him.

Not once did he come up to the surface to take a breath.

I would have been content to stand there and watch him forever, but I had to be at work in an hour and a half. I needed to get my ass in the water.

The metal of the ladder was cold on my feet as I lowered myself into the water. I hissed the moment my dick bobbed beneath the surface. The water was chilly, but compared to the lake, it felt like bathwater.

I made a mental note to do more research on open water triathlon swimming and dove in.

With my eyes closed, I focused on my technique, kicking my feet and using my arms to drag my body through the water. Swimming was the only time I found my muscular body to be a hindrance to my performance. I didn't have that lean swimmer's physique, and that made this so much harder.

My hair stuck to my face while I swam, making the periodic visual checks I should have been doing nearly impossible. Like a dumbass, I'd forgotten my swim cap and goggles.

I was almost to the opposite end of the pool when my body slammed into something soft yet solid.

FUCK!

Cyrus's voice.

I'd heard his voice in my head.

I splashed and sputtered, trying to tread water and catch my breath and being simultaneously terrified.

Cyrus popped out of the water and stared at me. "Are you all right?" he asked in that fucking British accent.

"Yeah," I said, flipping my hair out of my eyes. "Are you?"

"I'm fine." He was floating in the water without issue, his tentacles open in a wide parachute below his waist.

Wild.

"Did you, uh, did you talk to me in my head? Was I imagining that?" The words rushed out with a light spray of salt water as I began to panic. "Can you read my mind?" I blurted out.

Cyrus stared at me for several beats, his eyes unblinking and his mouth a thin line, but then the corners of his lips turned up slightly and his fins began to vibrate with laughter.

Heat spread over my cheeks and I slapped the water, splashing Cyrus in the face. "You fucker."

Beads of water rolled off his slick skin as he smiled, revealing sharp teeth that looked like something you'd see on a piranha.

It was slightly terrifying, but not nearly as terrifying as the prospect of him being able to read my mind. If that was the case, he could have heard everything I thought about him at the party—everything I thought about *everyone* at the party.

Relief washed over me when he said, "I can't read your mind. But I can communicate with you using *my* mind. Telepathy." He tapped his temple with one of his webbed fingers. "It's theorized that my kind evolved the trait in order to communicate underwater. It also comes in handy when I'm trying to let Fallon know I'm ready to leave the bar."

I tilted my head in confusion. "Are the two of you, like, a couple or something?"

Cyrus barked with laughter as if it were the funniest thing he'd ever heard.

"Ah, shit, mate. That's hilarious." He sighed and caught his breath. "We're roommates. Not lovers. I'm into men, but he isn't my type."

I bit my lip and nodded.

So, Cyrus was gay, too.

An uncomfortable silence stretched out between us. I wasn't sure if I should mention what happened at the party and apologize for my behavior, or pretend like it never happened and not bring it up.

It was Cyrus who bridged the gap in conversation.

"So, uh, how is training going?" he asked. "I see you forgot your goggles." He raised the bumpy protrusions above his eyes that I assumed were a kraken's version of eyebrows.

"Yeah, and my swim cap." I laughed awkwardly. "So I'd say it isn't going well."

"I saw you watching me," he said with a smirk.

Fuck.

I might as well fess up to it.

"I mean, I was. You make it look so easy. And it must be when you're built for swimming. I drag ass through the water."

"I was watching you for a bit before you ran into me." He looked away from me and smiled. "You're a shit swimmer," he mumbled under his breath.

I grunted and swam over to the side of the pool, crossing my arms over the edge. Treading water while we talked was exhausting.

Cyrus swam up beside me and used his tentacles to haul his body out of the water with ease. I was in awe as I watched them ripple and writhe in a swirling mass of blues and greens. His coloring reminded me of a raging sea, which made sense for a kraken, I guess. It really was pretty.

He positioned himself so he was sitting on the ledge, his tentacles dangling into the water.

"You know, I may not be an expert, but I could train you," he offered. "Help with some of your mechanics. If you'd take the help, that is."

I looked up at his alien-like face, his fins lightly flapping, and those unblinking eyes. "You'd do that? Even after what happened at the party?"

He dipped his head, almost like he was ashamed. "I'm sorry. For touching you without your permission. Sometimes my tentacles have a mind of their own."

I couldn't believe what I was hearing.

He was apologizing to me?

When I was the one who acted like a complete and utter dick to him?

"No, I'm sorry," I blurted. "I shouldn't have acted that way." I lowered my voice, even though it was only the two of us in the pool. "Sometimes I'm weird about touch and, like, affectionate gestures."

Cyrus raised his head and stared at me. "I completely understand."

"I just, um, I appreciate you not saying anything to Atlas."

"I heard from Atlas that the two of you got off on the wrong foot."

"We did," I said. "But I'm trying."

"I know you're protective over your sister, but I can tell you from experience, Atlas is a great guy. One of the nicest I've met in my seven hundred years. After all he's been through, he deserves happiness."

"Tegan does, too, and I'm starting to realize that they found that in each other." I sighed and squinted up at Cyrus as salt water dripped down my forehead and into my eyes. "Look, if the offer still stands, I could really use some help in the swimming department."

A wide grin spread over his face. With those sharp teeth, it was almost menacing—*almost*. "Well, Reece Rollins, you've got yourself a swim coach."

Seven

CYRUS

"CYRUS, ARE YOU OUT OF YOUR MIND?" FALLON SQUAWKED from where he sat at the kitchen island.

As usual, I was preparing lunch and he was sitting on his ass watching me, expecting the food to just appear in front of him.

"This is Reece we're talking about. Tegan's asshole brother Reece. He gives you one weak-ass apology about his behavior at the party and you just forgive him?" Fallon cocked his head from side to side and wiggled his talons. "Oh, Reece. It's fine. I forgive you. I'll train you," he mocked in a terrible British accent.

"First of all, that is a terrible impression of me—"

"I thought it was pretty good," he said under his breath.

"Second of all, he said he's trying. His sister is marrying our best friend. I'm simply"—I turned around to face him and held my arms out—"trying to extend an olive branch of sorts."

"I'm telling you, man. This is a bad idea." He let out a long whistle and bristled his feathers.

I whipped back around and continued to aggressively chop the vegetables for our stir-fry.

Fallon's reaction to the news made total sense, given his understanding of the situation between Reece and me. But there was no way I was ready to reveal the fact that he was my mate. I was still coming to terms with it myself.

And if the news got back to Reece?

It would be disastrous.

He was just now starting to warm up to the idea of Atlas being his sister's fated mate.

Having that bomb dropped on him when he least expected it?

I was positive it would lead to instant rejection.

There was nothing in the world worse than being rejected by your mate. It was likely I wouldn't survive it. My lifespan was tied to Reece's now. For the rest of Reece's lifetime, I'd have to struggle with a broken heart, knowing that my mate was out there and wanted nothing to do with me. Only to pass when he passed, alone and never knowing true love.

It would be a miserable existence.

And, to be honest, I wasn't sure I wanted to live through that.

Coaching Reece would give him an opportunity to get to know me better, and perhaps with time, he would develop feelings for me.

But maybe that was wishful thinking.

I jostled the wok with my hand while using my tentacle to stir the dish with a wooden spoon, focusing all my attention on the stir-fry instead of debating with Fallon.

"Cyrus," he said from behind me, "I worry about you. That's all. You've been going through it lately."

I stilled, my fins perking up.

Other than not painting, I'd thought I was acting normal. Had it really been that obvious I was struggling?

I didn't give Fallon enough credit. He could be tiring, but he was a good friend.

I plated our food, setting a steaming bowl of stir-fry in front of him before taking a seat beside him at the island.

"Thank you." Fallon clicked his beak with excitement.

"You're welcome. It's hot."

I shook my head as the impatient griffin brought a forkful of stir-fry up to his beak.

"I know you worry, but I'm a grown man, Fallon. One who is centuries older than you are, in fact. I've just—lost my way a bit. It feels like everyone else around me is growing and changing, and I'm stuck in the same place."

"Even though you're older than me, I'm still allowed to be concerned about you. I mean, I get it. Being single as fuck and watching our buddy meet someone and fall in love fast. It sucks."

I laughed around a mouthful of food. "Fallon Ridgewing, Briar Glenn's biggest player, is lamenting about being single? I never thought I'd see the day." I reached out with my tentacle and playfully nudged his shoulder.

He shrugged, his wings making the gesture look ridiculous. "What can I say? Summer will be over before we know it and then it's cuffing season."

I stared at him and tilted my head in confusion. *These kids and their slang.* "What in the goddess's name is 'cuffing season'?"

Fallon let out a chirpy laugh and fluttered his wings slightly. "Cuffing season is basically the fall and winter. The cold months when people don't want to be single and so they jump into relationships."

"But why 'cuffing'?" I asked.

"You know, like 'handcuffed.' Being tied down."

I nodded my head in understanding. Maybe I'd have someone of my own to warm my bed this cuffing season.

Gods, I was getting ahead of myself.

"Shit," Fallon mumbled with a noodle dangling from his beak.

"I gotta get going or I'm gonna be late for work." He bolted off his stool and grabbed his preworkout drink from the fridge. "So, when's your first training session with him?"

"Monday. We'll be training a few days a week."

Fallon clipped his bag around his neck and tilted his head in my direction. "*Diving* right into it, I see."

I rolled my eyes, and he warbled with laughter.

"I had to," he said once he caught his breath. "Thanks for lunch, bud. I'll see ya later."

Fallon opened the front door, yelling over his shoulder, "And get some painting done! I can't afford the rent by myself!"

Cheeky fucker.

He was well aware I had enough money stockpiled for *multiple* lifetimes, but he loved to tease me.

Fallon was right, though, I did need to do some painting. And thanks to my new muse, my well of creativity was practically overflowing.

After cleaning the kitchen, I shuffled down the hall to my studio. The afternoon sun filtered through the wide windows, lighting up the space and filling it with warmth.

It was perfect for what I wanted to paint.

The *only* thing I wanted to paint.

I grabbed a pencil and pulled my stool in front of one of the blank canvases lining the wall. I closed my eyes and thought back to how Reece looked as he stared up at me from the ledge of the pool: those emerald eyes shimmering bright, the freckles dotting his muscular forearms, and the way the water dripped off his beard down into the pool.

Despite the fact that I'd been around for a long time, I wasn't always certain of *everything*, but I was certain that Reece Rollins was one of the prettiest men I had ever seen.

With his macho exterior, he probably wouldn't want to hear that, but it was the truth. You could be masculine and pretty. They weren't mutually exclusive.

As I finished the final line of my sketch, my phone buzzed from where it sat on the cart that held my paints.

My tentacles clenched tight to my arms, almost forcing me to drop my phone.

I couldn't believe what I was seeing.

It was like he knew he was on my mind.

Unknown: Hey, Cyrus. It's Reece. I got
your number from Atlas. Are you
available to meet a little later in the
morning for training Monday?
Around 10 am?

Reece Rollins—my mate—had asked for my phone number.

I was so giddy, I felt like my hearts were going to burst out of my chest.

The other morning at the gym was such a whirlwind that I'd completely forgotten to exchange our contact info.

I saved his number in my phone, then typed out a response.

Cyrus: Hello! 10 a.m. works for me.

I hesitated before hitting send.

Should I add "Have a nice day"? "See you Monday"?

Shit.

Even if Fallon was home, it wasn't like I could ask him for advice on this. It would be a dead giveaway that I had some sort of interest in Reece. "See you Monday" was probably my best bet.

Cyrus: Hello! 10 a.m. works for me.
See you Monday.

I hit send and stared at my phone, still in shock that somewhere in Briar Glenn, Reece was choosing me, of all people, to message.

His response was almost immediate.

Reece: See you then. Have a nice day!

I smiled at my phone before setting it back down on my supply cart.

It would be a nice day.

Because today I was going to paint another portrait of the most beautiful man I had ever seen, and next week, I'd get to spend time with him.

Sure, I'd be giving him the adult triathlon version of swim lessons, but it was still time with him.

Time with my mate.

As I started to mix the color palette for today's painting, the merman portrait from the other day caught my eye.

It really was a gorgeous piece. Gallery worthy, even.

I snatched my phone from the cart with one of my tentacles and rang up Eduardo.

He answered on the first ring.

"Cyrus, I've been worried about you. I thought you might be dead." He huffed.

"Nope, very much alive. I've been in a bit of a slump, but I think that's over now. Can I send you some photos of my recent work? I think I want to put on a show."

Eduardo screamed with excitement, and I smiled.

I was back.

Eight

REECE

TUCKING MY PHONE INTO MY POCKET, I SMILED. IT WAS COOL that Cyrus was flexible, considering he was the one doing me a favor.

"What's got you smiling?" Jimenez asked as he opened the passenger door of our work truck and passed me my iced coffee.

This was part of our daily ritual. Every afternoon after lunch, we'd stop at Briar Glenn's only coffee shop, the Busy Bean, to get our caffeine fix to carry us through the rest of the day. We alternated who paid, and today it was Jimenez's turn.

"Nothing. Uh, just in a good mood today, that's all." I took a sip of my coffee and started the truck, hoping that he didn't press me on the subject.

"Are you sure you don't mind covering for me on Sunday? I know it's sort of last minute—"

"Nah. It's cool. Cyrus said he'd meet me at the pool around ten on Monday, so it works out."

"You know, I chatted with him a little bit at the party. He's a nice guy. Not bad-looking, either." Jimenez took a swig of his coffee and raised his perfectly shaped brows.

"Is this really happening right now? You're telling me you find Cyrus attractive?"

He shrugged and looked out the window. "I don't know. It's something about the tentacles. I saw this anime once—"

I slammed on the brakes, almost sending coffee flying all over the interior of the truck. "Stop it. Stop it right now. I don't want to hear about any freaky cartoon porn or how you think that Cyrus is hot."

Jimenez looked over and flashed me a shit-eating grin. "I didn't say he was hot. That was all you, boss."

"Jimenez! I did not!" I barked.

I didn't think Cyrus was hot, and I didn't need my coworker busting my balls about it.

I stomped on the gas, sending the truck speeding down the road toward the park while Jimenez busted out laughing.

"Chill! I was just playing around. You're gonna get us pulled over," he said, and cackled even louder.

"Fuck off," I grumbled under my breath.

I pulled into our usual spot, adjacent to the athletic fields, and got out of the truck.

"Hey, I'm sorry. I know you're sensitive." Jimenez walked around to where I was leaning against the truck.

"It's been a lot. The shit with Atlas and my sister, what happened with Cyrus at the party."

Jimenez gave me a thoughtful smile and leaned against the truck beside me. "The stuff with Tegan, it's getting better. I know the two of you used to be close. She probably misses that just as much as you do."

I swirled my finger through the condensation forming on my

coffee cup. "You're right, but I was still a total dickhead to Cyrus at the party."

"Damn, dude. You're really caught up on that, aren't you?"

I was. Which was very unlike me. Normally I didn't care if I looked like a dick, but Cyrus was just so kind.

"You apologized and he forgave your ass, right? Plus, he agreed to coach you," Jimenez said. "It seems like he's trying to move past it, and you should, too. But if it's really bothering you, you could do something nice for him to show your appreciation and work toward making amends."

"Like what?"

"I don't know. Maybe take him to lunch or something after training. Get to know the guy a little bit. He *is* one of Atlas's best friends. You're gonna be spending a lot of time together over the next few months. Might as well make the best of it."

Sipping my coffee, I nodded.

Cyrus and I would be spending a lot of time together. Time that he wasn't being compensated for in any way. The least I could do was take him out to lunch a time or two.

What kind of food did he like?

Calamari was probably out of the question.

I chuckled at my own joke and looked over at Jimenez, wondering if he'd heard me. His deep brown eyes were fixed on the centaur couple playing Frisbee in the field like they did every afternoon.

"You wanna join them for a game, Jimenez?"

"Nah." He laughed and shook his head. "They're just nice to look at."

"Do you think they're mates?" I asked. Every time I saw the two of them, they looked so happy together.

"I'm not sure. I don't really know anything about centaur mating habits."

"Would you ever want that kind of connection with someone?" Mating bonds. Love. None of it had ever been on my radar.

"What?" he asked. "A mate?"

"Yeah."

Jimenez smoothed his thumb over his lower lip, nodding slightly before fixing his brown eyes on me. "Yeah, I think I would."

I opened my mouth to say something smart, to criticize him about being a hopeless romantic, but shut it just as fast. I was curious about what he had to say. Sure, Jimenez was young, but he was also pretty wise.

He continued. "Your sister has a mate and you see how happy they are together. Yeah, it might have been fast, but you're telling me that if someone brought you that kind of happiness, you'd push them away?" He shook his head. "You'd have to be out of your mind not to want what they have. Mate or not, who gives a fuck? Love is love."

Everyone around me was opening their lives to love and mates. Meanwhile, I was the same miserable prick I'd always been, with nothing to show for it.

"Dammit, Jimenez. Why do you have to be so fucking smart?" I huffed, crossing my arms over my chest.

He shrugged his shoulders and smiled. "It's both a blessing and a curse. Someone's gotta call you out on your shit."

Even if I didn't say it, I was thankful that he did.

Nine

CYRUS

"HEY, BUDDY!" ATLAS GREETED ME WITH A SMILE AS I SHUF-fled through the doors of Leviathan. He leaned across the front desk and waved me over to him.

"Chai feeling sick again?" I asked.

Atlas frowned and nodded in confirmation.

Chai was one of the trainers at the gym, a young minotaur who had been missing a lot of time due to some mysterious illness. Atlas had taken to covering the front desk in her absence, though a wolven greeting you with a sharp-toothed smile the moment you walked through the door had a bit of a different effect.

"Poor thing," I said. "She can't seem to catch a break."

"Yeah, she's going through it. I think Tegan and I are going to swing by her house and check on her later this week. Are you training Reece today?"

"Indeed, I am. He's meeting me here at ten." My tentacle unraveled from my arm and pulled on the bright red whistle hanging from my neck. "I even got this bad boy. Wanted to be profes-sional, you know."

Atlas chuckled and shook his head. "Oh, man. I'm sure Reece is going to love that. You better watch yourself with that one, Cy."

My tentacles clenched tight to my forearms. *Oh, I'd watch myself with Reece, all right.*

It was an innocent enough comment, but the fact that he was my mate had my mind reeling with all sorts of possibilities.

"Cyrus? You all right?" Atlas leaned in closer, his head tilted and his bright yellow eyes searching my face.

Oh yeah, Atlas. Just having sexual fantasies about your soon-to-be brother-in-law. No biggie.

I cleared my throat awkwardly and shrugged my shoulders. "I'm fine. I'm, uh, just a little tired. Fallon got in late last night and woke me up."

Not a huge stretch from the truth. Fallon did get in late last night after sampling his current flavor of the week. So much for cuffing season . . .

"Okay, well, you know I'm here for you if you ever need to talk, right?" he said, his ears drooping slightly.

My friends were the best, but this concern over my mental state working its way into every single conversation needed to end.

"Right. Right. I'm aware. And, uh, I meant to tell you, and Fallon, too, that I've been painting again. I rang Eduardo about a gallery show the other day."

Atlas flashed me a wide grin, the pointed tips of his teeth peeking out from beneath his lip. "Right on, bud!" He reached across the counter and shook my shoulder. "I knew you'd kick that painter's block. Do you have a theme for the show?"

"Not yet. It's kind of a hodgepodge right now, but I think I'll be able to tie it all together."

Realization dawned on me.

What in the goddess's name had I done?

I was going to exhibit a gallery full of paintings of Reece Rollins and hope that no one noticed?

I'd already sent Eduardo photos of my current pieces. There was no way he'd let me back out now.

Besides, the gallery wasn't *in* Briar Glenn—the town was much too small for that. It was in the art district of the neighboring town, Rock Harbor, about a forty-minute drive away. And it wasn't like my friends came to all of my shows anyway.

It would be fine.

Everything would be fine.

I was getting myself worked up over nothing.

I'd handle it when the time came. For now, I had more pressing matters. Like molding Reece Rollins into an Olympic swimmer.

"Well, I should probably head over to the pool. I want to do a few laps to recharge before Reece gets here. Say hello to the missus for me, will you?"

At that, Atlas smiled and his body swayed with the wagging of his tail. "Will do. And, Cy, good luck. You know where to find me if you need me."

Why was he so bloody worried about me and Reece? I could handle him just fine.

I gave him a little wave with my tentacle and shuffled off down the corridor that led to the pool.

As usual, the pool room was empty. I could count on my tentacles the number of times I'd run into other swimmers here, but that's what made it the ideal place to train Reece.

I'd also heard from Fallon that it was the ideal place for *other things*, too. Damn voyeur.

I fixed my wide eyes on the clock.

It was only nine thirty, so I had plenty of time for a swim

before Reece arrived. Even though I'd be in the water for some of his drills, I planned to spend the majority of the session on the pool deck to monitor his form. From what I'd seen the last time we were in the pool together, we had a lot to work on.

I scuttled to the edge of the pool as fast as I could before diving in and barely making a splash, the water gliding over my body. I propelled myself through the water like a torpedo, the lengths of my tentacles undulating, the thin skin that connected them opening like a parachute and then closing again.

As the salt water absorbed into my skin, my body hummed with pleasure.

The pool wasn't the churning depths of the open ocean, but it was still a comfort, one I was thankful for each time my body needed a little pick-me-up.

I swam the length of the pool, twisting and twirling in the water until my three hearts were pounding. I drifted to the bottom, lying on my back and blinking up at where the sunlight filtered down through the water while my heart rates slowed.

My mind drifted back to my mate. All I could think about lately was Reece.

He had looked breathtaking emerging from the pool. Water trickled down his body and collected in the fluffy happy trail that disappeared beneath his swim trunks.

I wanted to run my tentacle along it before sliding it down his shorts, wrapping it around the stiff length of his cock, and giving it harsh strokes.

It had been so long since I'd been intimate with someone.

Sure, I'd had partners. Tentacles were actually quite popular amongst humans, but I'd never felt that *connection*.

If you had told me centuries ago that a handsome but prickly redheaded human would be my mate, I would have laughed.

But here we were.

I noticed a shadowy figure staring down at me from the edge of the pool.

Reece was here for our training session.

I shot toward the surface, giving him a wide smile the moment my head crested out of the water.

"Fuck, you're impressive in the water." He shook his head and the corners of his lips turned up in a slight smile.

To most people, it probably wouldn't seem like that big of a compliment. I was a kraken, after all. But hearing it from Reece. Hearing it from my mate . . . you would have thought he'd hung the stars and named one after me.

"Thank you." I let out a shy laugh and hauled myself out of the water with my tentacles. Reece stood next to where I sat on the edge of the pool, and I stared up at him. "I watched a bunch of videos about swimming techniques last night and I have some ideas on how we can improve your form."

What I really meant was I was up until three a.m. watching swimming instructional videos for triathletes in preparation for this, but he didn't need all the details.

Reece scrubbed a hand through his beard and looked down at me. "I, uh, I really do appreciate this, Cyrus."

"It's no problem. Truly. Why don't you get changed and we'll get started?"

He nodded, then walked off toward the locker room.

Again, I was hit with disbelief. Reece Rollins was my mate, and today we would be spending time together. Alone.

Gods, he looked so good, too. But not nearly as good as he did when he emerged from the locker room a few minutes later.

Reece walked over to me in his swim trunks, his well-toned abs tapering to that delicious happy trail.

"Do you have your swim cap and goggles this time?" I teased, sliding the whistle back and forth along my neck nervously.

"Yes, Coach," he responded with a wry smile curling his lips.

Coach. I liked the sound of that.

He pulled the cap out of his pocket and slipped it onto his head before putting on his goggles. "Look okay?" he asked as he tucked a few stray strands of light orange hair into the cap.

I bit back a laugh. With his swim cap and goggles on, he looked a bit like me.

"You look great but, um, what's with the trunks?" I asked, my gaze gliding down his body unapologetically. He didn't seem to notice, though.

Reece looked down, tugging at the loose material of his trunks. His brows pinched together, an adorable furrow forming between them. "What about them?"

"Well, you already have a lot of drag because of your muscles. If we can eliminate any additional drag, you'll swim faster. So, you know, wearing trunks that are a little more fitted is great for reducing drag." It was basic fluid dynamics.

He put his hands on his hips and bit his lip. "So, like a banana hammock? I really don't want my junk hanging out there."

My laughter echoed across the empty room. While I'd enjoy seeing it, that wasn't exactly what I had in mind. "Goodness, no. They make something called jammers. They're essentially compression shorts you can swim in."

How was it that I'd figured this out in one night of research, but he was totally unaware of what jammers were?

I got the impression that Reece just automatically assumed he would be good at something. No research needed.

It made sense that someone like him would have unwavering self-confidence.

Must be nice.

Reece puffed out a relieved breath. "Fuck, thank goodness. I have a tri suit, but I can't really use that for pool training. I'll order myself some jammers after we finish up." He shifted his weight from leg to leg, flexing his toned calves. "Um, speaking of, when we're done training, I was wondering if you wanted to get lunch together? You know, as a thank-you."

Had my mate just asked me out?

I mean, technically, it was a platonic lunch date. But the fact that he asked and that we'd be spending time together outside of training was enough to make my hearts flutter.

I couldn't help the wide smile that spread over my face. "That would be very nice, thank you. Did you have somewhere in mind?"

He pursed his lips, his mustache curling down over his mouth. It was adorable. Like a grumpy walrus. "My first thought was sushi because I'm on a meal plan right now, but I wasn't sure if—"

My fins flapped as I laughed. "Reece. I'm a sea creature. Fish eat other fish all the time. Sushi is perfect."

His face turned pink as he rubbed his hand over the back of his neck. "Sushi it is, then. What are we doing today?" Reece fixed his gaze on my whistle, the bright green of his irises intensified by his goggles.

"I was thinking I'd have you do a few laps back and forth, get a better sense of your form, then we'd work on corrections and move to a few drills. How long do we have before the triathlon?" I asked.

"Well, it's July now, so that gives us about three months." His expression dropped slightly.

It was obvious he was nervous about this part of the race and doubted his abilities, but I was determined to help.

"Hey," I said, stepping closer to him. I had to remind myself not to touch him, even though my instincts as his mate were urging me to comfort him. "We have plenty of time. We're going to get you where you need to be. You've got this."

He nodded and I gave him a reassuring smile before moving toward the edge of the pool.

I brought the whistle up to my lips and gave it two harsh blows, the shrill sound bouncing off the walls of the open room.

"Fuck," Reece whispered under his breath and clenched his jaw.

"What are you doing just standing there?" I asked. "Get your ass in the pool."

Gods, I could already tell I was going to love this.

Ten

REECE

FOR THE NEXT TWO HOURS, CYRUS SAT ON THE EDGE OF THE pool and gently criticized me for how much of a shit swimmer I was.

And that whistle. That fucking whistle.

There was a part of me that wanted to shove it down his throat, but there was another part of me that appreciated how seriously he was taking this.

I mean, Cyrus had done his research on triathlon swimming drills, as well as the appropriate training gear.

Plus, his advice was actually helpful.

Sure, my body hurt like hell, but I could already tell that with his modifications to my form, I was improving.

"Great job today, Reece," he said as I climbed out of the pool on shaky legs.

I was exhausted and fucking starving, but for the first time in a long time, I felt a sense of accomplishment. It meant a lot to me that a skilled swimmer like Cyrus thought I'd done a good job.

"Thank you," I mumbled as water dripped down my body.

After I pulled off my goggles and swim cap, Cyrus tossed me a towel.

As I ran it down my chest and over my stomach, I caught Cyrus watching me out of the corner of my eye.

Poor guy was probably jealous.

In all honesty, though, he had a great body. Broad, strong shoulders, muscular pecs, and a waist that tapered into a V shape before fanning out into his tentacles.

It was probably from all the swimming.

This shit was a workout, that was for sure.

He was still staring as I wrapped the towel around my waist. Being the center of his attention, those wide eyes fixed on me, made me feel unnerved—flustered even.

"I'll, uh, I'll get changed and we can go. I'll drive if that's okay?"

"Yeah, that sounds good." He put his arms behind his back and shifted on his tentacles.

Gods, this was going to be interesting.

I changed as fast as I could. On the off chance Cyrus agreed to lunch, I'd packed clothes for going out rather than my usual summer athleisure attire, opting for a short-sleeve Henley, khaki shorts, and boat shoes.

It was funny I even cared, though, considering Cyrus was essentially always in the nude.

What a weird concept.

I wondered what was underneath that parachute of tentacles.

How did he go to the bathroom?

Did he have a cock?

What the actual fuck?

Was I really thinking about Cyrus's cock?

I shook my head and walked out to the pool deck, where Cyrus was waiting for me by the door.

When he heard my boat shoes clopping against the concrete, he looked in my direction and flashed me those piranha teeth. "Are you sure you don't mind driving?" he asked, looking me up and down.

Fuck.

He was totally checking me out.

I didn't blame him. I looked fucking good. But still, we had an agreement as coach and trainer. I didn't need shit getting weird.

"I don't mind at all," I said. "It was my idea anyway."

We walked side by side down the hallway to the front lobby.

"How was training?" Atlas asked from behind the desk.

I puffed out a harsh breath. "You didn't tell me this guy is an absolute hard-ass. I haven't had a workout like that in years. That whistle is going to haunt me in my dreams."

Atlas barked out a laugh. "I told Cyrus you were going to *love* the whistle."

"I think it helped Reece take me seriously," Cyrus said. "He's already improving. By the time the triathlon rolls around, he'll be the best swimmer in Briar Glenn."

There was something about Cyrus's praise that made me feel warm inside. I couldn't tell if I was proud of myself or if I was happy that *Cyrus* was proud of me. Maybe it was a little bit of both.

"That title belongs to you, but I'll gladly take second-best swimmer," I said. "Shit, I'll take completing the swim with a decent time and moving on to the rest of the race." I smiled, and as if on instinct, I grabbed Cyrus's shoulder and gave it a playful shove.

His skin was so soft and cool underneath my palm, but he wasn't slimy like a fish. It was actually kind of nice. I felt like even more of a dickhead for how I'd acted at the party, because here I was, giving Cyrus my own innocent little touch.

Atlas looked at where my hand gripped Cyrus, and he raised his eyebrows, his muzzle curling up in a sly grin.

Shit.

I pulled my hand away and cleared my throat. "Well, we'd better get going."

My body went rigid.

Really, Reece? We?

Atlas smiled even wider. "Oh yeah? Where are you going?"

"We're going to that sushi place over in Rock Harbor. You know, the one Fallon loves," Cyrus chimed in.

Did he not get what this looked like?

Or did he just not care?

He was checking me out earlier by the pool, so . . .

"I'll let you two get going, then," Atlas said. "Have a nice lunch."

We said our goodbyes, and the moment we were in the parking lot, Cyrus broke the silence. "Was it just me or was he acting weird?"

I stopped dead in my tracks and whipped around to face him. His deep teal coloring was even more impressive in the sun, and I could see myself reflected in the depths of his wide dark eyes. "Are you fucking oblivious, Cyrus? Atlas thinks this is a date or something."

"Well, is it?" Cyrus asked with a straight face.

"Fuck no!" I blurted out, and he laughed, the translucent fins along his neck vibrating.

"Then why does it matter what Atlas or anyone else thinks?"

"It matters because I don't want Atlas telling my sister I'm putting the moves on his friends. I want to make it clear that we're just two bros going out to get sushi."

Those sharp piranha teeth were on full display with his smile. "Two bros, you say? I didn't realize I was going to lunch with Fallon."

"Oh, fuck off. Don't even compare me to that giant chicken."
I rolled my eyes. "Get in the car."

Cyrus's fins flapped slightly as he stifled a laugh. He climbed
into the passenger seat beside me, tucking his tentacles into the
footwell before clicking on his seat belt. I was curious how this
was going to work, but Cyrus seemed to manage just fine.

"You're insufferable, you know that? Giving me shit in the pool
and out of it. A guy can't even catch a break when he's trying to
do something nice for you."

"Yes, poor Reece. Getting a taste of your own medicine. That
must be very difficult for you."

"I really am trying, you know." My voice was a shy whisper.

"Hey," he said with a kind smile. "I know you're trying. I
wouldn't be here if you weren't."

ROCK HARBOR WAS THE CLOSEST BIG CITY TO BRIAR GLENN.
Sure, it was no New York City, but there were still towering business offices and cramped one-way streets. The college, waterfront,
and hospital made it an appealing place to live and work. They
also made it loud and crowded. I tended to avoid Rock Harbor at
all costs, but Kyodai was my favorite sushi restaurant. For good
food, I'd make an exception.

I parked in the closest parking garage, and Cyrus and I walked
down the sidewalk toward the restaurant. Well, I walked. Cyrus
propelled himself along on his tentacles.

I looked over at him. "Do you mind if I ask you something?"

He shook his head. "Not at all."

"Doesn't it hurt? Your tentacles rubbing on a hard surface like
that?"

He raised one of his tentacles to show me the underside. His skin was paler there, a light, almost white blue with rows of quarter-size suction cups running down its length. "The suckers on the underside serve as little feet, gently pulling me along. As long as I stay hydrated, it doesn't hurt at all."

"Cool," I murmured. It was weird as fuck, but there was no way I was going to tell him that.

When we reached the front door, Cyrus grabbed the handle with a tentacle, holding it open for me.

"Thanks," I said, and stepped inside.

Kyodai was a sleek, modern sushi restaurant. A rotating bar sat in the center of the room, with sushi chefs working inside it. They prepared the sushi rolls and set them on the little conveyor belt for customers to grab.

For a weekday, the place was packed. People dressed in business attire sat at the bar, and college students filled the booths that lined the room.

We walked up to the hostess station and a young minotaur greeted us. "Welcome to Kyodai. Just the two of you today?"

I nodded. "Yep."

"Would you like to sit at the rotating bar or in a booth?" the hostess asked.

I turned and looked at Cyrus for an answer. I wasn't sure how tentacles would work on a barstool, but I figured it was best not to be presumptuous.

"We'll take a booth, please," he said.

There was so much about Cyrus that was a mystery to me. For some reason, he piqued my interest, and I wanted to learn more about him.

We shuffled into the booth, with me on one side and Cyrus on the other.

"Someone will be over to take your drink order shortly. Enjoy your meal." The hostess set our menus down and returned to the podium at the front of the restaurant.

Cyrus held his menu in his webbed hands, with one tentacle wrapped around each of his arms. The ones he kept wound around his forearms were slightly smaller than the tentacles he used to move, but they were still about the size of my wrist before tapering to a rounded tip.

Why were those tentacles different from the ones he used to move?

Maybe because they were meant to be used as another set of hands?

Gods, he was interesting.

Cyrus hummed, reminding me that we were at a restaurant together and I was just sitting at the table, rudely staring at his tentacles.

"I don't even know what to pick," he said, scanning the menu. "I haven't been here in ages and everything sounds so good."

I bit my lip and shifted my attention to my menu, needing to fixate on something other than Cyrus. What was with this new-found fascination with him?

"So, uh, are you a sushi guy or a sashimi guy?" I asked. "I like both, but I tend to prefer sushi. If someone says they don't like the California roll, they're a liar."

Cyrus snorted. "I didn't expect you to be so passionate about sushi."

"What can I say? I enjoy good food. Sweets are my kryptonite, though."

Just as Cyrus was about to say something, the waitress walked up to our table.

"What can I get you to drink?" she asked as she pulled her notepad out of her pocket.

"I'll have a water," I said.

She smiled at Cyrus. "And for you, sir?"

"Could I have a water and a pot of green tea for the table, please?"

"Of course," she said. "I'll be right back with those."

"Thank you," Cyrus and I said in unison as the waitress turned on her heel and walked away.

We sat there for a moment staring at each other.

"So, you're a painter," I said. "We didn't really get to talk much about that at the party. Ya know, because I was a jackass."

Cyrus crossed his arms and leaned over the table. "You keep dwelling on that bit. I told you it's fine."

I huffed and shook my head. "It isn't, though. I saw the look on your face, Cyrus. My reaction hurt you." I leaned against the back of the booth, my eyes fixed on a pair of harpies at the rotating bar.

For some reason, I couldn't bring myself to look at Cyrus. Maybe it was embarrassment over my behavior at the party. Maybe it was because I hated how easily he forgave me and how willing he was to help me.

"It *did* hurt me," Cyrus said calmly, his voice low and soothing. "But you took the time to apologize and explain yourself. You're making an effort to get to know your sister's mate and his friends. You're making leaps and bounds already."

I huffed and rolled my eyes. He acted like that was some impressive feat rather than me using him for my own benefit and then trying to make up for it. I was a piece of work who didn't deserve his kindness. "You're so fucking positive, you know that?"

He shrugged and gave me a small smile. "When you've been around for centuries, you tend to let go of the small stuff."

"Gods. Centuries. I can't even imagine. I'm thirty-five and I already feel like I'm falling apart."

"Thirty-five? Really? You look like you're still in your twenties." He raised his bumpy eyebrows, his coy smile spreading into a wide grin.

I could feel my cheeks turning red.

What the fuck was happening here?

One little compliment from Cyrus and I was blushing like a fucking schoolgirl.

"Oh, fuck off," I grumbled under my breath.

By some act of the goddess, it was at that moment the waitress arrived with our drinks.

"Here you go," she said, putting our glasses in front of us.

She set the fancy cast-iron tea kettle on a trivet in the center of the table and placed two dainty cups next to it.

The waitress took our order and quickly bustled off to the kitchen, leaving Cyrus and me alone once again.

I watched in awe as his tentacle unraveled from his arm and curled around the handle of the teapot, pouring the hot tea into the cup while his hand held it steady.

"Tea?" Cyrus asked as the tentacle reached across the table, the teapot hovering over my cup.

"Please." I stared with wide eyes as the tentacle poured my tea. "That's wild. The painting makes sense now."

Cyrus set the kettle down and laughed. "It's especially convenient for painting. I can use my hands and my tentacles."

Well, the whole tentacle-hand thing checked.

"Have you always been an artist? I'd imagine doing the same thing for centuries gets old pretty quick."

Cyrus's tentacle wrapped around his cup and brought it up to his thin lips. "Most of my passions have been art-focused. Sculpting, architecture, photography, but painting is my favorite. There's something satisfying about the act of applying paint to canvas and creating something out of nothing. Taking an image out of my brain and immortalizing it."

I didn't know what to say. That was some eloquent poetic shit.

"What about you?" he asked. "How did you come to work for the Parks Department?"

"I mean, I didn't have too many options. My dad worked for the Parks Department before me. The old man was actually my boss for a few years while I was in college. He pretty much decided this was what I was going to do."

Cyrus cocked his head, the bumpy blue skin of his brows wrinkling slightly. "But is that what you wanted?"

If I was being honest, I'd never really thought about it. I'd spent most of my life, at least until my father's passing, doing what he expected of me: excelling in sports, graduating at the top of my class, and taking over his position at the Parks Department.

When I tried to think about it now, I had no idea what I wanted.

I sat there for a second, rubbing the back of my neck while I watched the steam wafting from my cup. "I, uh, I don't really know. I mean, don't get me wrong, I enjoy my job. For the most part, it's pretty easy. But I've always felt like—like there's this void inside me. Like something's missing, if that makes sense?"

Cyrus took another sip of his tea and nodded. "It makes total sense. I hope you can find what you need to fill that void."

"If I haven't after thirty-five years, I don't think I ever will."

"Oh, you'd be surprised."

Before I could ask Cyrus to explain what he meant, the waitress made her way over to our table with a giant platter balanced over her arm. Colorful plates of sushi covered the entire tray. I didn't think we'd ordered that many rolls, but seeing them all laid out like that really put things into perspective.

"Sorry about the wait!" she said, setting the plates of sushi down on the table.

"That's quite all right," Cyrus reassured her. "We're not in a rush, are we, Reece?"

"No, not at all." I shook my head and stared at Cyrus as he beamed up at the waitress.

Gods, he was so fucking kind to everyone he met.

Even to assholes like me who didn't deserve it.

"Can I get you anything else?" she asked.

I grabbed my chopsticks and slid them out of the wrapper. "I think we're good, thanks."

"Enjoy." She gave us a little nod before she rushed off to another table.

"This looks amazing," Cyrus said as he broke apart his chopsticks with his hands, then passed them along to one of his tentacles.

The thick appendage curled around the delicate sticks and held them perfectly, clicking them together before reaching for a piece of sushi.

I watched as his tentacle carefully brought the sushi up to his mouth. Cyrus's lips parted to reveal two tongues, which wrapped around the food and pulled it inside.

My mouth must have been gaping open, because Cyrus laughed at me around his mouthful of food. "Ah, yeah. The tongues freak people out a bit, but they're actually quite helpful. Especially for certain *things*."

I could feel myself blushing once again.

Was Cyrus really telling me that two tongues were helpful when it came to oral?

I felt like I was in an episode of *The Twilight Zone*.

Never in my life did I think I'd be out to lunch with a kraken, hearing him talk about how good his tongues were for sucking dick.

I pressed my fingers into my temples and rubbed them hard. "Gods, Cyrus. I don't need to hear all this shit."

He shrugged while his tentacle used the chopsticks to pick up another piece of sushi. "Well, Fallon and I discuss these sorts of things. I was just trying to be friendly."

"Oh, it's friendly all right," I mumbled, and shoved a piece of sushi into my mouth.

This fucking kraken was doing things to me, and I didn't hate it.

Eleven

CYRUS

MY HEARTS SANG AS I WALKED THROUGH THE FRONT DOOR OF my apartment.

I'd spent an entire afternoon with my mate and made him blush several times, and I was under the impression he didn't find me quite as disgusting as I'd originally thought.

I'd caught him staring at my tentacles and tongues several times throughout our meal, and the look on his face when I told him about the other uses for my tongues—priceless.

Gods, he was adorable, and it was so easy to get him riled up, too. Some light flirting and the discussion of my unique anatomy, and Reece flushed bright red.

I knew what I'd be painting tonight.

"Fal?" I called out as I shuffled toward the living area. "You home?"

The apartment was dead silent.

I pulled out my phone and texted Fallon.

Cyrus: Should I expect you for
dinner?

Sure, I felt like his father most of the time, but I really did enjoy Fallon's company. He'd made the last few years of my life less lonely. Even if he was an annoying prick who didn't know how to cook or clean up after himself.

Fallon: Going out tonight after work.
Have a date. Don't expect me until
late. Atlas told me you went out to
lunch with Reece today. 👁 👄 👁
How did it go?

I snorted, thinking about my lunch with Reece. I knew Fallon was asking because he'd anticipated it being a disaster.

It was a shame he was such a gossip. I really wished I had someone I could talk to about all of this, but it wasn't worth the risk. Especially with everything going so well.

Cyrus: It was actually quite nice,
thanks. I think Reece and I are
becoming friends.

Fallon: No. Way. 😲 The two of you
are becoming besties?!

Cyrus: Don't be jealous. No one will
ever replace you, baby 😘

Fallon: 😄

Cyrus: Be safe. Text me if you need a
ride later. I'll be home painting.

Fallon: I certainly will, tentacle
daddy. 🐙

I laughed and shook my head. Fallon was too much. But I guess it made sense that if Atlas was wolf daddy, then I was tentacle daddy.

With Fallon gone for the night, I'd have the apartment all to myself. I could do anything I wanted.

Anything.

My tentacles propelled me over the carpet and down the hall to my room as fast as they could.

How long had it been since I jerked off? I'd been in such a deep depression that nothing had really done it for me.

But seeing Reece stare at my tongues and my tentacles, those forest green eyes shining bright with lust as a blush blossomed over his pale cheeks. The way water sluiced down over his abs and collected in his happy trail, not to mention the bulge it led to. My mate was truly the most beautiful man I'd ever seen.

He ignited something within me that had been snuffed out some time ago. It made me feel invigorated—alive.

I longed for the day I'd taste him, take his cock into my mouth, and tease him with my tongues, use my tentacles to explore that sensitive spot inside him and bring him the type of pleasure that only I could.

Fuck.

The tissue of my mating tentacle swelled, and I scrambled toward my nightstand. I fumbled through the drawers, searching frantically for my stroker.

My eyes caught on the yellow rubber toy and I snatched it up as fast as I could.

The mating tentacle I kept wrapped around my forearm unraveled, leaving behind a light sheen of lubricant.

I held the stroker in the palm of my hand as my tentacle circled the entrance, coating it with lube before plunging inside.

"Fuck," I groaned, sitting on the edge of my bed.

The silicone was soft and tight, gripping the firm length of my tentacle with each of its thrusts.

I focused my thoughts on Reece, what it would be like to slide my mating tentacle over the defined globes of his ass before slipping it inside him. The delicious stretch of his tight hole around the tapered length of my tentacle as I eased it inside.

Gods, I hoped he was vers.

He exuded machismo vibes, but from my experience, those were some of the most enthusiastic bottoms.

My tentacle bored in and out of the stroker, the suckers lightly popping and reattaching with each twist and twirl.

It wasn't enough to hurt, but it *was* enough to ramp up the pleasure. I was told it felt amazing on the prostate.

Fuck, how I yearned to play with Reece's prostate, to make him come so hard, he'd see stars.

The possibilities were endless.

I could fuck his mouth with one mating tentacle, fuck his ass with the other, and stroke his cock with my hand until we both came.

I bet he tasted like heaven.

My breath came out as harsh pants, and a warm tingle began at the base of my mating tentacle. It spread along the length until it reached the tip.

With a loud groan, I came, my tentacle spasming as it flooded the stroker with a stream of sticky cum.

"Fuck," I moaned as I flopped back on the bed, doing the best I could to keep my cum from dripping out of the stroker and onto my stomach.

Apparently, all it took to get me off was the thought of what my mate tasted like.

My phone buzzed on the nightstand.

"Goddamn it, Fallon," I grumbled as one of my tentacles snatched the phone.

Speak of the devil.

It was Reece.

Reece: I had a really nice time at

lunch today. Maybe we can grab a

coffee together soon?

Tears welled up in my eyes, and my hearts thumped wildly in my chest.

This had to be some sort of dream.

Reece Rollins, my mate, wanted to spend more time together.

Cyrus: I'd like that.

I clutched my phone against my chest and cried, letting the tears drip down my face and over my fins.

An orgasm and a text message and I turned into a sobbing mess.

But these were happy tears.

For the first time in a long time, I had hope. I had a sense of purpose.

I had something—someone who made my life worth living.

And that felt pretty damn amazing.

Twelve

REECE

"OH, YOU FUCKING LIKE THAT, DON'T YOU," CYRUS RASPED *against the shell of my ear, the soft pads of his lips tickling my skin with each of his words. "I knew you wanted me to fuck you from the moment we met. It's the tentacles. It's always the tentacles."*

One of the thick tendrils snaked up my abdomen, over my chest, and around my neck. It lightly squeezed the sides of my throat, just tight enough to make speech difficult.

"Tell me what you want, Reece," he whispered as he kissed along my jawline, right where my beard met the column of my neck. His tentacles wrapped over my chest and waist, and he pulled me tighter against him.

The arousal I felt over being at Cyrus's mercy was heady, and my cock was so fucking hard.

I wanted him.

No, I needed him.

"Please fuck me," I grated out, the words strangled by the pressure on my neck.

Cyrus let out a dark chuckle and nipped playfully at my earlobe, pulling hard enough for me to hiss, but not nearly hard enough to draw blood. His webbed hands slid down my body until they caught on the straps of the lace thong around my hips.

"Mmm," he hummed. "Did you wear this just for me?"

I'd always had an interest in lingerie—the feel of the fabrics, the stark contrast of lace against a masculine form—but I'd never been with someone I felt comfortable wearing something like that around.

At least, not until now.

I gave a slow nod and Cyrus's tongues darted out, licking the side of my face in one slow stroke.

"We're going to have a lot of fun playing together." Cyrus tugged the strap of my thong and I moaned as it snapped against my skin with a sharp sting.

He pulled down the thong, freeing my cock from the confines of the lace, rubbing slow circles over my hip to ease the sting.

"Look at you," he said as one of his tentacles traveled around the base of my cock. "You're so fucking pathetic. So horny for me."

"Cyrus," I groaned as he pumped my cock with soft, slick strokes.

It was so smooth, and the suckers added a pleasant dragging sensation each time they attached to my skin.

"Gods, Reece. Your cock is a fucking work of art, you know that? So perfect." Cyrus swirled his hips against my ass in unison with the strokes of his tentacle. "And this body. I'm going to enjoy worshipping it. Making you come again and again."

I whimpered and leaned against him, pushing my ass out, practically begging him to fuck me.

"So impatient," he purred as one of his tentacles slid down my back and teased along my crack.

The slick tip found my hole and swirled gently around the entrance, coating it with lube. A moan slipped past my lips as it breached my tight entrance.

"That's it. That's what you needed, wasn't it?" Cyrus asked as the tip of his tentacle swirled inside me.

"F-fuck yes," I sputtered, my voice hoarse because the tentacle still gripped my neck. "Harder. Please."

Cyrus let out another laugh, his fingers tangling in my hair before he wrenched my head back. "Oh, you want it harder? Deeper, hmm?"

"Please, Cyrus." I wasn't above begging, at least not for this, not for him.

The tentacle ventured deeper, stretching me around it as it widened, until what I presumed were suckers rubbed against the rim of my hole.

"Tell me you want them."

"I want them," I panted.

"Want what?"

"Your suckers. I want your suckers inside me." The tentacle stroking my cock squeezed tighter and I groaned. If—when—Cyrus started playing with my prostate, there was no way I was going to last.

"Good boy," he said, and the tentacle lurched forward, twisting and turning as the suckers breached my entrance again and again.

It was like a series of anal beads that could go on and on forever. I'd never felt anything like it.

"Shit!" I moaned and trembled against Cyrus's body.

"See, there's nothing to be afraid of. You're getting tentacle fucked and you love it, you needy little mess. But I know what you want. You want to feel my suckers on your prostate, don't you?"

The tentacle inside me continued to thrust in and out, twirling as it did so.

I wasn't capable of coherent speech, so I simply whined and nodded my head against Cyrus's harsh grip on my hair.

"All right, I guess I'll let you come," Cyrus huffed.

His grip on my neck tightened as the tentacle inside me found my prostate. It swirled mercilessly over the fleshy bead before one of the suckers attached to it—and attached hard.

"Ahh. Fuck," I panted, trembling against Cyrus as the suction teased my prostate.

The tentacle on my cock stroked faster and another coiled around my balls to hold them in a tight grip.

"Come for me, baby," Cyrus said and pressed his soft lips against the patch of skin behind my ear.

A tingling sensation started in my balls and a strangled noise crept out of my throat.

My body jolted as I came, and thick spurts of cum shot out of my cock, coating Cyrus's tentacles.

"Yes," he moaned.

Slowly, the tentacle around my neck loosened and gently massaged the area where it had strangled me.

I slumped against Cyrus as the last waves of my orgasm washed over me.

"You did so well," Cyrus whispered against my neck. He crossed his arms over my chest, holding me tight against him. "And when you're ready, we'll do it again."

"FUCK!" I BOLTED UPRIGHT AT THE SOUND OF MY ALARM, MY mind feeling fuzzy and disoriented.

A pillow was pressed tight to my crotch, and when I slid it away, there was a sizable wet patch covering the front of my briefs.

"Oh no. Fuck no. No. No. No," I groaned, recalling the dream I had before my alarm woke me up for training.

I threaded my hands through my hair and fell back against my pillows.

This couldn't be happening.

I'd had a wet dream.

About Cyrus.

I didn't even know where to begin when it came to unpacking this.

I mean, these things happened to guys all the time.

I'd had plenty of wet dreams about my friends when I was in high school and even fantasies about weird shit.

But maybe Dream Cyrus was right.

Maybe it was the tentacles.

It's always the tentacles.

What was it Jimenez said the other day about anime? I grabbed my phone from the nightstand and did a quick search for tentacle porn.

There was image after image of tentacles filling orifices. Mouths, pussies, asses. If there was a hole, someone had thought about a tentacle going inside it.

I scrolled down until an anime video titled "Yaoi Tentacle Monster" caught my attention.

My finger hovered over the clip before I slammed it down hard on my phone screen. I needed to do this.

I had to know.

In the animation, a slender guy was being restrained and spread open like a starfish by a giant tentacle monster.

A tentacle monster that looked terrifying.

It was nowhere near as attractive as Cyrus.

Tentacles slithered over the guy's body until one filled his mouth, another filled his ass, and one stroked his cock.

As the monster worked him over, the guy whined and groaned, his body bucking against the restraints. I guess to the right person it was hot, but I didn't find it particularly attractive.

I tossed my phone away and clenched my eyes shut, but my thoughts drifted back to my dream.

Of how assertive Cyrus had been, like he was when he trained me.

How his tentacles would feel wrapped around my throat and stroking my cock.

The soft press of his lips against my skin, and how he would feel inside me.

My cock hardened and strained against the damp material of my briefs.

Fuck.

This was happening.

It wasn't just the tentacles.

It was Cyrus.

Thirteen

CYRUS

"ARE YOU SURE EVERYTHING'S ALL RIGHT?" I ASKED REECE AS he ran his hands through his wet hair. He'd been a little off recently, avoiding eye contact with me and seeming slightly disinterested in training.

"Yeah, I'm fine. I'm just tired, that's all. Uh, I know we had coffee plans, but can I get a rain check on that? I want to get a nap in before my shift starts. I'd try while we're on rounds, but Jimenez never shuts his damn mouth."

I'd been riding such a high from lunch with him the other day that this felt like a major blow. We'd taken a huge step forward and now it felt like we were taking two steps back.

Maybe the flirting had been too much for him?

But he was the one who texted me about getting coffee . . .

My expression must have told him what I was thinking.

"Hey." Reece reached out and grabbed my arm, his thumb brushing lightly over my tentacle. "I promise everything is fine. I didn't sleep well. That's all." He gave me a soft smile before he pulled his hand away.

I expected him to wipe his hand on his shorts, like he'd done at the party after we shook hands, but there was none of that.

My mate had offered me a comforting touch and wasn't repulsed by it after the fact.

I nodded, the tentacle he'd touched clenching and relaxing, almost like it was pleased with his attention. "Yeah, wouldn't want you to be tired for your shift. And if you ever need to cancel swim practice, just shoot me a text."

He looked down at his feet and shook his head, his cheeks reddening slightly. "Nah, I wouldn't do that. I have a race to prepare for."

He meant that he wouldn't do that to *me*.

It was all starting to make sense now.

The way that Reece looked at me, the shy smiles and blushing cheeks, asking me out for coffee.

Was it possible Reece was interested in me?

As much as that thrilled me, I couldn't help but wonder how that made him feel.

Yes, I wanted to be close to my mate, but if he needed space to process things, I was happy to provide him with that.

I'd waited centuries for him, and I'd give him as long as he needed to work through his feelings.

"You get some rest. And, uh, if you're bored on rounds later, I always have my phone. If you want to chat." My tentacles clenched my arms tight with anticipation.

"Yeah, I'll shoot you a text for sure. I'll see you tomorrow."

"See ya then."

He gave me a little wave before hefting his bag over his shoulder and walking out of the pool room, but not before Fallon slipped past him.

"Sup, man?" Fallon tipped his head at Reece as he trotted by, his tail flicking behind him. "Yo, Cy," he said, and whistled at me. "How's it going?"

The griffin's feathers were slightly disheveled and his beady eyes were rimmed red.

"It's going. Long night?" I asked as he came to a stop beside me.

He shook his head and clicked his beak. "It was wild, bro. I hooked up with this super hot chick."

"Oh? Is she cuffing season material?" I raised my eyebrows at him, but I already knew what the womanizer was going to say.

"Nah, man. There's no way. She was way out of my league. It was a one-night-stand type of deal."

"Did you get her number?"

He looked away and tapped the concrete with his talon. "I, uh, I sort of left before she woke up."

"Fallon, what the fuck? That's low, even for you."

"There's no way a chick like her would be into me long term. It was a one-time-for-curiosity's-sake type of thing."

"You're projecting. What Atlas and Tegan have isn't a curiosity's-sake type of thing."

He laughed under his breath. "Yeah, but those two are fated mates. It's different. Hot chicks like to fuck me out of curiosity. They want to see what I have going on down there, not spend the rest of their lives trying to kiss someone with a beak. I get it."

Fallon's anatomy was unique. With his talons and beak, there were certain parts of intimacy he couldn't offer his partners. In the fourteen years I'd known him, he'd never had a long-term relationship. Just random hookups.

It was rare for him to be so vulnerable. Usually, he carried himself with unshakable confidence. He must have it bad for this girl.

I crossed my arms over my chest, giving him what I hoped was a disapproving look. "I think you should have been a gentleman and said goodbye. Maybe she would have given you her number."

"Cy, I've been through this time and time again. It's better this way."

"If you say so," I sighed, and we both stared at the calm water of the pool.

"How's it been with Reece? Is Ranger Dick following your advice?"

Normally, I'd find a nickname like that funny. However, hearing Fallon speak about my mate that way enraged me, but I did my best to control my anger. Fallon didn't know he was my mate, and he certainly didn't know the real Reece Rollins. "He isn't a dick, Fal. The whole asshole facade is a front. He's actually quite sensitive."

"Just be careful about getting close to a guy like that. You know he's trying to prove himself with Tegan. He could be using you to look good."

I was fucking livid now.

My color darkened to a deep blue and my fins flared as I rose up on my tentacles until I towered over Fallon.

"Whatever theories you have about Reece, you're wrong. I appreciate the fact that you care about me, but Reece and I are friends, and I won't tolerate you speaking negatively about him." My voice was a sharp hiss, the words slipping out through bared teeth.

"Noted," Fallon said, holding his talons out defensively.

I took a deep breath to slow my heart rates and lowered down on my tentacles. It wasn't often I lost my temper, but some primal part of me felt fiercely protective of my mate.

"I'm sorry. I didn't mean to lose my shit. I just think there are a lot of misunderstandings when it comes to Reece. He's created this persona of himself that isn't who he actually is."

"If that's what you think, Cy, I believe you. Maybe we can have a boys' night soon. Me, you, Atlas, Reece, maybe Kael. Oh, and Javier!"

Even with the disastrous results from their first meeting, Fallon had been dying to hang out with Javier again. And the idea of Reece coming over to our place, seeing my mate in *my* home, it would be a great opportunity to close some of the distance he'd been putting between us.

"We should. I think it would be good for Atlas and Reece to spend some time together. He might feel more relaxed without his sister around."

"Consider it done. I'll talk with wolf daddy and get it all set up."

I snorted. "That reminds me, we have to have a talk about 'tentacle daddy.'"

Fallon checked his phone and whistled. "Well, would you look at the time? I have to get to work!"

I laughed as he walked backward out the door.

"I'll see you at home, tentacle daddy!" He chirped with laughter as he disappeared into the hallway.

Fourteen

REECE

MY STOMACH CHURNED AS I WALKED THROUGH THE FRONT door of Leviathan Fitness. I was on edge about seeing Cyrus, about being around him, and was acting like I wasn't having all of these absurd dreams about him.

I felt bad for canceling our coffee date the other day, but there was no way I could sit across from him and make small talk.

Oh, hey, Cyrus! Nice tentacles you've got there. Wanna shove them up my ass?

There was definitely chemistry between us, or at least I thought there was, but I'd never had these kinds of romantic feelings for someone. It terrified the fuck out of me.

And I wasn't even sure if Cyrus was *actually* into me.

He could just be messing with me.

Gods, if I was rejected by the first person I pursued a romantic relationship with, I don't think my ego could handle it.

I stopped in front of the pool room and took a deep breath, willing myself to calm down before I stepped through the doorway.

As usual, Cyrus was already there, his smooth body gliding gracefully beneath the surface of the water. He didn't seem to notice me, so I slipped into the locker room as fast as I could.

Fuck, he looked good when he swam, the lengths of his tentacles rippling as they propelled him through the water.

"Motherfucker," I grumbled as I struggled to pull my jammers over my now semi-erect cock. The things were already tight as fuck, but when you were packing what I was, it was about a thousand times more difficult.

I could already tell today was going to go poorly.

There was no way I could keep doing this to myself.

Sure, I wanted to place well in the triathlon, but this was about more than that. This entire thing with Cyrus was forcing me to examine things about myself that I wasn't sure I was ready to tackle. There was also the fact that he was my sister's mate's best friend. Tegan would flip her ever-loving shit if I made a move on Cyrus.

I'd have to tell Cyrus I didn't need his help anymore.

After practice today, I'd come up with some excuse and try to end things as painlessly as I could.

When I returned to the pool deck, Cyrus was floating on his back in the center of the pool.

"Hey there," he said as I approached the edge. "Feeling well rested today?" With ease, he spun forward so that he was facing me and gave me a bright smile.

"Sort of." I rubbed the back of my neck and shifted my gaze from Cyrus. "I've been having a hard time sleeping."

"Hmm." Cyrus nodded. "Well, I guess we're going to have to train harder." He smirked and jetted over to where I was standing. "I thought today I'd watch you from the bottom of the pool. Really get a sense of how your form has progressed and what we can do to improve it. Sound good?"

"Yeah." I shrugged. "If you think it'll help." At least with him in the water, I wouldn't be subjected to that fucking whistle.

Cyrus tilted his head, his wide eyes narrowing slightly. "Is something bothering you?"

Gods, he was a perceptive fucker.

"Nope." I jumped into the pool, coating Cyrus with a spray of water.

"You're such a wanker," he said the moment my head broke the surface.

"No point in denying it."

Cyrus dove underwater and I stared as his parachute fanned out beneath me.

Laps. Up and back. Focus on form. He spoke to me in my head, his sultry British accent spreading warmth throughout my body. I could already feel my cock straining against my jammers, but if Cyrus noticed, he didn't comment.

How in the fuck was I supposed to focus like this?

I got into position and took a few deep breaths to get my mind straight, but before I could even kick off the wall, Cyrus chimed in my head again.

Are you training or taking an afternoon dip? We don't have all day.

What the fuck was his deal today? Was he upset with me about the whole coffee thing? This was even more of a reason to call this whole thing off.

Whether he was teasing or serious, I channeled my annoyance into productivity, pushing off from the wall as hard as I could. My body slid through the water, and before I lost momentum, I started to make big strokes with my arms and gently kick my feet.

There was so much to focus on. Was my core activated and my body taut? Were my hands and arms in the correct position? Were my hips aligned with my body? And of course I had to breathe.

All things considered, I felt like I was doing well as I closed in on the opposite end of the pool. Much better than I was before I started working with Cyrus.

Apparently, that wasn't the case.

Your legs are sinking, I heard Cyrus say telepathically. *Straighten up.*

On my swim back to the other end, I lowered my head like he taught me, hoping that would fix the problem.

Stop. Stop. Stop! he shouted. His words pounded into my skull, making me panic mid-stroke.

I choked on water, coughing from the burn of the salt. Cyrus shot out of the water next to me, his bumpy brows pinched together in a scowl.

"How are you not getting this?" he asked. He sounded as frustrated as I felt. "These are basic principles. Did you even watch the videos I sent you?"

My chest felt tight, and not from water inhalation. The way he was chastising me reminded me of my dad. I couldn't tell if I was hurt that Cyrus was acting that way or if it pissed me off. From the sinking feeling in my stomach, I think it was the former.

Once I could finally speak, I rasped, "Of course I did."

"Good. Now get into position and do it again!" he snapped, then disappeared beneath the surface.

FOR TWO HOURS, I WAS SUBJECTED TO CYRUS'S SCRUTINY. Over and over, he'd chime into my brain and chastise me on my form, my lack of focus, et cetera, until I decided I'd had enough.

It was too real for me. Too much of a reminder of the things I'd endured during Little League, my high school lacrosse games, and when I first started working under my father at the Parks Department.

Without a word, I swam over to the side of the pool, climbed the ladder, and headed straight for the locker room without even offering Cyrus a glance.

"What was that, Rollins?" Cyrus asked as he burst through the door of the locker room. "It's like everything we've been working on went right out the window."

I whipped around to face him and held my arms out. "What's with you, Cyrus? You were riding my fucking ass the entire session."

He shuffled closer, rising up onto the tips of his tentacles so he stood slightly taller than me. The normal light blue-green tone of his skin had been replaced by a deep blue, almost black color.

"I was riding your ass because you were acting like you don't even want this," he hissed through sharp, clenched teeth.

I stepped into his space so we were chest to chest, my breath coming out as labored pants. "You don't know shit about what I want."

"Then why don't you fucking show me?" Cyrus snarled, and one of his tentacles darted out to smack the locker right next to my head.

I glared at him, my heart racing as a confusing mixture of adrenaline and arousal coursed through my body.

Cyrus was scary when he was angry, but he was also sort of hot.

Was I really going to do this?

The answer was a resounding yes.

I lurched forward, wrapped my arms around his neck, and slammed my mouth against his so hard, our teeth clacked.

"Fuck," he groaned, and parted his lips, letting my tongue slip inside without hesitation. Like he'd been waiting for this.

Generally, I didn't kiss. That was a part of my whole casual touch thing, but this? This wasn't kissing. This was hot, heady desire stoked by his lips on mine and the possessive strokes of his tongues.

Cyrus pinned me against the lockers, the cool metal stinging my exposed back as he pushed his hips against mine. His tentacles wrapped around my legs, spreading them apart while his hands explored my body. He was everywhere. Hands and tongues and tentacles, touching me in ways I'd only dreamt of.

"Is this what you wanted?" he asked through frenzied kisses, thrusting his hips into my already hard cock. "Is this why you couldn't focus?"

"Yes. Holy gods, yes," I moaned as Cyrus kissed his way down my collarbone.

The party. The tension. The dreams.

So much had led up to this moment between us. A moment that a month ago would have seemed like an impossibility.

But there we were—kissing, touching, and dry-humping each other like we couldn't get enough.

"Tell me." Cyrus broke our kiss to stare at me. His cheeks were flushed dark blue and his chest heaved against mine with each word he spoke. It was comforting to know he was just as affected by this as I was. "Tell me where you want to go with this, Reece."

I'd never felt as vulnerable as I felt at that moment, so *exposed*.

"I want you to fuck me." My voice was a barely there whisper. But it was loud enough for Cyrus to hear.

"Oh, thank fuck," he gritted out before slamming his mouth to mine again. Those twin tongues stroked against mine possessively, more of a claiming than a kiss. "Where?" he asked, and gripped my cock through my jammers.

"Ahhh." I groaned against his lips and he laughed. "The shower stall?"

"Mm-hmm," he mumbled.

Before I knew what was happening, Cyrus was carrying me,

the muscular lengths of his tentacles supporting our combined weight and shuffling us toward the stall without breaking our kiss.

"Holy fuck!" I tightened my grip on his neck.

I knew he was strong, but I didn't think he was that strong.

"You like that, Rollins?" he asked as his tentacles slammed the door to the shower stall open and we stumbled inside.

"Yes," I hummed, kissing his face and neck, putting my lips on any part of him I could reach. "So fucking hot."

There was something about Cyrus's presence that comforted me. With him, I wasn't concerned with being the best. I could just *be*.

"How are we doing this?" I rasped.

In all honesty, I had no fucking idea about kraken anatomy. I mean, I'd had those dreams, but for all I knew, Cyrus could be packing a monster cock under that parachute.

He broke our kiss and ran his webbed hand along my jaw. "Well, I didn't anticipate having this conversation today, but I don't really have any holes that are fuckable. So, if you want to top, you can fuck my mouth."

Shit.

I bet those tongues would feel amazing milking every last drop of cum out of my cock, but that wasn't what I wanted right now.

I wanted Cyrus to fuck my brains out.

"No," I huffed, getting impatient. "I told you I wanted you to fuck me." I rotated my hips against his. "Do you have a cock under there or . . . ?"

Cyrus laughed again and unraveled the tentacles he kept wrapped around his arms. "I don't have a cock, but I have these." The tentacles wriggled in the air playfully. "My hectocotylus, my mating tentacles."

Oh my gods! Those are his cocks!

"So, you're fucking telling me the first time we met, you touched me with your cock." Realization hit. "You fucking touch everything with your cock!" I shouted a little too loudly for two people who were about to fuck in a semipublic place.

Cyrus pressed his palm to my mouth. "Will you relax? It isn't the same for my kind. Now, do you want me to fuck you or not?" He raised one of his bumpy eyebrows in question.

Yeah, it was weird—different—but even with that little detail about his tentacles, my cock was still throbbing. I still wanted him more than I'd ever wanted anything in my entire life.

I nodded and he slid his hand away. "Where do you want me?" I asked.

Cyrus smiled, pecking me on the lips one last time before his tentacles spun me around to face the shower wall.

The tile was cold on my cheek as I struggled to pull down my jammers. The wet material stuck to me like a second skin.

"Let me help you," Cyrus purred in my ear. He slid his hands down my chest and over my stomach before slipping them beneath the band of my jammers.

"Motherfucker," I groaned as he worked them off my waist.

My cock jutted forward, smearing precum on the shower wall as his tentacles pulled the swimsuit down over my muscular thighs. Cyrus pressed against my back and gripped my cock, using the palm of his hand to spread my precum down my shaft before giving it a few slow pumps. His soft palm gliding over my cock felt like heaven, and I rocked my hips, demanding more.

"Your cock is just as pretty as you are, Reece," he said, his lips grazing my temple with every word. "I can't wait to suck you off and watch that handsome face as you come undone. Would you like that?"

Fuck yes, I would.

I couldn't bring myself to say it, though. My mouth was too preoccupied with the grunts and groans Cyrus seemed to effortlessly pull out of my body with his touch.

He pumped faster and a tentacle slid up my chest before settling on top of my nipple. The suckers coating the underside latched on and I let out a low moan, throwing my head against Cyrus's shoulder and thrusting into his hand.

"You would like that. Look at you." He laughed against my neck before dragging the pointed tips of his teeth over my skin.

"Cyrus, please," I whimpered.

I'd dreamt about this. I'd beg and plead for it if I had to.

"All right, all right, Rollins. It's coming." The firm length of his mating tentacle slid down my crack, but my ass clenched tight, stopping it from reaching my hole.

"Relax for me," he whispered, rubbing his free hand along my jaw. "It's self-lubricating. It'll go in nice and easy."

Self-lubricating.

I took a deep breath, focusing on the feel of Cyrus's hand on my cock and the warm flutter of his breath against my neck as the tip of his tentacle circled my hole, coating it in a layer of lube.

It pushed in slow and steady, making my breath hitch when it was finally inside.

Fuck.

It was so smooth. The familiar stretch was there, but there was none of the resistance that came with a human cock, at least not yet.

"Breathe, darling," Cyrus instructed. "You're doing so well."

Darling.

I'd never been called something so sweet.

Cyrus nuzzled against my shoulder as the tentacle worked its way in deeper. With him, there was no feral thrusting or the slapping of skin on skin that I was used to. Cyrus's body remained still as he calmly fucked my ass, sliding his tentacle in and out while I melted against the shower wall. The only tell that he was enjoying this as much as I was were his ragged breaths against my back.

"You're almost to the suckers," he said, his voice tight. "Do you want them?"

My thoughts went straight to my dream and what those fleshy anal beads felt like slipping in and out of me again and again. It was enough to have my balls tightening up and a tingling sensation forming at the base of my spine.

"Please," I whimpered through clenched teeth. "I don't know how long I'm going to last, though."

Living out this sexual fantasy was proving to be a lot for me.

"Shh," Cyrus whispered, stroking my jaw again. "That doesn't matter. I want you to enjoy this. I want it to be good for you."

And it was. More than good, actually.

When was the last time I'd been with someone who actively wanted sex to be enjoyable for me? It was usually just random hookups where both parties selfishly chased their own release as fast as possible.

This was different, though, just like everything with Cyrus was.

He put my comfort and my pleasure before his own.

Cyrus pushed in farther, my tight entrance throbbing as the soft suckers ventured deeper.

"Cyrus," I moaned, arching my back and thrusting my cock into his fist.

"That's it, my needy boy. I'll give you what you want."

He continued stroking my cock with rough tugs, and the moment the tip of his mating tentacle pulsed over my prostate, I came with a loud groan. My thighs quaked and my hips jerked, coating his hand and the shower wall with streams of cum.

"There it is," Cyrus said as he kissed along my neck, stroking me through my orgasm until I went limp against his chest.

Fifteen

CYRUS

I GENTLY SLID OUT OF REECE BEFORE FINISHING WITH A LOW moan, my mating tentacle spasming and painting the dimples on his lower back with thick streaks of cum.

Considering he had work after this, I thought coming *on* him instead of *in* him was the polite thing to do. Although the thought of my cum leaking out of him all day, marking him as mine, appealed to me on a primal level.

"Can I clean you up?" I asked, reaching in front of Reece to start the shower.

"Sure," he mumbled. He was clearly in that postorgasm haze, satiated and sleepy, meaning I'd done my job.

The waterfall showerhead coated us in a light spray of warm water, rinsing away our cum and the lube left behind from my mating tentacle. I pumped body wash out of the wall mount dispenser into my hand, creating a sudsy lather before I rubbed it over the corded muscles of Reece's body.

"Fuck," he groaned, leaning into my touch. "That feels nice."

"I'm glad you think so. Aftercare is important."

Reece let out a shy laugh. "I, uh, don't have much experience with that."

Well, I have a lot to make up for, then.

When we were all clean, I shut off the tap and turned us around until my back was braced against the shower wall and Reece rested on my chest.

I couldn't believe this was happening.

My mate had initiated this between us.

He'd wanted this.

Wanted me.

"Is this okay?" I asked, knowing how he felt about touching.

"S'good," he mumbled and brought his muscular arm up to wrap around the back of my neck. His fingers softly brushed my fins and I shuddered.

Lying collapsed on top of each other in a shower stall wasn't exactly romantic, but it was the best aftercare I was able to offer at present.

"Sorry if I went a little overboard today with training," I whispered, his wet hair tickling my lips.

Reece shook his head against my chest. "You didn't go overboard. It just—reminded me of something. Well, someone."

"Of who?"

His deep laugh echoed off the tile walls. "Gods, Cyrus. You really want to make me come harder than I have in my entire life, then grill me about my childhood trauma?" His fingers absentmindedly trailed over the fins along my neck. "Can we at least go out to dinner first? Or maybe fuck in a bed?"

"I want to make sure I do better next time, is all. We don't have to talk about it right now." I ran my hand along his stomach and through his happy trail. "And I'd very much like to take you out to dinner and then fuck you in an actual bed."

"Awfully presumptuous of you to assume that this is going to happen again." There was a playful edge to his voice, but his comment still made me stiffen up.

"Well, is it going to happen again?"

Reece turned so he was facing me, propping himself up with his elbow on my chest. "I mean, I'd like it to." He paused for a second, digging his teeth into his lower lip before he glanced up at me with those emerald eyes. "I like you, Cy. No matter what I keep telling myself or how hard I try to deny it, the thoughts I have about you won't go away. Something about you, about this, is different."

"Did you ever think it might be you that's different, too? You've grown so much, Reece."

He looked away and smiled. "You think so?"

"I mean, the Reece Rollins I first met would have never let me fuck him in a shower stall."

His cheeks turned crimson and he rubbed his fingers along his temple. "Shut up."

"Come here, my little tentacle slut." I used my tentacle to bring his head forward until his mouth connected with mine.

"Fuck you," Reece grumbled against my lips.

"I'd happily go again." And I could, as many times as my mate wanted.

"As much as I'd enjoy that, I need to get going or I'm gonna be late for work," he said, slowly pulling away.

"Right, right. Parks Department stuff. Got it. Forgot that some people have normal jobs."

Reece stiffly rose to his feet, and I shuffled to a standing position next to him.

"Here." I passed him his jammers.

"Thanks."

He cracked open the door of the shower stall and stuck his head out, checking to make sure the locker room was clear.

Satisfied, he slipped out of the stall with his jammers covering his cock, and I followed behind him.

I still couldn't believe this had happened, and even though Reece admitted to wanting to do it again, I wasn't exactly sure what this meant for the two of us. Obviously, I knew this didn't make us a couple, but how were things going to go moving forward?

I was admiring the way Reece's ass flexed as he pulled on his briefs when he turned around to face me.

"Listen . . ." He scrubbed his hand along the back of his neck.

I clenched my jaw, bracing for impact.

There was no way something good was going to come out of this. If he wasn't ready, he wasn't ready . . .

"I want to keep training with you, and"—he motioned between the two of us—"I want to keep doing *this*." His voice was a shy whisper, his cheeks flushed bright red. "But I'd like it if we could keep this between the two of us."

I blinked rapidly, in total shock at what my mate was saying. I opened my mouth to speak, but Reece cut me off.

"I don't mean forever, but for right now. I, uh, this is all so new. I need some time to wrap my head around things."

"I understand completely."

I'd give him an eternity if he needed it. I was just happy he didn't immediately regret this.

Reece pulled his shirt over his head and stepped into my space. "Thank you."

He stared at me for a moment before sliding his hand along the back of my head and pressing his lips to mine in a quick kiss. "I'll text you later, okay?"

"I'd like that." My tentacle trailed along his arm as he pulled away.

"Bye."

"Bye," I said softly.

He gathered his things, then slipped out the door, leaving me alone in the locker room.

"Fuck," I mumbled under my breath and sat down on the bench between the rows of lockers.

My hearts raced, a warm happiness radiating from my chest to the tips of my tentacles.

I'd fucked my mate for the first time in the shower stall of my best friend's gym.

I couldn't believe this was happening.

Reece's strange behavior over the past few weeks finally made sense.

He had been avoiding me because he was attracted to me.

It was like a weight was lifted off me, and for the first time in a long time, I felt lighter. I was beginning to think that maybe my hopes and dreams about what Reece and I could be weren't so far-fetched after all.

Sixteen

REECE

"WHAT'S GOT YOU IN SUCH A GOOD MOOD TODAY?" JIMENEZ asked as I passed him his iced coffee. It was my turn to treat.

"What do you mean?" I said, taking a sip of my coffee, forcing myself not to smile.

Yeah, I'd had a pretty fucking great morning, but I wasn't about to kiss and tell.

At least not yet.

And definitely not to Jimenez. He was the closest thing I had to a best friend, and while he seemed trustworthy, his sister was best friends with my sister. I didn't want to risk things.

"I don't know," he said. "You were, like, whistling and shit when I picked you up. It's very out of character for you."

"What are you, a detective or some shit, Jimenez? I had a good training session this morning, that's all."

Fought with my trainer. Kissed him. Got tentacle fucked. You know, a typical Wednesday. Nothing too crazy.

"All right, all right. Where am I going?" he asked as he pulled the work truck onto the main road that ran through Briar Glenn.

"The parks have been pretty clean. Why don't we head back to the office for a little bit? I need to catch up on some paperwork."

To be honest, we spent the majority of our time on the clock cruising around, checking on the parks and playing fields.

It wasn't the most exciting job, but someone had to do it.

"Sounds good, boss man. I wanna browse my dating apps anyway."

"Jimenez, what the fuck are you doing on dating apps?"

The guy was handsome. Funny. Kind. It surprised me that no one had locked him down yet.

"It's rough out here, man." Jimenez glanced over at me. "I keep swiping and swiping, but I can't find someone who checks all the boxes, you know? I swear if I see one more person holding a dead fish in their profile pic . . ." He clenched the steering wheel tight and shook his head. "Are you seeing anyone?"

The question made me stiffen up.

"You know I don't date. I have enough shit going on in my life as it is." It was true, I had a lot going on, but Cyrus fit right into my life. Well, other than the whole secrecy thing.

"You really don't, though. You never get lonely?" He pulled the truck to a stop in front of city hall before looking over at me.

I thought about it for a moment.

Yeah, I missed having sex on the regular, but I'd never felt a deep enough connection with anyone to want to keep them around for more than just the occasional hookup.

And I'd never been in love, that was for fucking sure.

But presently, there was someone in my life I enjoyed being around. Someone who made me laugh with his stupid fucking flirting and made me come with his stupid fucking tentacles. It just so happened that person was my sister's mate's best friend, which complicated things.

"I mean, sometimes I do, but I figure if I meet someone, I meet them. I'm not going to force anything."

Jimenez shot me that winning smile, all white teeth and perfect fucking dimples. "I didn't know you were such a romantic, boss."

"Oh, fuck off, Jimenez."

I stepped out of the truck and headed into city hall with Jimenez following behind me.

Constructed during the town's founding, city hall was one of the oldest buildings in Briar Glenn. There had been some slight updates and additions over the years, but for the most part, the building kept its original historical charm. Our office was there, along with the mayor's and all the various municipal departments that kept Briar Glenn running.

"Hey, Bonnie," I said, giving our receptionist a little wave.

She was a sweet old lady with a white bouffant updo and big bug-eyed glasses who had to be well into her seventies. She'd been working here since I was a kid, and even though I was technically her superior, I treated her with the utmost respect. I wouldn't be nearly as good at my job without her.

"Hello, Reece, Javier." She flashed us both a pleasant smile, but it quickly disappeared when she noticed our coffee cups. "I see you just got done with your afternoon coffee run."

"Ah, shi—" She gave me a disapproving look. Bonnie hated it when I cussed. "Shucks, Bonnie," I said, correcting myself. "I'll call you next time for your order."

"Please do. Oh, and Reece," she said, "I pulled the permits you requested for the triathlon. They're on your desk waiting for your approval, then I'll give them to the mayor to sign."

"Thanks, Bonnie. I don't know what we'd do without you."

"See ya, Bonnie," Javier said, and we made our way to our office.

The Parks Department was sequestered in the back of the building, one giant room separated into two separate workspaces. Javier's desk was in the main space, by the printer and filing cabinets, and my office was behind a heavy wooden door.

Javier sat down in his chair and started up his computer.

"You all good out here?" I asked.

"Yep." He pointed to a stack of papers on his desk. "I'm gonna file these maintenance reports, then take a little afternoon nap."

We didn't get an official lunch break, so I really didn't give a fuck if he wanted to take a nap at his desk. I'd been known to do the same.

"Sounds good. I'll be in my office if you need anything."

I stepped inside my office and sat down at my desk. Just like Bonnie said, the permit paperwork was there, neat and organized, with little flags on each page notifying me where to sign. That woman deserved a raise and all the coffee her heart desired.

I scribbled my signature and set the papers aside to return to her later. For the next thirty minutes, I worked on my computer, filing reports and filling out time sheets, making sure everything was documented. If I wanted to push the mayor to hire someone else for the department, I had to bring him documentation of all the overtime Jimenez and I had been pulling.

Buzz.

Buzz.

I quickly snatched my phone from where it sat on my desk.

About time.

I'd been waiting all fucking morning for Cyrus to text me.

I guess I could have texted him first, but I didn't want to seem too desperate.

I leaned back in my chair and peeked through the glass panel of my office door. Jimenez was slumped over his desk, mouth gaping open with light snores slipping out. It was probably the only time the guy wasn't attractive.

Confident I wouldn't be bothered, I unlocked my phone and read the message.

> **Cyrus:** Hey there. I thought you were
> going to text me. I was getting
> impatient.

I bit my lip and grinned down at my phone screen. Apparently, we were both playing the waiting game. I felt a slight sense of satisfaction that Cyrus was the first one to crack. Call it my competitive spirit or whatever.

> **Reece:** Maybe I wanted you to text
> me first.

> **Cyrus:** I get you off AND I have to
> text first? I can already tell that
> there's going to be an uneven
> distribution of work here.

> **Reece:** What can I say? I'm a pillow
> princess 🙍

There was some truth to that statement.

Don't get me wrong, giving was great, but so was receiving with the absolute least amount of work necessary.

> **Cyrus:** I gathered as much. What are
> you doing right now?

> Reece: Sitting in my office. You?

> Cyrus: Thinking about how good your
> ass felt stretched around my
> tentacle, if I'm being honest.

"Fuck," I mumbled, and ran my fingers through my hair. One little reminder of what we'd gotten up to this morning was all it took to have my cock standing at attention.

> Reece: You felt so fucking good. I'm
> pretty sure I have marks on my
> nipple from your tentacle.

> Cyrus: Oh yeah? Show me those
> nips.

I snorted. *Nips.*

> Reece: I'm at work.

> Cyrus: Show me.

I leaned back in my chair and craned my neck to get another look at Jimenez. He was still fast asleep.

Was I really going to send Cyrus nudes while I was at work?

Yes, yes, I absolutely was.

I quickly closed the blinds to my office, clicked the lock, and started to unbutton my shirt.

This was crazy.

But it was also exciting.

I liked it when Cyrus was dominant and demanding. It made me want to please him.

I stood in front of the mirror and opened my shirt. Light purple sucker marks trailed across my chest before turning into a deep purple bruise right over my nipple.

The fucker had given me a purple nurple.

I was going to have to wear a compression shirt in the pool until these faded. All it would take was one look from someone at the gym to know what the two of us had gotten up to.

My phone buzzed again.

Cyrus: I'm waiting.

I flexed my arm, pushed out my bruised pec, and snapped a picture. Before sending it over, I added the caption Look what you did to my fucking nipple.

Cyrus replied almost immediately. That's a good boy. Fuck. I can't wait to suck on those nipples while I jerk your cock.

"Shit," I hissed and palmed my dick through my pants.

I mean, the door was locked and Jimenez was passed the fuck out. And I was the boss. I didn't need to explain myself.

I bolted over to my desk and threw myself down onto the chair. My fingers fumbled with my belt, and I cursed under my breath as I fought to pull down my zipper.

"Fuck," I groaned the moment my hand made contact with my already throbbing cock.

A bead of precum formed along the slit of my head as I worked my cock with slow strokes. With my free hand, I typed out a message to Cyrus.

Reece: I'm touching myself under my desk.

Fuck, I loved being a tease.

Cyrus: Show me.

It was too easy. I knew he'd play along.

I set my phone to record and sent Cyrus a video of me smearing my precum over my head with my thumb before giving my cock two quick jerks. You could hear my heavy breathing in the background of the clip.

Cyrus: So obedient. So fucking filthy.
Stroke that cock and imagine me bending
you over your desk and fucking you.

I loved seeing this side of Cyrus. It was such a stark contrast to his usual playful demeanor.

I leaned back in my chair and dug my teeth into my lower lip, thinking about what it would feel like with those tentacles pinning me to my desk while Cyrus used his suckers to massage my prostate. What it would feel like as each row of suckers worked in and out of my ass.

My balls were already tingling with the urge to come.

Reece: I wish you were inside me
right now.

My phone buzzed with a message from Cyrus. It was a link to a blue-green silicone dildo.

A silicone dildo that was shaped like a tentacle.

Cyrus: Send me your address. I want
you to use this and think of me.

Fuck. My kraken—boyfriend?—was sending me a tentacle dildo to use and think of him. I was positive there would be stipulations with this gift, in the form of me sending Cyrus videos of me fucking myself with it.

And I was more than okay with that.

"F-fuck," I stammered, and came with a deep groan, catching the thin ribbons of cum with a tissue before they could drip down onto my pants.

My phone vibrated as my body jerked with the last few waves of my orgasm. I wiped my hands, tucked my cock back into my pants, and threw away the cum-soaked wad of tissues before opening my phone.

It was another text from Cyrus.

Cyrus: Did you come?

Holy fuck, did I.

                                        Reece: Yeah

Cyrus: What were you thinking
about?

                          Reece: Using my new toy for you.

Cyrus: Good boy.

Good boy.

His praise sent heat rushing straight to my cheeks. I'd gotten off to him twice today, and that still wasn't enough.

My phone vibrated again, but this time it was a phone call.

"Fuck," I mumbled to myself when I saw who was calling.

Tegan.

Why was she calling me?

She never called me.

And why did it have to be right now? I felt like I'd just been caught in the act. Like she knew that something was going on between me and Cyrus. I knew that wasn't the case, but the fear was still there, lingering in the back of my mind.

I accepted the call and cleared my throat. "Hello?"

"Hey!"

"What's up?" I asked. "Is everything okay?"

"Everything's fine!" Tegan rushed to say. "I, um, I just wanted to see if you wanted to come over to Mom's on Saturday. I have to grab something out of the garage and Mom's going to make dinner."

"Oh!" I said, sounding just as shocked as I was. We were going from barely speaking to making plans. I wasn't mad about it, though. "Yeah! Sure."

"Cool. Um, I'll see you there around four?"

"Sounds good," I said.

"Okay, bye!"

"Bye."

I threw my head back and groaned, because what the fuck had I gotten myself into? I'd just fucked Atlas's best friend and made plans to do it again, and now I had to be around her while I was keeping this giant secret. Guilt tied my stomach in a knot, but there was no way I was cutting things off with Cyrus. As terrified as it made me, there was potential between us. Feelings I'd never felt before. For now—for him—I'd happily live in this lie.

Seventeen

CYRUS

SINCE OUR FIRST GLORIOUS FUCK, I'D BEEN OVER THE MOON. While it wasn't the romantic encounter of my dreams, it was still progress with my mate. With every waking moment, I was consumed by thoughts of him. Fantasies of our future together. Vivid memories of the warmth of his skin and the steady tempo of his beating heart against my chest.

Because of his work schedule, we hadn't been able to squeeze in another training session this week, but we did exchange frequent text messages. Just the usual What are you up to? and How was your day? It was almost like we were in a real relationship.

I grinned at the pair of vibrant green eyes staring back at me from the canvas. I was putting the finishing touches on yet another painting of Reece when my phone started to vibrate.

Atlas was calling.

Interesting. I was more of a text message kind of guy, and he was aware of that . . .

I tapped the phone screen with my tentacle, putting the call on speaker. "Hello."

"Hey, are you home?" he asked.

"Yes, why?"

"I was wondering if I could come over for a little bit and hang out."

I set my brush down and stared at the partially painted canvas sitting in front of me. I wasn't really busy. My creative well had been overflowing since I met Reece. I could finish this painting anytime, but it was rare that one of my oldest friends wanted to get together with just me. "Uh, sure. I'm not doing anything."

"Are you hungry?" I could hear his wolfish grin through the phone.

I snorted. "Are you?" I asked, already knowing the answer.

"Of course I am. I was going to see if you wanted me to bring some food."

"I have stuff here I can make us."

He chuckled, a deep rumbling laugh. "I was hoping you'd say that."

"I figured." Like Fallon, Atlas enjoyed my cooking. "Do you remember the passcode?"

He paused for a moment before giving me an awkward, "Yes?"

I rolled my eyes. "I'll text it to you. Just let yourself in."

"Okay. See ya in a few."

I quickly cleaned up my supplies and turned my easel away from the doorway on the off chance Atlas made his way into my studio. It was unlikely, but I'd rather he didn't get an eyeful of his future brother-in-law's naked body.

Just as I was shuffling out into the hall, the front door opened, and Atlas stepped inside. *Gods, was he sitting outside the complex when he called?*

"Hey, buddy," he said. His ears perked up and his tail started to wag, gently slapping against the wall.

"Hey," I called out over my shoulder as I scuttled to the kitchen with him following behind me. "No Tegan today?" I asked. The two were practically attached at the hip.

Atlas sat on one of the stools at the kitchen island. "She had a few things to catch up on at the bakery, then she's going over to her mom's to sort through her garage."

I leaned against the counter and stared at him with a cocked brow. "And you didn't offer to help her?"

Atlas was a big muscular wolven—the ideal assistant for that sort of task.

He shrugged. "She told me Reece would be there to help. I think she was looking forward to spending some time with him alone."

Well, that was certainly an improvement from where things had stood between them a few months ago.

"Interesting," I said under my breath.

"As pissed off as he makes her, I know she misses having a relationship with him."

"Of course she does. It's the same on his end as well." Worried I'd said too much, I quickly tacked on, "You know how complex sibling relationships can be."

Atlas sighed and shook his head. "That I do." He had two older brothers, and while they got along, they weren't exactly close.

"So, what are you in the mood for?" I asked, turning away from him to open the fridge.

"What do you have?"

I moved some things around, sorting through the groceries I'd picked up after training Reece the other day. "I have pork belly, so we can have ramen. Or there's some leftover shredded chicken for enchiladas."

Before I could list anything else, he said in a rush, "Oh, let's have ramen."

"Ramen it is."

It was so much easier cooking for him now that he'd healed his relationship with food and with his body. If I had to calculate macronutrients for another one of my recipes, I was going to scream.

I grabbed all the ingredients with my hands and my tentacles and spread them out on the counter.

"Are you sure you don't mind cooking?" Atlas asked. "We can always get something delivered from the diner."

"Nonsense. I wouldn't have offered if it was a hassle. I need to eat, too."

I pulled a stockpot out of the cupboard, filled it with a container of chicken broth, then set it on the burner to boil while we chatted.

"I guess when Fallon's not available, I'm the second choice for hanging out," I said with a smirk.

His ears drooped, his puppy dog eyes widening. He was really playing up his cute doglike qualities. "Aw, come on. It's not like that at all."

"I'm joking. It just isn't often that the two of us hang out like this." I set to work chopping up the mushrooms and scallions.

"Well, you and Fallon live together, so we don't exactly have a lot of opportunities to hang out without him."

"True." I couldn't even recall the last time it was just the two of us. A quick conversation in his office at the gym didn't count.

I dropped the noodles and vegetables into the broth, letting them boil while I sautéed the pork belly. The savory aroma of sizzling fat wafted off the pan, filling the apartment. Fallon was going to be pissed when he got home; ramen was one of his favorites.

When the noodles were cooked to perfection, I sat two giant soup bowls on the counter and ladled generous servings into each. Considering Atlas's appetite, I added a few extra pieces of pork belly to his bowl.

"Fork or chopsticks?" I asked.

"Uhh, fork, please."

I should have known. When we were in college, I tried to teach him how to use chopsticks, but it was a complete and utter failure. His massive hands just weren't dexterous enough to use chopsticks without breaking them.

"Here you go," I said, placing a bowl, soup spoon, and fork in front of him.

He leaned over the bowl and took a deep inhale of the steam rolling off the soup. "It smells so good."

"Of course it smells good. I made it." I sat next to Atlas at the island, watching as he slurped up a forkful of noodles. "How is it?"

The rapid *thump thump thump* of his tail gave it away before he could even speak. "Delicious. And even more delicious because I didn't have to make it."

I laughed and shook my head. "When Tegan started that raging inferno at the engagement party, Reece informed me that she isn't much of a cook."

"She's not, but I'm not much of a baker, so it works out."

It begged the question, what was Reece like at home? As into fitness as he was, I was certain he prepared his own meals. But what were some of his favorite dishes? Sweets, obviously. But what about actual meals? There was so much about him that I didn't know . . .

"Maybe I should get you and Tegan cooking lessons as a wedding gift," I suggested.

"That's not a bad idea, actually."

"Does it feel odd being engaged again?"

He shook his head. "Everything with Jade feels like a distant memory at this point."

"I'm really happy for you." I'd told him that so many times already, but I meant it. He went through so much with Jade that he deserved happiness with his fated mate.

"Thanks, buddy." He took a bite of his ramen and hummed at the taste before he asked, "How are things going with Reece?"

I nearly choked on my food. "What?"

Surely there was no way he knew that something was going on between me and Reece. Yes, we'd hooked up at the gym, but there weren't cameras in the locker room. And it wasn't like he kept tabs on all the times Reece and I got coffee together. If he asked around town, he could gather as much, but he wasn't really the nosy type.

"How's training going?" Atlas asked. "I heard you blowing that whistle nonstop the other day. I'm sure he loved that."

He certainly loved what came after.

"Uh, it's been good. He's improving . . . slowly."

"I really appreciate you doing this for me."

Doing this for him? Guilt made my chest feel tight because I wasn't doing this for him. I was doing this for me because Reece was my mate. If he wasn't, I probably would have told him to fuck right off.

"While I'm happy that this is bridging the gap between you, Tegan, and her brother, I'm not just doing it for you. It gives me something outside of painting. Something outside of my friendship with you and Fallon. A purpose of sorts."

"You've been different since you started working with him."

"Have I?" My heart rates ramped up, but I did my best to seem unaffected outwardly. It didn't come off sounding accusatory or that he was implying anything. Still, it made me nervous.

Atlas scooped up another spoonful of soup and nodded. "You've been more upbeat. You're painting again."

"Well—" I paused for a second to gather my thoughts, trying

to think of what to say without giving anything away. "When you've lived for as long as I have, sometimes you lose your way. Then something happens that reignites your passion for life, and I think that's where I am right now."

"So you're telling me that becoming a swim coach has reignited your passion for life?" he asked skeptically.

"Something like that," I murmured against a piece of pork belly.

"Do you know when your show will be? I'm sure Eduardo has been chomping at the bit for an exhibition."

What was this, twenty questions? I couldn't remember the last time Atlas grilled me like this.

"Uh, I'm not sure, really." Eduardo and I had discussed a date in the fall, after the triathlon, but nothing was set in stone. I didn't want to give Atlas an exact date. Not that I expected he'd try to attend, but on the off chance he mentioned it to Tegan and she encouraged his support, I wanted to be as ambiguous as possible.

"Did you come up with a theme yet?"

Oh, yes, an entire exhibition dedicated to your brother-in-law. Dick out. The whole nine.

I shrugged, biting back a smile. "Why? Still considering posing nude for me?" I nudged him with one of my tentacles.

He laughed and shook his head. "I mean, it would make a great gift for Tegan, but no."

"How's the wedding planning going?" I asked, shifting the conversation away from me.

"We booked the venue. We're having it at the same reception hall as the mayor's daughter. The wedding where we ran into each other again."

"Oh, I love that. A nice full-circle moment for the two of you."

His tail thumped. "We thought it was cute, too. We're actually going to have everyone over for dinner once we get more of the details ironed out."

By details, I assumed he meant them announcing—or asking—us to be part of the wedding party. I knew Fallon would be Atlas's best man, lifelong friends and all that, and I'd be a groomsman, but what did that mean for Reece? I was hopeful Tegan would include him, but in the absence of their father, would he walk her down the aisle or would he be another groomsman?

I knew the whole thing was an archaic tradition, but I was certain Reece would want the honor of walking her down the aisle. Could they get their relationship to that point before the wedding, though? I was hopeful—as long as things between Reece and me didn't come out before then.

"Well, you know I'm happy to help with whatever I can," I said, forcing a smile.

"I appreciate that, Cy."

We ate and talked, catching up on everything until our bowls were empty.

"Well, I'm gonna get going," Atlas said after a while, scooting his stool away from the counter.

"You're welcome to stay for a bit," I offered. "We can load up the PlayStation and I can kick your ass in a few FIFA matches."

Atlas laughed. "I appreciate the offer, but I want to do a few loads of laundry and clean the kitchen before Tegan gets home from her mom's house."

"Ah, domestic bliss."

I walked Atlas to the door.

"Thanks for dinner, buddy," he said, wrapping me in a hug.

I knew some men were uncomfortable when it came to hugging their friends, but Atlas was very much a hugger.

"Anytime." I patted his back a few times before pulling away.

"It was actually quite nice hanging out without Fallon's big mouth interrupting us every other word."

"It was. We'll have to do it again soon. I'll see you at the gym this week."

"Yep, I'll be there!"

I shut the door behind Atlas and slumped against the wall. Lying to him felt wrong. I knew he wouldn't have a problem with things between Reece and me. He was very forgiving and accepting, but I didn't want to put him in a position where he had to hide something from his mate. Their relationship was built on trust. I wasn't going to ask that of him. At least not yet.

Eighteen

REECE

"MA," I CALLED OUT AS I STEPPED THROUGH THE FRONT DOOR of my childhood home. "I'm here."

Remi was on me within seconds, weaving through my legs and rubbing his naked face on me. He was my mom's cat, a rescue sphynx that reminded me of a shaved nut sack. A freaky little thing with big ears and wide alien eyes.

My dad didn't like animals, so we didn't have any pets when I was growing up, but as soon as he passed, Mom adopted Remi. With Tegan and me living our own lives, I assumed the house was just too empty for her. I was happy she had Remi to dote on. She had all sorts of sweaters and clothes for him. Today he was dressed in a fuzzy orange turtleneck that looked absolutely ridiculous.

"Hey, buddy," I said, patting his butt. He stretched, sticking his naked tail straight up in the air. I was more of a dog person, but he was pretty fucking cute. "How ya been?" I gave him a few scratches under his chin, feeling contented purrs rumble out of him. For a little guy, he really got that motor running.

"Hey!" I looked up to see Tegan popping her head out from the kitchen at the end of the hall, a smile spreading across her face.

I grinned back at her, feeling my heart warm at how excited she seemed to see me. "Hey, Tegs."

I made my way down the hall, passing the gallery wall of photos of me and Tegan from our childhood. In so many of the pictures, she was smiling while I had a permanent scowl etched on my face.

How was it that two kids from the same family had such different childhoods?

I took a deep breath, forcing a smile when I walked into the kitchen.

"Where's Atlas?" I asked. From what I'd gathered, the two of them did everything together.

"Oh, um, he had some stuff he needed to catch up on at the gym," Tegan said. "He said to tell you hello, though."

"Hey, sweetheart," Mom said, wrapping me in a tight hug. A set of oven mitts covered her hands, and she softly patted my back. "I just got dinner in the oven. I figured we could eat when you're finished in the garage."

"What are you making?" I was asking the important questions.

Mom took off her oven mitts and set them on the counter. "Lasagna."

"Your favorite," Tegan said with a smirk. She might have been our father's favorite, but our mom had always had a soft spot for me.

I took a minute to look between the two of them. My sister really was the mirror image of our mom—just without the glasses. By some miracle, I was a pretty even mix of both of my parents. If I had looked exactly like my dad, I wouldn't be able to look at myself in the mirror.

"Well," I said to Tegan, "you ready to get this shit show started?"

She sighed. "I suppose."

"Try not to move too much around in there," Mom said. "I have everything arranged just how I like it."

Somehow, I knew that was a lie.

"Sure thing, Mom," Tegan said. She looked at me and rolled her eyes, making me laugh.

We walked out the back door and made our way around the side of the house to the detached garage. Mom used it for storage now, but when Dad was alive, he kept an old project car in here. He never worked on the thing, and it sat there for years collecting rust and dust. After he passed, it was one of the first things we got rid of. I swore I heard my mom murmur "Good riddance" under her breath when the tow truck finally pulled away.

The garage had an old manual door, so I grabbed the handle and pulled it up, cringing at the sound of the metal clinking against the tracks. A shimmering wave of heat poured out of the garage and onto the asphalt. Of course we were doing this on one of the hottest days of the summer.

"Oh my gods," Tegan said as the two of us stared in disbelief at the sight in front of us.

The garage was jam-packed. Boxes were stacked three to four high, arranged in rows that made the garage a cardboard corn maze. A barely used treadmill was tucked against the wall, and an old deep freezer was jammed in a back corner—completely unreachable. What was the point of keeping it if she didn't use it?

"Does she get rid of anything?" Tegan asked.

"Apparently not. What are we looking for again?"

"The box of stuff from Mom and Dad's wedding."

"Did she check the attic first?" That seemed like the sort of thing that would be better suited for a closet, someplace climate controlled, rather than a hot garage. I guess it made sense, though. Mom was never really happy in their marriage. Tegan was probably the only reason she hung on to those mementos.

Tegan nodded. "Yep. She said it wasn't up there."

"Fuck." Not that climbing around in the attic would have been much better. I'd hit my head on the rafters up there more times than I could count.

She put her hands on her hips, stared at the garage full of junk like it personally offended her, and puffed out a breath. "Fuck indeed."

I couldn't help but laugh. It was moments like this that reminded me we were siblings.

"I guess I'll start with this side and you start with that side?" I suggested.

"Sounds good."

I started to make my way through the piles of boxes and plastic storage bins. As chaotic as things looked, everything was labeled and sorted into groups that sort of made sense. At least in a way that would be logical to Pam Rollins.

Sweat dripped down my back as I sorted through the stacks of boxes.

Coffee mugs. Dad's old tools. Craft supplies. Ancient sports equipment. Easter decorations.

When was the last time Mom even decorated for Easter?

Just when I was about to give up hope for my side of the garage, an old Staples box caught my attention. *Wedding Shit* was scrawled on the side in my dad's chicken scratch handwriting. I snorted because, even in death, I was reminded of what a prick he was.

"I found it, Tegs," I called out to my sister.

"Oh, yay. I found something, too."

I picked up the box and brought it out to the driveway. Tegan tugged a bin over, the sound of the plastic scraping across the pavement making my jaw clench. She could have just asked me to carry it for her.

"What's that?" I asked.

She tapped the bin. A piece of painter's tape with my name on it was stuck to the lid. "Your memory box," she said matter-of-factly.

"Memory box?"

"Yeah, Mom made us both one. I already took mine to the cottage, but I'm assuming she told you to come get yours and you never did."

I snapped the top off the bin. Inside were my pictures from Little League, Ninja Turtle action figures, and the baby blanket my nana made. The fabric was thin and pilled with age—and from being carried around everywhere when I was a kid. Until my father started making fun of me, that is.

"What am I supposed to do with all this?" I wasn't exactly a sentimental person, and there were some memories I desperately wanted to forget.

"You hold on to it, and then when you're old, you"—she paused—"show it to your kids."

Kids.

A relationship had never been on my radar, let alone kids. Not that there was anything wrong with kids. When Atlas and Tegan had them, I'd happily step into the role of fun uncle. But as far as parenting children of my own went? It scared the shit out of me. No matter how much I convinced myself I wasn't my father, the thought was still there, lingering in the back of my mind, that I'd be like him. Parent like him.

It was enough to put me off the idea altogether.

And, as a gay man, the path to parenthood wasn't exactly an easy one. It wasn't like it could just happen.

I continued rummaging through the box, pulling out a chipped Pokémon picture frame. Inside it was a faded picture of me and Tegan standing on a muddy embankment by the lake. An old rope swing hung off a tree in the background. Back in the '90s, that thing was the highlight of our summer. By the time I started working at the Parks Department, it was long gone. Deemed a safety hazard, and for good reason.

I had to have been about ten when the photo was taken, my face still chubby and boyish. That would make Tegan around five.

"What's that?" Tegan asked, peeking at the photo.

"Us at the lake when we were kids." I tapped the glass, pointing at the rope swing in the background of the photo. "I think Mom took this when I finally got you to do the rope swing. Do you remember that?" I asked, a smile tugging at my lips at the memory.

How the fuck was that twenty-five years ago? I remembered how loud Dad cheered for her. Despite my jealousy over his reaction, I was pretty damn proud of my sister for conquering her fear.

She shook her head. "I only know about it from Dad telling the story over and over again."

"You were so proud of yourself when you finally did it on your own."

"I wouldn't have had the courage to do it without you standing on the bank encouraging me."

I laughed, nudging her shoulder. "I thought you said you didn't remember."

"That's the only part I remember," she said, nudging me back.

"Did you find it?" Mom shouted from the side of the house. She joined us in the driveway, eyeing the boxes we'd pulled out.

"Yep," Tegan said, tapping the box labeled *Wedding Shit* with her foot. "And Reece's memory box."

Mom tsked at me. "I told you to come get that last summer when I started the house remodel."

"I forgot, okay?" I glanced at the picture one more time before laying it in the bin on top of my baby blanket. "I'm a busy guy."

"Mm-hmm. Busy my butt," Mom huffed. She stepped inside the garage and poked around the boxes. "I don't even know what's in here."

Tegan and I looked at each other, biting back our smiles, because of course Mom had no idea what was in here. We watched her mill around the stacks, mumbling to herself as she took stock of all the junk she'd accumulated over the years.

"Reece," Mom called out from the back of the garage. "Come help me with this box."

I let out a sigh and shuffled through the aisles. She was standing next to a stack of boxes, pointing to one on the bottom. Because of course it was on the bottom.

I moved everything to the side, hoisting the box into my arms. "Fuck, this is heavy," I grunted. "Is this your brick collection?"

"Oh, hush," she said as I set the box on the asphalt. "That's what all those muscles are for."

She ripped a piece of dry rotted tape off the box, clapping excitedly when she saw what was inside.

"All my records." That explained why it was so heavy. She flipped through the titles and let out a little shriek. "Ah! I've been looking all over for this thing." She pulled an old flannel shirt out of the box, one I remembered her wearing all the time when we were kids. With it being in the garage, she was lucky a mouse hadn't gotten ahold of it.

I said, "Did you come out here to take a trip down memory lane or . . . ?"

"Oh," she said, shoving the flannel back into the box. "I came to tell you that dinner's ready. Why don't you move this stuff for Tegan and me? Then we can eat."

AFTER I PUT MY BOX IN MY CAR, TEGAN'S IN HERS, AND MOM'S record collection in the living room, I joined them at the table for dinner.

My mother had already plated me a generous serving of lasagna and a big hunk of garlic bread. I took my phone out of my pocket and set it on the table before sitting in the same spot I'd sat in for the last thirty or so years. Sure, the house and the furniture were different now, but it was still my spot.

"What do you want to drink?" Tegan asked.

"Oh, I can—"

Before I could get up, Tegan was already at the fridge. "Water? Iced tea?"

"Is it sweetened?" I asked.

"Unsweetened," Mom said, "and there's Splenda on the table for you."

Tegan set my tea on the table and took the seat across from me—her spot.

"Thanks, Tegs."

"You're welcome. It's the least I can do for you since it was like a million degrees in there."

My phone vibrated and I snatched it off the table, biting back a smile when I saw who it was from.

Cyrus: You'll never guess who just
left my house.

Reece: The Little Mermaid?

Cyrus: No, you dinglehopper. Atlas.
He stopped by for dinner.

Reece: That explains why he isn't
here then.

Cyrus: He mentioned that he
thought Tegan wanted to spend time
with you alone.

Reece: Really?

Cyrus: Mhm. How are things
going?

Reece: They're going okay. Tegan
seemed excited to see me.

Cyrus: I'm happy to hear that. Do you
have any plans after you leave your
mother's?

My lips twitched with a smile.

Reece: Yes. Going to check out a
glory hole in one of the truck stops
along the interstate.

Cyrus: Oh fuck off. Why would you
need a glory hole when you have my
mouth?

Fuck. He couldn't talk to me like that when I was around my family.

> Reece: I'm joking. Why? Are you free later?

> Cyrus: I was thinking that we could meet at the pool. Have a little quickie.

"Who are you texting?" Tegan asked, making me jump.

I shoved my phone into my pocket, feeling like a kid who just got caught texting in class. Honestly, this was way worse, considering *who* I was texting.

"Oh, uh, Javier," I rushed to say. "Just about something at work."

"I like Javier," Mom said. "It's a shame the two of you work together. You'd make a cute couple."

I grimaced at the idea. Two months ago, I would have agreed, but since things had taken off between Cyrus and me, it felt weird to imagine myself hooking up with anyone else. "Even if we didn't work together, Javier isn't my type."

Apparently, my type was blue and muscular, with a pointy head and long thick tentacles. A dry sense of humor and a laugh that made me feel dizzy.

The complete opposite of Javier.

Tegan snorted. "You know Reece doesn't do relationships, Mom."

She sighed. "I'm going to keep holding on to hope. There's someone out there for you, honey."

"Yeah, Mom," I said. "I'm sure there is."

"Speaking of Javier, how have things been at work?" Mom

asked. I could have kissed her for steering the conversation away from my love life.

I swallowed a bit of lasagna and shrugged. "It's been okay. Lots of campers this year compared to last. I think I'm going to ask the mayor to put another ranger in the budget for next summer. Javier and I are working ourselves to the bone."

Mom nodded. "The revitalization initiative is getting Briar Glenn a lot of attention."

"Mm-hmm," I agreed. "Lots of tourists."

"We should go camping sometime," Tegan suggested.

"Yes," Mom said, pointing at Tegan with her fork. "Just like when you two were kids."

I stared at my mother, my brows drawing back. "You want to go camping?"

"Of course not." She wrinkled her nose. Once a year my dad would drag all of us on a weeklong summer camping trip. Sure, we were right down the road from our house, but my mother was miserable the entire time. "I meant you, your sister, Atlas, maybe some of his friends."

"Oh, that would be fun." Tegan sounded genuinely excited.

Hmm. Us and Atlas's friends. That included Cyrus. There was no way I could stay in a tent with Cyrus with my sister and Atlas sleeping in the tent next to us. And what if Fallon went, too? It would be fucking weird if he shared a tent with us. It wasn't like I could insist that everyone have their own tent.

I couldn't spend any longer panicking about tent logistics because my mom and sister were staring at me expectantly. "Uh, sure. We can do that. Maybe in the fall, once the park slows down."

As things stood right now, I was way too busy with triathlon prep, work, and stealing moments with Cyrus. I didn't have time to add anything else to my calendar.

Tegan beamed. "I'll talk to Atlas, and we can set something up."

"Sounds good." We were quiet for a few minutes when it dawned on me that I should ask Tegan about the wedding. Show a little interest in what was going on in her life and her relationship.

"So, what did you need out of Mom's wedding stuff, Tegs?" I asked. "Don't tell me you're going to wear her old dress." My parents' yellowed wedding photo still hung in the hallway, and there was no way that long-sleeved high-neck lace monstrosity our mom wore was even remotely close to Tegan's dream dress.

She laughed and shook her head. "I'm not going to wear it, but I'm going to use it for something."

Knowing how our mother felt about her marriage to our father, it seemed weird that my sister would want to celebrate that in any way, shape, or form. I guess to her, it was important to incorporate something from their wedding into her own.

"That's cool." Our mother gave me her mom look, practically daring me to say something that might upset Tegan and ruin whatever delusions she had about our parents' marriage.

Smooth, Reece. Real smooth.

"It's going to be really cute," Tegan said.

"How's the rest of the planning going?" I asked, not knowing a single thing about wedding planning.

"It's going well. I think we're going to have everyone over again soon to go over the details," Tegan said. "Just you guys and some close friends. We didn't get to spend time with everyone at the engagement party."

"How could you when the entire town was there?" I teased.

Tegan looked at our mother. "Well, the person organizing the party went a little overboard."

"Sue me," Mom said around a mouthful of lasagna. "It isn't every day your daughter gets engaged."

"Mom, we are already mated."

Mom waved her off. "Don't act like you haven't dreamt of getting married, Tegan Marie."

I laughed and shook my head. This was what I missed, the banter between us. Without Dad around, it was so much easier for Mom and me to be ourselves. We didn't have to spend an entire meal walking on eggshells. That told you everything about Don Rollins you needed to know.

Mom put her elbows on the table and rested her chin on her hands. "It makes me so happy seeing the two of you getting along."

"It makes me happy, too," Tegan said.

The bright smile on her face made my chest feel tight, and all I could do was nod my agreement.

If things continued like this, I was going to have to tell her eventually.

I just hoped she'd hear me out when that time came.

Nineteen

REECE

"FUCK," I GROANED, THROATY AND LOW. STAYING QUIET WAS difficult when Cyrus was deep-throating me within an inch of my life.

Harder, he said, the word a warm purr at the base of my skull. He didn't have to ask me twice.

I tightened my grip on his head, really thrusting my hips and pressing Cyrus's hot mouth to my pelvis. This was my reward for a job well done during training this morning, and I was going to take advantage of it.

That's it, he purred in my head. *Use me. Show me how well you fuck.*

"Shit," I grunted.

My balls were so tight, and I could feel the tingling sensation of my orgasm building at the base of my spine. He was just so fucking good. Good at taking my cock in his throat and good at talking dirty.

"Cy—I'm gonna come."

He adjusted his hands, grabbing my ass and increasing the

pace. One of his tentacles wrapped around my balls, applying gentle pressure that tipped me over the edge.

I came hard, thighs quaking and body jolting. Cy sucked me through it, dragging his tongues over my shaft until I was completely spent.

When he pulled off my cock, I was already reaching for him, grabbing his arms to bring him chest to chest with me. I wrapped one hand around the back of his head before crushing his lips to mine, licking and sucking and tasting myself on his tongues. My other hand ran up his chest and glided over his soft skin and defined muscles.

"Fuck, I can't get enough of you," I murmured against his lips.

"You have no idea how happy it makes me to hear that."

He pulled away from me, chest heaving as he wiped his mouth with the back of his hand.

"Are you sure you don't want me to get you off?" I asked, feeling like an asshole because I was the only one who got to come.

Cyrus shook his head, his lips tipping up with a satisfied smirk. "It's all right, darling. Your pleasure is my pleasure."

"All right . . ." I trailed off. Part of me felt guilty for being a pillow princess, but he really did enjoy getting me off.

He passed me my jammers, then stuck his head around the corner, making sure the coast was clear before we headed out to the main locker area. As usual, it was empty.

I turned away from him to grab my bag from my locker when he said, "You have such a lovely ass."

"Is it?" I asked, glancing behind me to look at my sculpted glutes.

"Yes. I want to fuck it with my tongues soon."

"Cyrus," I hissed. "You stop that right now."

He crossed his arms. "You're the one who said you can't get enough of me."

I pulled on my boxer briefs and started to put on my uniform. It was a typical Parks Department uniform: khaki, stiff, and ugly as hell. Cyrus stared at me while I buttoned my shirt and tucked it into my pants.

"What?" I asked with a laugh. He was really fawning over me this morning. I wasn't mad about it.

"You just look sexy in your uniform, that's all." He told me that every time he saw me in it, but I didn't think I'd ever get tired of hearing it.

"Oh yeah?"

"Mm-hmm. You and Javier should do a Parks Department calendar."

"Like a sexy one?"

He nodded.

"Are you telling me you want to see Javier with his shirt off?" I mean, I used to enjoy that, too, but the thought of Cyrus admiring Javier like that sort of pissed me off.

Was this what jealousy felt like?

"Not particularly. I just thought that would be less awkward than having you model for a calendar just for me."

"Why do you need a calendar when you can have the real thing? I'll send you pictures anytime you want."

"You're going to regret that."

"Never." I ran my hand through my damp hair, pushing it back. "Look okay?"

"Handsome as always. Are we still on for coffee?" he asked.

"Yep. I told Jimenez I was going to be in late today."

"You're skiving out on work to spend time with me?"

I shrugged, trying to seem indifferent, but I really wanted to savor every second with him that I could.

He gave me a knowing grin, bringing a hand to his chest. "I'm touched."

"Shut up. You ready?" I asked.

He shifted on his tentacles, his blue eyes darting to the ground, then back up to stare at me. "I was thinking, maybe we could invite Atlas to get coffee with us."

"You want to invite Atlas to hang out with us?" I asked skeptically. With the whole secret relationship thing Cyrus and I had going on, it wasn't like we got to spend a lot of time together. Especially not in the open. And he wanted to let Atlas intrude on that time?

"Well, he's my friend and your sister's mate-slash-fiancé. I figured it would be a comfortable atmosphere for you to get to know him better." He quickly added, "I'm sure he'll tell Tegan about it, too."

I bit my lip, mulling it over. Atlas was a nice guy, and he was Cyrus's best friend. It would certainly look less suspicious if we invited him rather than just the two of us having coffee all the time. Extra brownie points with my sister would be nice, too.

"Yeah, all right."

Cyrus's face lit up, and damn, if I knew it was going to make him that happy, I would have agreed to it right away.

When I was finished getting ready, Cyrus led me down a back hallway toward Atlas's office. The door was open, and Atlas was sitting at his desk curled over his keyboard with his yellow eyes fixed on his computer.

I looked at Cyrus and he nudged me, tipping his head toward Atlas. *Go on*, his voice chimed in my head.

"Uh, morning, Atlas." The words came out all weird and strained.

Atlas's gaze snapped to the doorway, a smile wrinkling his muzzle when he saw that it was Cyrus and me. "Hey! Did you two have a good training session?"

"We did," I said.

Atlas leaned back in his computer chair. "That's great! You're gonna be in good shape for the triathlon."

"That's the plan," Cyrus said.

I was waiting for Cyrus to ask Atlas to join us when he discreetly nudged my foot with one of his tentacles. Looked like I was the one who would be asking.

"We're going to grab coffee at the Busy Bean. Did you want to come with us?" I asked.

His ears perked up, and I could hear the muffled *thump thump* of his tail. "I'd love to. I've been staring at spreadsheets all morning and I need a break."

"Cool."

We waited for Atlas to grab his things, then the three of us walked down Main Street to the Busy Bean.

It was living up to its name today.

Every parking spot in front of the shop was taken, and I could see there was a line at the register. Luckily, there were a few empty tables outside. With a whole day of working in the heat ahead of me, I would have preferred to sit in the air-conditioning, but I'd suck it up for more time with Cyrus.

We stepped inside the Busy Bean, and Cyrus shuffled along behind me.

Brian, the owner, was behind the cash register. He gave us a wave and a friendly smile when he noticed us.

"Hey, Reece, Cyrus," Brian said when it was our turn to order. "How are you this morning?"

His sunny disposition faded when Atlas stepped up beside us. *Interesting.*

I'd never seen someone react toward Atlas that way—other than me, that is. Judging by the clientele at the gym who chatted with him and the turnout for the engagement party, he was well liked.

"Atlas," Brian said flatly.

"Morning, Brian," Atlas said, smiling so big it made his eyes squint.

Yeah, there was definitely some bad blood there.

Brian seemed to shake it off, remembering that we were paying customers. "The usual for everyone?" he asked.

"Yep," Cyrus and Atlas said in unison.

"The usual drink for me, but . . ." I bent down, taking a peek inside the pastry case. Everything looked delicious, but there was one thing in particular that caught my eye. "Can I get a chocolate croissant, too, please?"

Eating a baked good from someone other than my mom or sister felt like a sin, but they didn't make croissants. At least, not like this.

"Sure thing," Brian said. "Is everyone together? Separate checks?"

"Together," I said.

Brian flipped the tablet around to face me, and before Cyrus could nudge me out of the way so he could pay, I was already tapping my card against the screen.

"Thanks, Reece," Atlas said as we stood at the end of the counter waiting for our drinks.

"It's my pleasure." I pinned Cyrus with a look and he grinned. Heat rushed to my cheeks and I forced myself to look away, the secret between us too much for me to handle with Atlas in our presence.

In a way, I liked sneaking around like this. As much as I didn't want to get caught, it was thrilling, sharing something between the two of us.

We grabbed our drinks and sat at one of the little café tables in front of the coffee shop. I was starving from swim practice, so

I dug into my croissant right away. It was heaven, flaky and buttery with rich chocolate wrapped inside.

Atlas watched me eat and cocked a furry brow. "Never would have taken you for a sweets guy."

"Oh, he loves them," Cyrus chimed in.

It made me pause mid-bite, because was that the sort of thing you'd know about an acquaintance? Or did Cyrus and I seem more like friends? I mean, I knew that sort of thing about Jimenez. I was probably overthinking it, but just in case, I decided to shift the conversation away from my eating preferences.

"So, what was that whole thing with Brian?" I asked Atlas.

"Did you know that before I asked your sister out, Brian asked her if I was her boyfriend? When she said no, he asked her out," Atlas said.

"Brian asked my sister out?" I said, spraying a few crumbs of croissant. That little shit. I told him when we were teenagers that I'd kill him if he ever made a pass at her.

Atlas nodded. "Yep. She said no, obviously. Ever since we became a thing, he's been a little cold to me."

Cyrus blinked at Atlas. "He's cold because you rubbed it in his face."

I looked at Atlas, my brows drawing back. For the Atlas I knew, that sounded a little out of character.

He shrugged. "I might have messed with him a little bit when your sister and I got coffee one morning."

"Damn," I said with a laugh. "He's going to spit in your coffee."

Atlas chuckled. "Your sister said the same thing."

"He's probably really upset that you're getting married. He's had a crush on Tegan since they were in middle school."

"Really?" Atlas asked, cocking his head. "She told me he was never interested in her until I came into the picture."

"That's because I told him I'd kill him if he ever asked her out." It was an empty threat, but it was enough to deter a guy like Brian. I guess with Atlas in the picture, he finally worked up the balls to make a move on her. *Too little, too late, bud.*

Atlas leaned back in his chair. "You really take the role of protector seriously, don't you?"

"Someone had to. But now that you're in the picture, I don't have to worry about it quite as much."

Cyrus was speechless, his mouth hanging open.

Did I say something wrong? I was just being honest.

Atlas stared at me for a moment before grinning. "I promise she's in good hands."

"I know she is." The more I got to know Atlas, the worse I felt that I'd given him and my sister such a hard time right out of the gate. He really was a great guy.

"Speaking of Tegan," Atlas said, "she told me she wants all of us to go camping."

Damn, she was not letting that go. I guess this was happening.

"I was thinking we could go in the fall. Once it cools down and things at the park slow down a little bit. I have plenty of equipment we can use. It'll be fun."

"What about you, Cy?" Atlas asked. "You down for camping?"

"I'm usually one for my creature comforts, but I could be persuaded," he said, staring right at me. "Maybe we can go right before the triathlon. You'll be finished with your training, so you can just relax."

Planning a camping trip wasn't exactly relaxing, but the weather would be perfect. "Uh, sure. Let's shoot for that."

Atlas took a sip of his coffee and his ears perked up. "Reece, I've been meaning to ask, what made you decide to sign up for a triathlon?"

"I like being the best," I admitted. It made me sound like a competitive asshole, but it was the truth. "Pushing my body to its limits. A triathlon seemed like a good way to challenge myself."

"That's how I felt about competing," Atlas said, "at least in the beginning."

"Competing?" I asked.

Atlas nodded. "I was a competitive bodybuilder for years."

"A five-time physique champion," Cyrus added. It was cute that he was hyping up his friend's achievement.

"That's wild," I said, eyes fixed on my future brother-in-law. Atlas was already jacked. I couldn't imagine the shape he was in when he was competing. "What made you give it up?"

He puffed out a breath. "I was just tired of it. Tired of being hungry all the time. Tired of the pressure of cuts and bulks."

While I kept a clean diet, I wasn't quite that strict with my meal plan. I was naturally lean, and I made sure I could fit my little sweet treats in and still maintain a calorie deficit.

"I could see that."

"If you ever decide you want to compete, let me know," Atlas said. "I'd be happy to train you."

I laughed. There was no way I'd put myself through that torture. "I appreciate the offer, but I get hangry enough as it is."

"You certainly do," Cyrus said quietly, staring at me from across the table with a sensual smile on his face.

What the fuck was wrong with him? Was he trying to blow our cover?

Atlas looked between us and slurped up the last of his iced americano. He could obviously sense the tension. "Well," he said, rising out of his chair, "I better get back to the gym."

"Someone has to make sure Fallon is actually training his clients," Cyrus teased.

Atlas rubbed his temples. "That fucking guy. I swear, if he wasn't my best friend—"

"Oh, don't give me that," Cyrus huffed. "You love him like a brother."

"I do," Atlas sighed. Fallon must have had some redeeming qualities if guys like Atlas and Cyrus valued his friendship.

"Thanks for coming with us," I told Atlas.

"Thanks for inviting me. We should do it again. Oh"—his eyes widened and his ears perked up—"every once in a while, we get together to play video games and hang out. Did you want to join us next time, Reece?"

It caught me off guard because I wasn't normally invited to those sorts of things. The closest thing I had to a friend was Jimenez, and we didn't hang out much outside of work. "Uh, sure. I'd love to."

Atlas's body started to sway, that tail of his going a mile a minute. He was obviously happy I'd agreed. "Cool. I'll let you know the next time we get together."

"Sounds good."

He tossed his empty cup in the trash, gave us a little wave, then headed down the street toward Leviathan Fitness.

I watched him walk off, waiting until he disappeared down the street to whisper-shout, "Were you *trying* to blow our cover?"

Cyrus scoffed. "Blow our cover how?"

"You know how! Those innuendos and those—those sultry looks."

"Sultry?" It was obvious Cyrus was trying to bite back his laughter. "I didn't know the word 'sultry' was in your vocabulary."

"Oh, fuck off."

One of his tentacles discreetly brushed against my leg. "You need to relax. I would never do anything to put things between us in jeopardy. Atlas knows I tease my friends. He's probably just shocked at how comfortable the two of us are together. Especially since you got off to a bad start with both of us."

Fuck, the truth hurt sometimes. I hated that I'd given them both such a bad first impression of myself.

When I didn't say anything, he continued, "All things considered, I think you and Atlas get along quite well, don't you?"

"We do," I admitted. "We actually have a lot in common."

He grinned. "Indeed you do."

"Shut up," I said, smiling right back at him.

I appreciated that he'd pushed me into this. That he wanted me to connect with Atlas.

We sat in silence for a few beats, watching cars roll down Main Street and the customers filter out of the Busy Bean. It would be time for me to get going soon, but I didn't want to leave Cyrus yet.

He took a deep breath and forced a smile. "You did well with training today. I think we should do an open-water swim at the lake soon."

My face pinched into a scowl. I'd swum at the lake a few times before I started training with Cyrus, but it was nothing like the training we did, or what I'd experience during the triathlon. Leisurely treading water wasn't the same as front-crawling as fast as I could for 750 meters in ice-cold water.

"You've got this," Cyrus reassured me, obviously reading my expression.

"Sure do," I said sarcastically.

"Fresh water isn't my favorite, but I could get in with you."

"You don't have to do that." The pool was one thing; the lake was another.

"But I would."

I imagined Cyrus jetting around the lake, swimming out to the buoy and back before I was even a few feet offshore. He was probably even more impressive in the ocean, cutting through the rough waves and diving deep on a single breath. Seeing him in his element would be like a dream.

"When's the last time you swam in the ocean?" I asked.

Rock Harbor was on the bay, but the only ocean access was a few hours down the coastline.

He rubbed his jaw and hummed. "It's been several years. I could swim through the bay out to the ocean, but the water isn't the cleanest."

I didn't blame him. Even with the massive efforts to clean up the bay, it was still pretty gross. You wouldn't catch me jumping in that water.

"You never ask Fallon and Atlas to drive down to the beach with you?"

He was taking a sip of his coffee and shrugged. "Fallon would probably go if I asked him, but I'd hate to trouble him—or trouble myself with him—just so I could swim in the ocean. Besides, the reason Leviathan has a saltwater pool is because of me. Atlas wanted me to have room to swim while I replenished my salt stores."

I'd been curious about that ever since I saw the gym logo and found out the pool was salt water. That was a pretty big accommodation to make for one of your friends. Add it to the list of things that made Atlas a good guy.

"What the fuck does that mean?"

"What?" he asked. "My saltwater stores?"

I nodded.

He laughed. "Basically, it helps maintain balance in my body."

Another interesting kraken thing.

"I see." I grabbed my phone off the table, checking the time. "Fuck," I groaned. "I don't want to go." It would be a few days before I got to see Cyrus again, and I wasn't ready to leave him yet.

Cyrus sighed. "I wish you didn't have to go, either." He spoke the first part, but then his voice echoed in my head: *I can hang back and you can walk back to the gym by yourself if you think it'll look less conspicuous.*

Someone laid on their horn, almost making me drop my coffee. It was Jimenez, pulling the Briar Glenn Parks Department work truck into a parking spot in front of us.

"Oh, fuck me," I said under my breath as Jimenez exited the car. I wanted to sulk about leaving Cyrus in peace.

"Skipping out on work to grab a coffee?" Jimenez teased. He looked like he always did during work, his khaki Parks Department uniform clinging to his chest and arms like a second skin, shifting and straining with each of his movements.

Jimenez tipped his head at Cyrus, giving him his signature handsome smile. Remembering my conversation with Cyrus from earlier and the whole "Parks Department calendar" thing, I wanted to wipe that smile right off his face with my fists. I didn't want anyone looking at Cyrus like that but me.

"Hey, Cyrus," he said. "How are you?"

My jaw tightened, my hands clenching into fists under the table.

Down, boy, Cyrus said in my head. *He's just being nice.*

He grinned at Javier. "I'm well, thanks. Reece, Atlas, and I stepped out for a coffee this morning, but Reece was just on his way out."

"Perfect," Javier said, jostling my shoulder. I fought the urge to shrug him off. He was the last person I wanted touching me right now. "We can head to the park from here and I can drop you off at your car later."

"Yeah. Perfect," I grumbled.

Javier pointed to the door of the Busy Bean, his stupid biceps flexing against his stupid tight sleeve. "Let me just grab a coffee and we can roll."

I waited for Javier to go inside before I murmured, "I'm sorry."

"It's not your fault," Cyrus said.

But it was. We had to keep this a secret because of me.

Apparently, now that the rush had died down, the Busy Bean was slinging out drinks right and left, because Jimenez was already on his way back with his coffee.

I stood up and stared down at Cyrus. "I'll text you later, okay?"

He glanced up at me with this painfully sad look on his face. *I wish I could kiss you goodbye.*

I mouthed, *Me, too.*

Javier stepped outside and slipped on his sunglasses. "Ready to hit up these parks, boss?"

I nodded. "I'll see you at our next session," I told Cyrus.

"See ya then." He tried to sound upbeat, but I knew this was hurting him. It made me feel like shit.

"Bye, Cyrus!" Javier said with a friendly wave.

"Bye," he murmured.

I spun my keys on my finger and headed toward the driver's side door.

"But I wanted to dr—" Jimenez started.

"Nope. Not today." I needed something to focus on other than the heartbroken look on Cyrus's face as we pulled away.

Twenty

CYRUS

 and joined each other for what we hoped were inconspicuous coffee dates. During the moments we weren't together, we spent our time texting, and I'd learned a lot about my mate.

His middle name was Michael and he loathed wearing socks; he said he hated the way they felt on his feet. He played lacrosse in high school, and he shaved his chest hair each time he took a shower to avoid the annoying prickle of regrowth.

They were tiny mundane things, but I enjoyed knowing them, knowing *him*.

And I particularly enjoyed the Reece Rollins he kept locked tight under that tough facade.

He was terrified of buzzing insects, swatting and cursing at them as if they threatened his very existence. On walks, he had to stop and pet every dog, and for being a triathlete fitness freak, he had quite the sweet tooth.

All of our intimate moments took place at the gym, and after sex, he'd snuggle up against me in the shower, running his fingertips over my fins while he stared into my eyes.

He was sensitive.

Nuanced.

And with each passing day, I could feel myself falling in love with him.

Sure, part of that inextricable pull to Reece was the mating bond, but it was also due to who he was as a person.

The sun was starting to rise as I pulled my car to a stop outside Reece's house. This morning we'd head down to the shore of the lake for his first open-water swim.

It was still summer, but here in the upper Northeast, the water was never really warm. According to my research, the average water temperature for the lake this time of year was eighteen degrees Celsius—brisk but not cold enough for him to need a wet suit.

The conditions of an open-water swim were different from the pool. The cold temperature of the water, the slight waves, maintaining his location. Anyone would find it intimidating, but if he was going to place well in this triathlon, we needed to start practicing under the conditions he was going to experience.

I was convinced he was ready. He'd been pushing himself quite hard now that I could use sex as a training incentive, but I'd seen his face when I suggested it.

Reece stepped out of the house dressed in his jammers and a hoodie, with the hood covering most of his head except for a tuft of red hair.

Gods, my mate was a stud.

I muttered a thank-you to the goddess as he slipped inside my car.

"Morning," I said.

"Morning," he grumbled back.

Reece wasn't much of a morning person. I knew he had an unhealthy caffeine addiction, and I'd promised to take him for coffee as soon as we were done with our session.

He scanned the empty street for a moment before he leaned over and wrapped his hand behind my head, pulling me in for a kiss. His lips caressed mine, slow and questioning—almost like he was asking for permission to kiss me out in the open like this.

It was more than okay.

It was everything I'd ever wanted.

I slid my hand up the column of his neck, buried my fingers in his hair, and deepened the kiss. Our tongues brushed together, giving me a taste of his minty toothpaste. This wasn't our normal frantic kissing. It was sweeter. Softer. Like we were savoring each stolen second.

"Well, that was certainly a development," I said with a dreamy sigh as he pulled away and fastened his seat belt.

"What? I missed you," he mumbled under his breath, pushing back his hood. "I can be sweet sometimes."

He squinted at me in the dim lighting before wetting his thumb with his tongue and running it over my eyebrow. "Were you painting?" he asked, showing me the dried flecks of gold on his thumb.

I wanted to say yes, to tell him I'd been working on a portrait of him in his Parks Department uniform, but he'd find out soon enough.

That is, if I ever worked up the courage to invite him to my gallery show.

Sometimes it was best to keep the muse and the art separate.

"Yeah, I'm working on a few different pieces. I've been quite inspired lately."

Inspired by the beauty of my mate—by you.

"I'd like to see your work sometime. You know, if you're comfortable sharing it with me or whatever. I know how people can be about their art."

A smile spread over my face, and my hearts sang over the fact that Reece was interested in seeing what I had created. For now, I'd hold off on the paintings of him, but I'd be happy to show him some of my older work. There was certainly enough of it.

"I'd love to show you sometime." I put the car in drive and started down the road toward the lake. "How are you feeling this morning?"

"Tired. Not ready to jump into that cold-ass water." He nestled deeper into his hoodie and I laughed.

"It's only going to get worse as we get closer to the triathlon. Best to get used to it now."

"Yeah, you're right." His hand snaked over the center console and came to rest on one of my tentacles, his thumb rubbing tiny circles over my smooth skin.

Without saying a word, I gripped the steering wheel with my left hand and grabbed Reece's hand with the other.

THE LIGHT OF THE MORNING SUN SHONE BRIGHT RED ON THE lake's surface as the waves lapped against the shore. Other than the two of us, the park was empty.

Reece stretched for a few moments before pulling his hoodie over his head, putting that perfect body on display.

"Shit, it's cold!" he bellowed, and threw his hoodie down by my feet.

"It's thirteen degrees Celsius, the average morning temperature for this time of year."

"Okay, but what's that in freedom units?"

I snorted. *Metric holdout Americans.* "Fifty-five degrees Fahrenheit."

"How are you not freezing?" He rubbed his palms over his biceps with rough strokes.

"My body thermoregulates. Nifty little kraken trick. Unfortunately, the trade-off is looking like this." I fanned my tentacles around me playfully and Reece stepped closer.

He wrapped his arms around my neck and pulled me to him, the pointed tips of his nipples rubbing against my chest. "I happen to think you're quite attractive," he said, and pressed his forehead to mine.

I had trouble believing a gorgeous man like him found a creature like me attractive.

"Reece Michael Rollins has the hots for me. I better alert the masses," I teased, using humor to cope with my own insecurities.

He blushed slightly, his tongue peeking out from under his mustache to wet his lips. "Soon, Cy. It isn't gonna be like this forever."

To be honest, I didn't mind if it was. As long as we could keep going with whatever this was between us, with whatever made my mate comfortable, I was happy.

"I'll be here. Take all the time you need, darling."

He brushed his lips against mine, his hands traveling down to where my back met my tentacles, and lightly thrust his cock into my hips.

"You're stalling," I mumbled against his mouth with a laugh. "What if someone sees us?" For the second time today, he'd sought me out when we were out in the open. Where anyone could see us. As happy as it made me, I knew how important it was to him that we keep this between the two of us.

"They won't. But yeah, I am stalling."

"If you're a good boy and do your swim, I promise I'll get you a coffee and get you off."

"Fuck," he groaned into my mouth before pulling away.

He could be such a brat. But he was *my* brat.

"Do you want me to get in with you?" I asked as Reece pulled on his swim cap and goggles.

"Nah, I won't subject you to that. Just have a towel ready for me when I'm done."

He stepped closer to the water, hissing the moment it hit his toes.

"You need to just get it over with. Jump right in." It was easy enough for me to say that from the comfort of the shore.

Reece clapped his hands together twice, and with a hoarse yell, he jumped into the lake.

"Motherfucker!" he howled the moment his head popped up from below the surface. "S'fucking cold."

"The sooner you start swimming, the sooner it'll be done, Rollins!" I yelled, my voice echoing out over the lake.

Reece got into position, and I started the timer on my phone as he swam out to the buoy.

He'd made leaps and bounds in his training. It was evident in how his arms moved and how his body cut through the water.

With steady strokes, he pushed himself, but as he reached the center of the lake, he suddenly cried out and his head bobbed underneath the water.

I watched for a moment until he resurfaced, his arms flailing wildly as he yelled out to me.

Panic set over me as I tossed my phone and rushed to the edge of the lake.

I'm coming. Hold on. I'm coming. I spoke to him in his head, trying my best to calm him, to keep my voice steady and even.

But I was absolutely terrified.

I plunged into the cool water, the muscles in my tentacles rippling as I shot off toward Reece.

A swim that took him a considerable amount of time was

nothing for me, and I was able to find him easily with his thrashing and sputtering.

I breached the surface and wrapped him up in my tentacles, pulling his back tight against my chest, holding on to him for dear life because, fuck, there was no way I could lose him. Not yet. Not before I told him everything.

"I'm here, darling. I've got you. I've got you," I said.

"C-cramps," he stammered. "I c-couldn't kick."

His legs had seized up, and in his panic, he'd sucked in a decent amount of water.

My mate had been in danger, and I'd just been standing on the beach watching.

"Shh. I've got you," I whispered in his ear as I swam us back to shore.

The moment I could stand, I rose on my tentacles and carried Reece up onto the shore.

"Fuck," I shouted once I got a better look at him.

He was shivering and coughing like mad.

I scuttled to the parking area and started my car, cranking the heater and grabbing extra towels.

"Shit. Shit. Shit," I mumbled, rushing back to Reece, covering him with towels, and pulling him into my arms.

At the moment, I didn't give a fuck if anyone was around to see us.

"I am so, so sorry," I mumbled with my lips pressed against his temple. "I should have swum out with you." My voice was strangled. I was on the verge of tears.

"S'okay, Cy. Not your fault." He snuggled closer against my chest, and my tentacles tightened their grip on his body.

He didn't understand, though.

He was my mate, and I wouldn't be able to live with myself if something happened to him.

We sat like that for a few minutes, huddled together on the cool beach as the morning sun crested above us.

Under other circumstances, it would have been beautiful, romantic even, but I felt like shit.

"Thank you for swimming out to get me." Reece strained against my tentacles and stretched out his legs. "I think I can make it to the car now."

I nodded, handing Reece his hoodie, and we wordlessly trudged across the beach to my car.

"I think I'm going to withdraw," Reece said the moment I slammed the car door shut.

His hood was pulled over his head and he stared at the lake with a blank expression on his face.

"Reece." I slid my hand over his thigh, and he looked at me with bloodshot eyes. "Today was a one-off thing. I know it was scary, but I don't think you should withdraw from the race."

"That was shit, Cy. What's the point of entering if I'm going to have a shit time?"

He'd worked so hard preparing for this.

We'd worked so hard preparing for this.

And he was going to quit?

"This isn't about cramping or almost drowning, is it?"

He didn't answer me; he simply turned and looked out the window.

"If you don't talk to me, Reece, I can't help you. And I *want* to help you. So please, please talk to me. Don't give me that hard-ass bullshit that you feed everyone else, because I know better."

He finally faced me, his cheeks flushed red and tears already forming in the corners of his eyes. "Do you know why I got out of the pool that day?"

I'd had a lingering suspicion for some time now, but I shook my head no. I wanted—no, needed—to hear it from him.

"The way you were training me, yelling at me, it reminded me of him. Reminded me of my father." He rubbed his eyes, smearing the tears over those perfect light red eyelashes. "My entire life, he raised me to be the best. It was a given. Expected of me. And if I wasn't, the old man rode my ass about it. But for Tegan, it was different. He was always telling her how proud he was. How amazing she was."

Tears streamed down his cheeks and he sniffled.

"I did everything he wanted to the best of my abilities, and it was never enough. No matter what I did, I could never make him love me. A lot of my issues are because of him. He'd berate me, belittle me, make fun of me. That really fucked me up, Cy." He let out a pained laugh. "You know, there was a part of me that was happy when he passed. I feel like shit actually saying it out loud, but it's true. It was like this weight had finally been lifted. I could let go of all of his expectations. But when we were training that day, it was like all those inadequacies got stirred up again. I was that same broken little boy."

Reece had been through so much. His father's continuous verbal abuse had done serious damage, and he'd developed that prickly demeanor as a defense mechanism. He'd coped the best way he knew how . . .

"And with you, Cy," he continued, "at first I didn't even give you a fucking chance. I was such a dickhead to you. I didn't deserve your help or your kindness, but you gave it to me anyway. I started to have this attraction to you. I told myself we were just fuck buddies or whatever, but it's grown into so much more than that."

He glanced over at me, his face bright red, those green eyes looking the prettiest I had ever seen them.

"I enjoy every second we spend together, whether you're fucking me or blowing that fucking whistle at me. The things I feel for you—I've never felt that way about anyone before. It scared me at first, but I'm not scared anymore. I have feelings for you, Cyrus, and I'm sorry it took a near-death experience for me to admit that."

I lurched over the center console and wrapped my arms around him tightly.

Seeing him like this broke me. My mate had been carrying all of this for so long.

"You're going to do great. You know that, right?"

"But what if I don't?" he asked, his head buried in the crook of my neck.

"As long as you give it your all, that's what matters." I ran my fingers along his wet hair, placing a soft kiss on the top of his head. "That's something to be proud of."

Twenty-One

REECE

"SHIT," I MUMBLED UNDER MY BREATH, HOLDING ONE SHIRT then the other against my chest.

Someone once told me the Henley shirt was the top equivalent of gray sweatpants, and I'd held on to that, loving the way the thin material stretched tight over my broad chest.

I knew Cyrus was a fan of that, too.

Since my near-death experience and slight emotional breakdown, things had been going great between us. I could be vulnerable around Cyrus in a way that I couldn't with other people. I didn't have to hide my thoughts or feelings.

He felt *safe*.

There was no way we could do this forever, and I'd never ask him to. We'd have to go public with our relationship soon. But for now, I was content to keep what we had between the two of us.

I wanted to savor this period where we wouldn't have to answer any questions or deal with judgment.

I'd changed, and Cyrus was the driving force behind that.

I grabbed my phone and sent him a text.

Reece: I need your help. I don't know
what to wear.

I laughed to myself because there I was, asking someone who didn't wear clothes for fashion advice.

Cyrus: Send me pics.

I held up one shirt, snapped a pic, then repeated it with the other before sending them over to Cyrus.

Cyrus: Yeah, but send me one
without the shirt in the way. Shirts
are optional for boys' night. 💯

I snorted and rolled my eyes. Gods, he was such a horny fuck. Tonight would be my first time over at the apartment Cyrus shared with Fallon and would be our first time around a large group of people since we started hooking up.

I was nervous but also excited. Tonight, I was going to be the one teasing Cyrus.

When I was finally dressed, my beard freshly trimmed, and my hair pushed back in that messy way Cyrus liked, I grabbed my keys and typed out a quick text.

Reece: Leaving now. See you soon.

I stared at my phone for a second. Would adding a kiss emoji be too much? I mean, we kissed in person. We did more than kissing in person.

Fuck it.

Reece: Leaving now. See you soon. 

Cyrus: See you soon, darling. 😘

Darling.

I could feel my cheeks heating like they did every time he called me that. I wasn't used to pet names or being with someone who made me *feel* things.

It was at that moment I realized this was something different. That what Cyrus and I had was real.

And I was thrilled about it.

"YOOO. LOOK WHO'S HERE." FALLON WHISTLED AND CLAPPED me on the back as I stepped into the apartment.

Gods, he was such a fucking frat boy.

I could tolerate him for Atlas and Cyrus, but I'd never go out of my way to hang out with him one-on-one.

Jimenez was enough for me.

Speaking of Jimenez . . .

"Yooo!" he shouted from inside the apartment, raising his beer at me when I came into view.

"Hey." I gave him a slight tip of my chin.

I scanned the apartment, taking in its high ceilings and exposed brick walls. When I pulled up to the building, I knew it was going to be fancy, but this was nicer than I'd expected. Cyrus had to be footing the bill because there was no way Fallon could afford this on what he made at the gym.

My—whatever Cyrus was to me—the artist.

Speaking of art, the walls of the apartment were covered with paintings. Most of them were done with muted colors, but there was one that really caught my eye. It was a nature scene with a bright orange sun rising over a shimmering body of water. It reminded me of the morning Cyrus and I had spent together down by the lake several weeks before.

The morning where I'd almost drowned and then confessed my feelings for him.

"Cy painted that one a few weeks ago. It's good, isn't it?" Fallon asked, and ruffled his feathers.

I nodded, smiling to myself.

Cyrus was a shithead. Keeping these from me.

I wondered what other secrets he had.

"You want a drink, Reece?" Fallon asked with his head buried inside the fridge. "Atlas mentioned you don't like booze, so I had Cyrus pick up some seltzers and he made this fancy mocktail thing."

I fucking lived for mocktails.

And Cyrus knew that.

"I'll try the mocktail, thanks." I glanced at the living area before I took a seat at the kitchen island. "Where are Atlas and Cyrus?"

Jimenez joined me and leaned against the island. "They're out on the terrace. You gotta ask for a tour, man. This place is fucking nice."

"That's all Cyrus. This place is way outta my price range," Fallon said as he poured my drink. He held the pitcher with the scaly skin of his talons.

Shit.

He was pretty fucking good with those little chicken hands.

Fallon passed me my drink and made his way around the island. "Let's head out to the terrace." He said "terrace" in an awful British accent, obviously mocking Cyrus for the way he said it.

I knew he was trying to be funny, but it still made my fist clench.

Jimenez and I followed Fallon across the living room and through wide sliding glass doors that led outside.

The sun was setting, bathing the terrace that overlooked Briar Glenn in warm orange light. Atlas leaned against the railing, his muzzle scrunched up as he let out a barking laugh at something Cyrus said.

Cyrus.

Hearing that smooth British accent sent shivers down my spine.

He looked in our direction as we walked out onto the terrace, and when his gaze connected with mine, his mouth parted into a wild smile.

He was so fucking handsome.

Not in the traditional sense, sure, but in a way that was attractive to me.

The angular planes of his face, his soft translucent fins, the musculature of his body, his bright coloring, and *those tentacles.*

Nothing would ever compare to those tentacles.

"Hey there," Atlas said, extending his hand out to me.

I was expecting a handshake, but he pulled me in for a tight hug.

Holy fuck, he was strong.

I was shocked he hadn't accidentally suffocated my sister with one of his hugs.

"Hello, Reece." Cyrus's voice was so calm, it practically bordered on a purr. I watched as he brought his mocktail to his lips and winked at me.

That fucker.

And I'd been so sure that I'd be the one who would be doing the teasing.

The five of us sat on the fancy—or "posh," as Cyrus called it—outdoor sectional, drinking and shooting the shit.

I was surprisingly relaxed—until Atlas brought up the triathlon.

"How's tri training coming along, Reece?" Fallon asked, leaning forward in his seat. "I know you and Cyrus have been hitting it pretty hard."

Atlas glanced over at Cyrus, and I could have sworn he smirked, but it passed too quickly for me to be sure.

Was he onto us? I knew there were cameras in the gym, but the locker room and showers were safe. There was no way Cyrus would have mentioned to him what was going on between us without bringing it up to me first.

"There's, what—a month left until the race?" Atlas asked.

Gods, Atlas. Way to remind me.

Cyrus chimed in before I could answer. "Yeah, a month. Reece is going to do great. He's come a long way. A few more open-water swims and he'll be set."

I fought to school my expression. I didn't want to give anything away, but knowing that Cyrus believed in me made my heart sing.

"We'll all be there to cheer you on. I think your mom and your sister are making shirts for everyone." Atlas wiggled his ears.

I choked on my drink. "Are you fucking serious?" I coughed.

"Mm-hmm, it's true. Selene was telling me all about it," Jimenez said with a laugh.

"S-Selene?" Fallon gave Javier a sideways glance.

"Yeah, my sister. She's one of Tegan's best friends," Jimenez said while absentmindedly scrolling through his phone.

"I thought Declan was Tegan's best friend." Fallon tapped his talons against the armrest of the sectional.

Jimenez shrugged and kept scrolling. "I don't know, man.

They're all close. They have sleepovers and shit all the time. Well, at least they did before Atlas came into the picture."

"Trust me, they're still around all the time. But Tegan's friends are my friends. Whatever makes her happy." The tip of Atlas's tail wagged ever so slightly.

He was head over heels for my sister. I felt like a jackass for ever being opposed to it.

While everyone chatted, I nursed my virgin mojito and did whatever I could to keep from staring at Cyrus.

He looked so good with the last rays of sunlight shining off his smooth skin. His tentacles gently swayed as he spoke, like how you'd tap your fingers or bounce your leg, and each time Atlas told a joke or rehashed a funny story, he'd throw back his head with a laugh, like everything that came out of his friend's mouth was the funniest thing he'd ever heard.

"I, uh, I gotta take a piss," I said, setting my drink down and rising off the sectional with a groan.

"Oh, I can show—" Fallon started to say, but Cyrus cut him off.

"I'll show him where it is. I wanted to give Reece a little tour anyway."

"That would be great." I followed behind Cyrus.

We were both silent as we walked inside and down the hall to the bathroom. My body tingled with anticipation. Sitting across from Cyrus all night and not being able to touch him had been complete torture.

He came to a stop at the bathroom and leaned against the doorway while I walked inside. I watched as he leaned back, his pointed head peeking down the hallway, making sure the coast was clear before he slipped inside.

I was on him the moment the lock clicked, pushing him

against the door and kissing my way down the finned column of his neck.

"You're so fucking sexy, you know that?" I mumbled against his smooth skin while my hands slid over his back, down to where his torso ended and his tentacles began.

"Am not," he whispered, and gripped my chin, forcing me to make eye contact with him. "Especially compared to you, you sexy fucking tease."

His mating tentacle unraveled and massaged my cock through my shorts. It was the kraken equivalent to frotting, and I lived for every second of it.

I whimpered, thrusting my hips to meet his tentacle, and Cyrus let out a dark laugh.

"Darling, you know I love it when you're a needy boy, but we can't. Not with all these people here. Is this how you want them to find out? Them hearing us fucking in the bathroom?"

I sighed and pressed my forehead against his, staring into his wide eyes. "You're right. I'm just horny."

He snorted and slipped one of his hands underneath my shirt, the tips of his fingers gently caressing the outline of my abs. "When are you not horny?"

"For you? Never."

Cyrus smiled and pressed his lips to mine, but he didn't go further than that, a quick kiss and nothing more. "Now that you've had some attention, do you want to see the rest of the apartment? Fallon's room is a fucking mess as usual, but I can show you my room and the studio."

I wanted to see his space, but I was more interested in seeing his art. I'd asked him to send me pictures of what he was currently working on, but he was always so damn secretive about it.

"I'd like that."

I groaned when Cyrus pulled away, adjusting my boner and doing what I could to make it less visible.

"There really isn't a good way to hide that thing." He smiled and raised his bumpy eyebrows.

"Cheeky fuck."

"Cheeky? Look at that. Not only am I rubbing you off, I'm rubbing off on you." His fins vibrated with laughter.

"Are you going to show me around the fucking apartment or are you going to stand there and make fun of me?"

"Yes, yes. Come on. You're grouchy when you don't get your way, you know that?" He held the door open, and when I went to pass him, he grabbed my shoulder.

"Might just have to spank that bratty behavior right out of you next time, hmm?" he whispered against my ear.

I froze and closed my eyes. "Fuck."

"Come on, then," he said, and shuffled down the hallway. "We'll start with my room and then I'll show you the studio."

Cyrus's bedroom was exactly what I expected.

It was masculine and modern, with an exposed brick wall behind the bed, and bright white walls covered with more moody paintings in various tones of blue and green. A record player sat on a shelving unit filled to the brim with vinyl: an extensive collection of all the '80s sad boy shit Cyrus loved.

"Damn." I spun a globe that sat next to the record player, watching the continents blur into swirling colors. "I knew your room was going to put mine to shame."

It wasn't that I was messy or dirty; design just didn't come naturally to me like it did to Cyrus. I kept my furniture to the essentials, and I was clueless when it came to home decor.

"I'm sure your place is lovely." Cyrus came up behind me, rested his head on my shoulder, and wrapped his arms around my waist. "But I'm happy to help you spruce it up a bit if you'd like.

In fact, I think I have some paintings in storage that would work well."

"You'd give me some of your art?"

Cyrus's work sold for thousands of dollars. He'd been featured in magazines and had gallery shows all over the world, and he wanted to give me some paintings?

"Mm-hmm." He nuzzled his face against my neck. "And every time you walk past them, you'll be reminded of me."

It made my chest ache. I didn't want to be reminded of him; I wanted to *be* with him.

"Cyrus, I—"

I had so many things I wanted to say. So many feelings, especially one feeling in particular that I wanted to express. Feelings that were strange and foreign to me, that had my heart beating fast and gave me the warm fuzzies.

They were there, and they were for Cyrus, but they scared the shit out of me.

When I didn't say anything, Cyrus held me tighter and kissed my cheek. It was like we were connected. Like he knew what I was feeling without me uttering a single word.

There was no way I could tell him how I felt. Not yet.

So I did the next best thing I could think of. Something that would give us a taste of what things could be like between us.

"Let's go away for a weekend," I blurted without giving the actual logistics of a trip like that any thought.

Cyrus went rigid behind me. "Do what now?"

I spun around to face him. "A weekend away. Just me and you." He stared at me with his mouth hanging open. He didn't seem convinced, so I started listing off the reasons why we should do it. "We can have sex in a bed and wake up next to each other. We don't have to worry about being seen together."

"I— But what about . . . ? Are you sure?" There was uncertainty in his voice, and I couldn't tell if it was because he was worried about blowing our cover or if it was because of me. That once again, he felt like he wasn't good enough to be involved with someone like me. It hurt knowing he thought so little of himself.

I grabbed his hand, giving it what I hoped was a comforting squeeze. "Just say yes."

Cyrus rolled his thin lips before revealing a shy smile. "All right."

"All right?" I asked, my voice pitching up.

He nodded, and I lunged at him, wrapping my arms around him and kissing along his jawline.

He tipped his head to the side, giving me better access. "How are we going to do this?" he asked, threading his fingers through my hair.

"I'll take care of everything," I murmured against his skin between kisses. "You just think of an excuse to slip away for the weekend." I sounded awfully confident for someone who had zero experience planning a weekend getaway.

"I think I can manage that."

"Good." I grinned, unable to hide how I felt. "I'm excited."

"Me, too."

"Now," I said, pulling away to look at him, "I believe someone told me they were going to show me their studio." There was no way I was leaving this apartment without seeing it.

"I'd hate to break a promise," he said, his lips tipping up with a soft smile. "Come on, darling."

He popped his head out of the doorway, checking that it was just the two of us in the apartment before leading me to the studio, his hand still holding mine.

Because of his webbing, we struggled to thread our fingers together, but it never really bothered me. I was just happy to be touching him.

It was crazy what a difference a few months could make. How one being could change your whole outlook.

"Here we are," Cyrus said as he pushed open the door.

"Shit," I muttered under my breath, and stepped inside the studio.

It was gorgeous.

Large windows lined one of the walls, and against the other was a row of canvases. Some were covered with drop cloths, but there were a few completed paintings out on display.

Cyrus leaned against a workbench covered with paints and brushes, and I headed straight for the paintings. They were mostly landscapes: forest scenes, coastal towns, and even a few places around Briar Glenn I recognized.

"Cyrus, these are beautiful," I said, glancing over at him. His arms were crossed over his broad chest, a shy smile turning up the corners of his lips, but I could tell he was beaming with pride.

"I'm glad you like them," he said as he shuffled over next to me. "For the first time in a long time, I'm feeling inspired." He reached down and grabbed my hand, the two of us staring at the canvases. "You crashed into my life when I least expected it, but also when I needed it most. You can be a dickhead, but you're *my* dickhead. My life is infinitely better with you in it, Reece Rollins."

My cheeks flushed and tears formed in the corners of my eyes when Cyrus brought my hand up to his lips.

"Come on," he said quietly. "We should get back to the party."

"Wait." I stepped in front of him.

I held his face between my hands and pressed my lips to his, kissing him like my life depended on it, using my actions to say what I couldn't admit to.

At least not yet.

Because my life was infinitely better with him in it, too.

Twenty-Two

REECE

IT WAS EASY ENOUGH FOR ME TO HIDE AWAY FOR A WEEKEND. But Cyrus? Not so much. With Fallon as his overbearing, overly involved roommate, there was no way his absence would go unnoticed, so Cyrus had crafted some lie about going out of town for the weekend to check out a new gallery. He'd purposefully picked a weekend that Fallon worked so he wouldn't offer to accompany Cyrus on his trip.

I tried not to feel guilty about it, but with each week that passed, the web of lies Cyrus and I were weaving got more intricate. I just hoped things wouldn't snap before I got to a place where I felt comfortable telling my sister the truth.

While I waited by the window for Cyrus, my body buzzed with excitement—either that or the two cups of coffee I'd slammed in preparation for the four-hour drive ahead of me. By some stroke of luck, I'd found an Airbnb with last-minute availability. When I booked the place, the host messaged me, saying we should head out early to avoid traffic on the bridge into town and that he'd let us check in early—free of charge. I appreciated that, and not because it lowered the chances of Cyrus and me getting caught but because it meant we could spend as much time together as possible.

It wasn't every day that we had an opportunity like this. I wasn't going to waste it.

A pair of bright white headlights lit up the street, and my breath hitched. There was only one person who it could be, and I was already raising the garage door by the time Cyrus pulled into the driveway.

Just the sight of him made me smile so wide, my cheeks hurt.

"Were you waiting for me?" Cyrus asked the moment he shuffled out of his SUV.

"Maybe," I said with a shrug. I was trying to play it cool, but I was already moving closer to him, sliding my hand over the smooth skin of his waist and pressing a kiss to his soft lips. It didn't take long for things to get heated, his tongues swirling against mine, and his tentacles wrapping around my arms and my legs, applying gentle pressure that rushed straight to my cock. I let myself grind against him for a second, showing him just how much I missed him.

He laughed, cupping my face and staring at me with his deep blue eyes. The smooth pad of his thumb swept across my cheek affectionately, making me lean into his touch.

"I take it someone missed me," he whispered against my lips.

I nodded because it was the truth. We'd trained together yesterday morning, so we'd only been apart for less than twenty-four hours, but somehow it felt like an eternity. The old me would have been freaked out by those types of feelings for someone, but with Cyrus it just felt right.

I gave him one last peck on the lips before I pulled away. As turned on as I was, I wanted to hit the road before traffic picked up.

Cyrus yawned, wiggling the tips of his tentacles like he was trying to wake them up.

It was fucking cute.

"Tired?" I asked.

"Mm-hmm," he hummed. "I was so bloody excited that I couldn't sleep. I ended up painting most of the night."

I'd been so restless, I'd only managed a few hours of sleep myself. "I wish you could have stayed over," I admitted.

"Me, too. But we'll get to spend the next few days together to make up for it."

"Did Fallon give you a hard time?"

Cyrus shook his head. "He thought it was odd, especially since I was leaving so early, but it didn't seem like he suspected anything. Honestly, he's probably excited to have the apartment to himself for the weekend. It's easier for him to bring women home when I'm not there. I did tell him that if he has a party, I'll pluck his feathers out one by one."

"He'd do that even though he works this weekend?" The guy was in his thirties. Wasn't he a little too old for that sort of thing?

"Do you think that work would stop someone like him? His best friend is his boss."

I chuckled. "Good point. I'll let you know if I hear anything about a party from Javier."

The two of them had been hanging out quite a bit since the engagement party. And by hanging out, I meant getting blackout drunk and picking up people at bars. I wasn't sure Fallon was a good influence on my friend, but Cyrus swore it was Javier who was the bad influence. We agreed to disagree on that one.

"What about you?" Cyrus asked. "Did you say anything to anyone?"

"Nope. It isn't like my sister and my mom check in on me or

anything. If they come by, they'll just think I'm not home. And if they call, I'll just feed them some bullshit excuse." Surprisingly, I didn't have any anxiety about the trip. I was going to spend an entire weekend with Cyrus, and I wasn't going to let anything kill my vibe.

"Perfect." The way he looked at me when he said it made my stomach flip.

"Are you ready?" I asked, moving toward the door.

"Just a second." He opened the back door of his SUV and pulled out a duffle bag.

"What's that?" I asked.

He didn't wear clothes. Hell, he didn't even carry a wallet . . .

"I brought some supplies for sketching and painting. You said we were going somewhere beautiful. Thought I could work on some sketches or watercolors while we're there."

Watercolors.

That was perfect for where we were going.

Cyrus followed me out the side door of the garage to where my car was parked on the street. I took his bag and set it on the back seat with my things, as well as the cooler full of food I'd packed for the weekend.

"It smells nice in here," Cyrus said when he tucked himself into the passenger seat. Because I had a normal car and not an SUV, it was a little cramped with him and all his tentacles. I hoped the long drive wouldn't be too uncomfortable for him. If things continued to progress, I was going to have to get a bigger vehicle.

That thought made me pause for a second. Because it meant that I saw this going somewhere. That I thought of a future with Cyrus in it.

My chest felt tight and my heart fluttered, a confusing mixture of fear and excitement hitting me all at once.

Was this what it felt like to be—I couldn't even bring myself to think it.

"T-thank you," I stammered, remembering that Cyrus had just made a comment about how good the car smelled. "I had it detailed for our trip."

"That was sweet of you." He clicked his seat belt and tapped his phone screen. "Do you want me to play some music?"

"Sure." I already knew what I was in for with Cyrus's taste in music. It would be some sad croony '80s shit, and even though I played it off like I was humoring him when we listened to it, I secretly liked it.

While Cyrus got the music going, I typed the address for the Airbnb into the GPS.

"Don't look," I told him, using one hand to shield the screen. I'd given him an idea of how far we'd be traveling, but I didn't tell him exactly where we were going. I wanted him to be surprised.

Cyrus yawned again, showing off that mouth full of sharp teeth. I had to really be into him if I let those razor blades near my cock.

"Fuck," he said. "Why am I so bloody tired?"

"Just lay your seat back and sleep."

"I can't do that. I want to keep you company."

"I've got music, and I had some caffeine. I'm good."

"Are you sure?" he asked.

"Don't make me tell you again," I said sternly.

He laughed and gave me a sleepy smile. "If you get tired, crack a window or wake me up, and I can drive the rest of the way."

"Okay," I said, even though there was no way I was going to do that.

Cyrus reclined the seat and one of his tentacles slithered across the center console to rest on my leg. By the time we hit the highway, he was already asleep.

AFTER FOUR HOURS ON THE SOUTHBOUND INTERSTATE, I pulled onto the narrow two-lane bridge that led to the peninsula where we were staying. It was your typical tourist town, with kitschy boardwalk attractions and overpriced vacation rentals built around the beach. This was one of the last warm weekends of the summer, meaning it was going to be absolutely packed.

The drive across the bridge felt like it took an eternity, and I let out a sigh of relief once my tires hit solid ground. It wasn't that I was afraid of bridges; I'd just never been on one quite that long. As I drove deeper into the peninsula, the trees lining the road tapered off into rolling sand dunes covered with long stalks of beach grass. According to the GPS, we were getting close to the Airbnb.

I couldn't wait to see the look on Cyrus's face when he finally got to swim in the ocean.

It was rare that I did nice things, let alone romantic things, but I hadn't let anyone in like I'd let Cyrus in. With him, it was so easy—well, easy after our first encounter together. I was going to have to live with that embarrassment for the rest of my life.

Cyrus had to be tired, because he spent the entire drive asleep in the passenger seat. As exhausted as I was, I was happy that he actually did what I asked of him. He was constantly doing shit for me: Training me for the triathlon. Treating me to coffee. Making me come undone. The least I could do was make sure he was well rested for the first day of our trip.

I cracked open my window and let the salty sea air drift into the car. Goose bumps pebbled my arm, and a tiny shiver raced down my spine. Even this far down the coast, there was a noticeable chill in the mornings and in the evenings now, the last bits of the summer heat fading to the cool temps of fall.

It would be time for the triathlon before I knew it.

The end of my training sessions with Cyrus.

What did it mean for our relationship after that?

Cyrus stirred, eventually setting his seat in the upright position.

"Good morning, sleepyhead," I said, taking my eyes off the road for a second to stare at him.

Sunlight kissed his skin, making his blue-green color shimmer like a calm sea. In a way, that's what he was. His presence was steady, allowing an inexperienced sailor like me to navigate the ocean of feelings I had for him.

Fuck. Cyrus's deep poetic nature was rubbing off on me.

He noticed me glancing at him out of the corner of my eye and he gave me a sleepy smile. "Where are we?" he asked.

I laughed and shook my head. "I told you that you were just going to have to wait. I want it to be a surprise."

Cyrus's brows drew back, his tiny nostrils flaring. "Well, I can already tell we're near the ocean. There's no disguising that smell. Or hiding the dunes."

Well, I guess it was sort of stupid to think I'd be able to keep it a surprise until we arrived. Why did he have to wake up before we got there?

It was fine. He was still happy. That's what mattered.

"Well, you said it's been a while since you swam in the ocean. I wanted to make that happen for you."

"You planned all this just so I could take a dip in the sea?" he asked, his voice tight.

I nodded. "I mean, that and because I wanted to spend time with you without looking over my shoulder."

When he didn't say anything in response to that, a knot formed in the pit of my stomach.

Was it a problem that I wanted us to be out in public together? Or did he hate the fact that it was a secret at home?

"Everything okay?" I asked.

"Mm-hmm," he mumbled. I looked over at him again, noticing the shiny glaze of tears lining his eyes.

"Hey." I reached for his hand, bringing it to my lips and placing a soft kiss on the back.

"Sorry," he sniffled. "I'm just very touched. I've never had someone do something like this for me."

I let out a heavy breath, letting my anxiety slip out with it.

So he wasn't mad about the whole secret relationship aspect of this. He was touched by the fact that I'd planned something nice for him based on a comment he'd made in passing.

"I, uh, I've never done something like this for someone before. I never wanted to until I met you."

It was the truth. Not once in my life had I ever felt the urge to do something romantic for a partner, but then again, I'd never had an actual partner.

Outside of fulfilling my sexual needs, I'd never actually felt something for another person. Not like the romantic attraction I felt toward Cyrus.

It was strange and it was scary, but the more time we spent together, the clearer it was that there was something going on between us. We were more than just fuck buddies.

"I—" Cyrus started.

I gripped the steering wheel tight, holding my breath while I waited for him to say whatever it was he was going to say.

"I appreciate you," he said after a few tense seconds.

It felt like I'd taken a punch right to my stomach, and I didn't know why. Was I expecting him to say more than that? It was sort of unfair, given all the things I hadn't been able to articulate.

I swallowed hard, forcing my disappointment down with it. "I appreciate you, too."

The GPS had me make a right turn, and we pulled up to the main house of the Airbnb. It looked just like it did on the listing, a white Cape Cod–style house with beachy turquoise blue accents.

I would have preferred to drive straight to the bungalow to check in, but an orc stepped out onto the porch to greet us. He was big and burly, dressed in a linen outfit with his black hair hanging down his back in a long braid. If I remembered his profile photo correctly, he was definitely the owner, but I wouldn't be surprised if he ran a meditation retreat or an ayahuasca commune out of this place on the side.

I'd try ayahuasca.

Maybe it would heal my childhood trauma.

Cyrus rolled down his window and waved with one of his tentacles.

"You made it," the orc said, smiling so wide the blunt tips of his tusks dug into his upper lip.

"We did," Cyrus said cheerfully, the sunshine to my grumpy.

"How was the drive?" the orc asked.

I really wasn't in the mood to socialize, at least not until I had another cup of coffee, but it was in our best interest to be nice to the host. Especially since he'd helped me out by taking a last-minute booking like this.

"Not bad at all," I said honestly.

He nodded. "You left early enough to beat the traffic. Any later in the day and you would have been parked on the bridge. I'm Brok, by the way. My partner, Rob, is still asleep, but I'm sure you'll see him around at some point during your stay. We have you set up in bungalow number three, the one closest to the beach.

Just follow the driveway straight down and you can park right out front. On the kitchen table you'll find a binder full of restaurants. There's also a little grocery store in town, but it's quite overpriced, so I hope you followed my advice and brought anything you might want to eat with you. Rob and I spend quite a bit of time out on the porch here at the main house, and you're welcome to join us. Just let us know if there's anything you need."

"Thank you so much," Cyrus said, beaming.

"Thank you," I added.

Brok nodded and started to head inside, but he stopped, turning back toward us again. "I know you've had a long drive. Can I get you anything? A cup of coffee? Tea?" he asked.

"Coffee, please," I rushed to say. I needed it like I needed air.

Brok disappeared inside the house, returning a few seconds later with two paper cups of coffee for us.

"Gods, thank you," Cyrus said. Two of his tentacles reached out the car window, carefully grabbing the cups from Brok. "I can't handle this one until he's had his coffee," he said, flashing me a teasing smile as he passed me my cup.

"My Rob is the same way," Brok said. "Thirty years later and I still get up early to start the pot."

"Thirty years together," Cyrus said in awe. "That's lovely."

They'd been together almost as long as I'd been alive . . .

"What I would give for thirty more," Brok said dreamily. "Anyway, I'll let you get settled in. Enjoy the beach."

"Thank you," I said.

Brok gave us a little wave as I pulled off down the driveway.

"He seems nice," I said.

"Very nice. And he's been with his partner for thirty years. Can you believe that?"

I laughed. "Thirty years is, like, a blink of an eye for you."

"It is, but I've never been around the same person for that long."

"Been around?" I asked. *What exactly did he mean by that?*

"Mm-hmm. Been around."

I cocked a brow. "Like, dated?" Previous dating history wasn't a topic we'd really breached, not that I really had much to discuss there.

"Why do you ask?" He flashed me a sly smile.

I shrugged again, trying to act casual but failing miserably. I shouldn't have cared, but the thought of him with someone else really pissed me off.

"Oh my gods," he laughed, obviously enjoying this. "You're jealous."

I shook my head, my cheeks already flaming. "I am not," I lied.

"You are, too. And don't even act like you haven't dated other people. I mean"—he gestured at me with his hands—"look at you."

"That's the thing, though. I, uh, I haven't dated anyone, really."

Cyrus was silent for a moment, his wide blue eyes staring at me. "You what?"

"I don't date. I just—fuck."

"So that's what you meant when you said you've never done something like this for someone before?"

"Yeah. All of this is new for me."

"Why me?" he whispered.

I put the car in park and looked over at him. I wanted to have his full attention for what I was about to say. "Because you're special to me, Cy. You do so much for me, and I wanted to give you back just a fraction of the kindness you've shown me."

He leaned over the center console and wrapped me in a tight hug. "Thank you, darling. You're special to me, too."

We got out of the car, but before I could grab our bags and the cooler, Cyrus's tentacles had already snatched them up.

"You could have let me help," I huffed as we walked up to the cottage. It was a replica of the main house, just on a much smaller scale. Perfect for the two of us.

"You booked the place, you drove, and you surprised me with the sea. The least I can do is carry everything."

I typed the passcode into the electronic lock, and we stepped inside the bungalow.

It was the size of a studio apartment, one big room with a queen-size bed, a tiny kitchenette, and a compact en suite. Light blue paint covered the walls, and every opportunity to use seashells in the decor had been taken. Seashell bedspread. Seashell shower curtain. Seashell tablecloth. Behind the bed? A painting of a sandpiper running along a beach covered in—you guessed it—seashells.

From the listing photos, I had an idea of what we were in for, but the place was really giving off snowbird-vacation-home vibes. The only thing it was missing were doilies and a basket of decorative seashell hand soaps—ones that weren't meant to be used.

I'm sure Brok and his partner were nice guys, but they desperately needed an interior decorator.

Cyrus set down our stuff and shuffled around the room, taking everything in. "Reece, this place is adorable."

With a smile on my face, I leaned against the doorframe, watching him check out the place. "I knew you'd like it."

I didn't, actually. I was worried it would be too tacky for someone like Cyrus, but it wasn't like I had a ton of options.

I flopped down on the bed, propping myself up on one arm to stare at him. "So, anything you want to do?" I asked, wiggling my eyebrows. My muscles ached from the drive, but with Cyrus, there was one thing I was always in the mood for.

"Swim," he said, staring out the window toward the ocean, totally ignoring my advances. "Let's go for a swim."

I chuckled and hauled myself off the bed. I should have known that was the first thing on the agenda. "Let me finish my coffee and I'll get changed."

Twenty-Three

♥

CYRUS

WHILE REECE CHANGED, I TRANSFERRED EVERYTHING FROM
the cooler to the fridge. Eggs, bacon, chicken breasts. I loved that
he had the forethought to grocery-shop and meal-plan for the
weekend. Not that there was anything wrong with eating out
while on vacation, but I wanted to cook a meal with him. I wanted
to experience all the things we didn't get to do in Briar Glenn.

"I would have done that, Cy," Reece said.

I peeked around the fridge door, taking in the sight of him—
shirtless—with his swim trunks hanging low on his hips. That
glorious happy trail that I loved so much ran straight down his flat
stomach, disappearing below the waistband of his trunks. It was
like a fuzzy little rainbow leading to the pot of gold at the end: his
cock.

My gaze raked back up his body to his handsome face. He was
smirking, obviously aware of the way I'd been shamelessly admiring him.

"Like what you see?" he asked, bringing his arms up and flexing his defined biceps.

How was it that the goddess had blessed me with a man whose body rivaled the Farnese Hercules? It was as if he'd been etched out of stone by one of the greats. At some point I'd have to add a sculpture of Reece to my growing collection of artwork dedicated to him.

The familiar tingle of arousal ran down my mating tentacles, so I shut the fridge and shuffled over to him. "Indeed, I do."

"Nope," he said, stepping back. "I tried that, and you shut me down."

Fuck. I *had* shut him down in favor of swimming, hadn't I?

"Right. Right." I moved back, putting some space between us before I could pin him to the bed and fuck him until he couldn't see straight. "Swimming. The whole point of this trip."

"Exactly," Reece said, and started for the door.

"Where do you think you're going?" I asked.

"You said you wanted to swim."

"Do you not see the sun? You're going to burn to a crisp."

"Oh fuck," he said, glancing down at his pale skin. "Good point."

"Exactly." He stood there staring at me. "Do you have sunscreen?" I asked.

"Nope."

"I knew it." I laughed and made my way over to my duffle bag, pulling out a bottle of SPF seventy sunscreen I'd bought just for this trip. As a kraken, I didn't need sunscreen, but Reece certainly did.

"How did you know?" Reece asked.

"Because I've seen you sunburnt several times this summer. Someone with your complexion is at a greater risk for melanoma. You need to start taking sun protection seriously."

"I'll get some of those UPF shirts just for you."

"Please do," I said, already making a mental note to order him a few. As much as I hated the idea of covering up his perfect body, the last thing I wanted was my mate's life cut short because of something preventable. "Hold out your arms for me."

Reece sighed but complied, raising his arms in a T shape.

I coated my hands with sunscreen and rubbed it over his shoulders, back, chest, and abs, until he was covered in a shiny layer of lotion.

"Let me get your face, too."

He closed his eyes, and I carefully massaged the sunscreen into his cheeks and scrunched forehead, and over the freckled bridge of his nose.

"You're going to put me to sleep massaging me like this," he mumbled.

"I just wanted to make sure it was thoroughly applied. Done."

I stepped back and he opened those vivid green eyes, their intensity nearly taking my breath away.

"What?" he asked, tipping his head to the side.

He was just so damn handsome.

"Nothing. All set."

Reece slung a towel over his shoulders, and we slipped out the door.

There were a series of handmade signs leading us over a boarded path that passed right through the sand dunes, down to a strip of private beach. Seagulls circled overhead, and foamy waves crashed against the shore, littering the beach with clumps of seaweed.

The morning sun hung high in the cloudless sky, already warming the sand.

"Good call on the sunscreen," Reece said, holding his hand over his eyes to squint at the ocean. "I would have—"

I couldn't make out the rest because the moment my tentacles hit the sand, I scuttled toward the water as fast as I could.

"Hey," Reece shouted from behind me, racing to catch up. "Wait for me."

I forced myself to slow down. He'd put so much thought into this, and I wanted us to share the moment. "Sorry," I said. "I'm just so bloody excited."

"Good." He grabbed my hand, and my hearts thundered in my chest. It was so unexpected, this casual display of affection from a man who didn't like being touched.

I gave his hand a little squeeze, and the two of us headed toward the water together.

A wave washed over the shore, and at the first brush of salt water against my tentacles, my body hummed with excitement.

The sea.

For the first time in years, I was going to swim in the sea.

And it was all thanks to my mate.

Reece and I ventured farther offshore, until the water was up to our waists, then our chests. Salt water surged through my body, making every cell feel alive and amplifying my good mood. A salt-water pool or bathtub soak was one thing, but this? It was heaven. It was like I was weightless. Like I'd become one with the ocean.

"Come here," I said, reaching for him with my tentacles.

I wrapped them around his waist and pulled him through the water until his body was pressed against mine.

"Are you happy?" he asked, staring into my eyes.

"Happier than you could ever know."

I released my tentacles and slipped underneath the water.

"Hey," Reece said. "Where did you go?"

The water was so murky, there was no way he could see me, but I could see him. Those long pale muscular legs slowly kicking in the water.

I swam around him a few times, flaring out my parachute, allowing my tentacles to graze his legs.

"Cyrus," he laughed. "I don't like you swimming under me when I can't see you. It freaks me out."

Why? I asked telepathically. *It's just me. I won't let anything get you.*

Reece shouted when I swam between his legs and lifted him out of the water so he sat on my waist while I floated on the surface. I was living for this. It was all the things I wanted to do with him at the lake in Briar Glenn and couldn't.

"I feel like I'm on a living surfboard," he said, staring down at me.

Water dripped off his full lashes down onto his slightly flushed cheeks. With all the time he'd been spending in the sun, freckles dotted the bridge of his nose and clustered in large patches across his broad shoulders. The next time I painted him, I'd have to flick my brush at the canvas to memorialize them in little flecks of paint for when the winter came and they inevitably faded.

I'd never tire of looking at him. Making art of him. Appreciating his beauty.

"How does the salt water feel?" he asked.

I closed my eyes, focusing on the way the waves lapped at the fins along my neck. "Heavenly. Thank you again for doing this."

I knew he wasn't the romantic type—that was my job—and this weekend had been such a pleasant surprise. It let me know just how special I was to Reece, that my hopes of my mate reciprocating my feelings were coming to fruition. I'd almost slipped earlier, telling him exactly how I felt about him, but I was too scared to say it.

The fact that we were here and things between us were moving in the right direction, that was enough for me. Everything else would fall into place in time.

"Cy?" Reece said, and my eyes shot open.

"Hmm?"

He leaned forward until his forearms were on my chest and his handsome face lingered over mine. "I asked if you want to go get breakfast. I'm starving."

"Oh, yes. Let's do that." As sad as I was to leave the water, we had all weekend to swim. All weekend to hug and hold hands and kiss and fuck without the worry of watchful eyes.

"Are you going to let me off?"

"Nope," I said, already jetting us back to the shore.

"Cyrus," Reece yelped, digging his fingers into my skin, trying to hold on for dear life as we shot through the waves with ease. His panic quickly shifted into amused laughter, making me laugh with him.

When the water was too shallow for swimming, I slid out from under him, and we walked onto the beach.

Reece grabbed his towel, shook off the sand, and wrapped it around his waist. "It's crazy to me that we're only four hours down the coast and it's this much hotter. The water was surprisingly warm, too."

I laughed. "Anything is warm compared to the lake."

"True."

"Is there anything you want to do after breakfast," I asked as we made our way back to the bungalow.

"I figured we could just chill today. Hang out on the beach. Maybe after dinner we can watch the sunset. How does that sound?"

"That sounds lovely."

Twenty-Four

REECE

WE SPENT MOST OF THE DAY ON THE BEACH, SWIMMING TO-gether in the ocean and relaxing in the sun. Well, Cyrus spent it in the sun. When I started to get too pink for his liking, he set up one of Brok's umbrellas and parked me under it for the rest of the afternoon.

I sat in the shade, watching him jet along the surface of the ocean before disappearing under the waves. He'd shoot out of the water and make a big splash as he dove back down, like a more graceful version of a whale's breach. Every once in a while, he'd look at me on the shore and flash me a sharp-toothed smile before his voice excitedly echoed in my head: *Did you see that?*

Cyrus was usually joyful, but this was unparalleled. It was like he was a little kid, making sure I didn't miss a moment of his antics.

I started to feel the effects of getting up at four a.m. around dinnertime, and when Cyrus noticed me nodding off in my beach chair, we finally packed it in for the day.

When I got out of the shower, I found Cyrus crouched over the counter, prepping dinner in what was probably the smallest kitchen I'd ever seen.

"What are you doing?" I asked.

"Making dinner," he said with his casual British snark.

I should have known he had some ulterior motive when he told me to shower by myself.

"Why don't you let me help?" This was the romantic getaway I'd planned and grocery-shopped for. I was the one who was supposed to be wining and dining him. At least, that was how it had played out in my fantasies.

Cyrus laughed. "There's barely enough room in here for me. If you help, we'll practically be on top of each other. Not that I'd mind being on top of you, but you've had a long day. The least I can do is make dinner."

I sighed. There was no way I was going to win this one. "All right. Well, I'm here for moral support."

"Thank you, darling. And thank you for making sure we'd have everything we'd need."

"You heard Brok. There's only one tiny grocery store here and it's massively overpriced. I figured it would be easier if I just brought everything with us." I noticed the plate of bare chicken breasts on the counter. "You gonna put something on that chicken?"

He whipped around, glaring at me with his hands on his hips. "Excuse me. I'm the one cooking here. If you're going to continue being a backseat chef, I'll have you wait out on the porch."

I let out a genuine laugh. "I'm sorry. I'm just not used to someone else cooking my meals. Well, other than my mother."

I sounded like a loser. A thirty-five-year-old man who just

admitted that the only other person who cooked for him was his mother.

"You better get used to it. Cooking is my love language." His back tensed up like he was bracing himself for how I was going to respond to that.

"I, uh, I've never really cooked for anyone else. But I enjoy it. And I'd like to cook for you." I scrubbed a hand through my wet hair, suddenly feeling shy. "That was my whole plan, actually."

"Shit," Cyrus hissed. "I'm sorry. That was inconsiderate of me. You've just had a long day, and you've done so much already—"

"It's okay," I reassured him. "There will be more opportunities for me to feed you this weekend."

"Better be feeding me that cock," he mumbled.

I went up behind him, skated my hand over his hip, and nuzzled my nose against the soft skin along his jawline. My cock wasn't even remotely hard, but I rotated my hips and pressed it into his back. "You can have that anytime you want," I whispered, feeling his breath hitch at my words.

He opened his mouth to respond, but before he could find his thoughts, I pecked his cheek and sauntered over to the kitchen table and sat down.

"You're cruel, you know that?" he tsked.

I took a sip of my water and shrugged. "Consider it payback for all the times you've teased me."

"Well, maybe I do deserve a taste of my own medicine," Cyrus said with a grin. He fished around in the fridge for a second before pulling out a bottle of my favorite barbecue sauce. "I'm assuming barbecue chicken is okay?"

I nodded. "Yes, please." It was exactly what I'd planned on making. Simple, fairly healthy, and delicious.

He coated the chicken breasts with the sauce, taking a minute to think when he was finished. "Is oven-baked okay?"

"Yep."

"Perfect."

Forty minutes later, Cyrus set a plate of barbecue chicken, steamed broccoli, and mac and cheese in front of me. Yes, I was health conscious, but a serving of mac and cheese every once in a while never hurt anything. Just like the occasional sweet treat. Life was about balance.

"Thank you," I said, already cutting into my chicken breast.

Cyrus took his seat across from me. "You're very welcome, darling."

The chicken was perfectly cooked, slathered in a layer of sticky, smoky barbecue sauce that melted in my mouth.

Cyrus stared at me intently while I chewed.

After I forced down a bite, I said, "Why are you looking at me like that?"

He laughed. "I can't watch you enjoy a meal I prepared for you?"

"I mean, you can." Heat rushed up my neck to my cheeks. I looked away from him and focused on a little sculpture made out of seashells on the entryway table. "I'm just not used to it."

"I never expected you to be like this."

I forced myself to look at Cyrus again. His elbows were on the table, his chin resting on his clasped hands. "Like what?" I asked.

"Well, you're extremely attractive. From the outside, someone would look at you and think you'd dated around. That you've been in plenty of relationships."

"I've just never been interested in anyone that way," I admitted.

He hid his face in his hands, looking so fucking adorable. "You're killing me, you know that?" he murmured.

I chuckled. "I was just thinking the same thing."

AT THE BACK OF THE BUNGALOW, THERE WAS A LITTLE PATIO that overlooked the ocean. We sat on the uncomfortable wicker sofa and snuggled together. The sun was setting over the ocean, a bright, almost fluorescent orange ball of light surrounded by soft purples and pinks.

"This view is gorgeous," Cyrus said, trailing his fingers over my thigh.

"Are you sure you don't want to go down to the beach with your art supplies?" I was barely hanging in there, but if he wanted to go down to the beach to paint, I'd happily lie on a towel next to him.

He shook his head. "There are some moments that are better captured with your memory than with your art."

"Always so poetic." I closed my eyes, letting my head fall back. "Am I?"

"Mm-hmm," I murmured.

"Tired?"

I slumped my head to the side so I was leaning against Cyrus's shoulder. "Just a little bit."

"Do you want to get in bed?" he asked.

I nodded. "Please."

"Can you walk, or would you like me to carry you?"

I laughed and blinked my heavy eyelids a few times. "I can walk."

We shuffled inside the house, and I stripped off my shirt and shorts, leaving me in nothing but my briefs.

Cyrus's eyes roved over my body appreciatively.

It was a shame I was tired.

"Sorry, Cy," I said when I caught him staring.

"It's all right, darling. It's only the first day. We have all weekend to have sex." He flipped the comforter back and patted the mattress. "Which side would you like?"

It dawned on me that this was the very first time I was going to spend the night with someone I was hooking up with.

At home, I slept in the middle of my king-size mattress, so I guess it didn't really matter which side. Either way, we were two large guys cramming onto a queen-size mattress. We were going to pretty much sleep on top of each other.

"I'll take this side," I said, climbing into bed on the side that was closest to me.

Cyrus took the other, the mattress dipping under the weight of his body. I knew he was strong, but I didn't realize just how heavy he was.

He kept his tentacles bunched together, respectfully keeping to his side of the mattress, like he wasn't sure if it was okay to touch me. Or maybe he was just giving me space to make the first move, to let me take things where I wanted them to go.

"Do you want to cuddle?" I asked quietly.

As someone who was averse to touch, it surprised me just how much I craved Cyrus's.

"Of course I do." He stretched his arm out across the pillows, making room for me to snuggle up against his body. His tentacles relaxed, draping over my legs and waist, applying gentle pressure like a weighted blanket.

Earlier in the afternoon, we'd cranked the thermostat down to make sure the bungalow would be nice and cool for bedtime. It was almost too cold, but with the blankets and the soft heat radiating off Cyrus, I was comfortable. I was at ease.

"This is the first time I've ever done this," I mumbled with my eyes closed. "And I'm glad it could be with you."

He stroked his thumb over the bare skin of my shoulder and placed a soft kiss on the top of my head. "Me, too. You have no idea how much." His voice was tight, almost like he was on the verge of tears.

This was so new for both of us. In the span of a few months, we'd become so much more than just coach and trainee.

I snuggled closer, focusing on the gentle rise and fall of Cyrus's chest. The way his smooth skin felt under my palm.

"Good night, Reece," he murmured.

"Night," I drawled, letting our connection rock me to sleep.

Twenty-Five

CYRUS

I WAS LYING NEXT TO AN ANGEL.

In sleep, Reece's normally stern expression was calm and serene. There was no wrinkle in his brow, no tic in his jaw. His red hair was a wild mess, catching the morning sun as it streamed through the window.

He was breathtaking.

"Do you want to keep staring at me or do you want to get up?" Reece grumbled with his eyes still closed. His already deep voice had more of a gravelly base first thing in the morning, one that made my tentacles curl.

"I was just enjoying the view."

His deep green eyes popped open, and before I knew what was happening, he rolled on top of me and straddled my waist. He braced himself on one hand and reached down with the other to cup my face, gently stroking his thumb over my cheek.

What I would give to wake up to him like this every day.

"Morning, Cy," he said, leaning closer, until his face hovered over mine.

I ran my hands up his chest, feeling the prickle of his hair re-growth under my fingers. "Good morning, darling. Did you sleep well?"

I knew the answer was yes. He was out the moment his head touched the pillow, and I didn't feel him move at all through the night. For the longest time, I'd just lain there next to him, watching the moonlight cast shadows on his handsome face.

"I slept great." He gave me a little peck on the lips before he rolled off me, and I frowned at the loss.

"Where are you going?" I asked, sitting up in bed.

With his back turned to me, he stretched toward the ceiling, making his muscles flex. He was so stunning, I had to remind myself to breathe.

"To make coffee," he said matter-of-factly, and sauntered to the tiny kitchen.

While Reece started the coffeepot, I shuffled into the bathroom to do my business. When I came out, he was standing at the stove—still shirtless—with a spatula in his hand. The familiar scent of bacon filled the air, the grease cracking and popping in the pan.

"Are you cooking bacon without a shirt on?" I mean, I did it all the time, but it was one of those "do as I say, not as I do" sorts of things.

He shrugged. "I didn't want to start with the eggs because I wasn't sure how you liked them."

I came up behind him, wrapped my arms around his waist, and kissed his neck, feeling his fresh stubble grate against my face.

A soft hum worked its way out of his throat, and he tipped his head to the side, melting into me. "There's coffee in the pot for you."

"Thank you," I said, pecking him on the cheek before making my way over to pour a cup.

A mug was next to the machine as well as hazelnut coffee creamer. My favorite flavor. He must have been paying attention when we ordered at the Busy Bean. The machine was still brewing, but there was just enough in the carafe for a cup. For a caffeine fiend like Reece to offer me the first cup of coffee was almost like an admission of his feelings for me.

"You didn't have to do all this," I whispered. Once again, I was feeling touched to the point of overwhelm by all of my mate's kind gestures.

"How many times do I have to tell you? I know I don't have to. I do it because I want to."

I made my coffee and sat down at the tiny kitchen table.

Reece peered over his shoulder at me. "You never did tell me how you'd like your eggs."

"Oh, over easy, please."

He scrunched up his nose.

"What's that look for?" I asked with a laugh.

"Over easy grosses me out. Why would I want my eggs all wet and drippy?"

"Have you ever tried it?" I didn't know everything about Reece, but he could be quite—particular.

"Nope, and I don't plan to." He cracked two eggs in the pan and quietly stared at them for a moment before he finally said, "Over easy was how my old man liked his eggs."

Well, that explained part of his aversion to them.

"How do you like your eggs?" I asked.

"Scrambled or in an omelet." So, very much the opposite of wet and drippy.

"What kind of omelet?"

"Western." He popped two pieces of bread into the toaster, then leaned against the counter to look at me. "I, uh, I liked sleeping in bed with you," he said, rubbing one hand over his bed head.

I grinned, feeling like my hearts were going to explode over how adorable he was being. "I liked it, too."

"I—I wish it was something we could do more often," he admitted. The slightest hint of pink rushed up his neck to his cheeks.

"Me, too, but we don't have to rush things."

He crossed his arms over his chest, his fingers gently drumming against his biceps. "After the triathlon, I want to tell Tegan."

I was taking a sip of my coffee, and I almost spit it out all over the seashell-patterned tablecloth. "Oh?" I choked out.

He glanced down at the floor for a second before giving me this sweet, shy, hopeful look. "I mean, if that's okay with you."

"Of course it's okay with me," I rushed to say. I didn't want him to feel pressured, but it was hard to temper my excitement.

"I appreciate you being so patient with me. I know I'm asking a lot of you."

Little did he know, he could ask me for anything, and I'd happily comply. I'd follow him to the ends of the earth. I'd wait forever if he asked me to.

"It's no problem at all."

The toast sprang out of the toaster and Reece whipped around to plate my food.

"Here you go," he said, setting it in front of me.

He made himself a cup of coffee and joined me at the table.

I stared at my plate and then at the empty space in front of him. "Aren't you going to eat?"

He shook his head. "I'm going to go for a run on the beach this morning, so I'll eat when I'm done."

"I hate that you went through all this trouble just to make me breakfast."

"Cyrus, I wanted to do this for you. This is what—" He stopped mid-sentence, pursing his mustache over his lower lip. I was on the edge of my seat, waiting for some type of admission. A label. Clarification on exactly what this was.

But I wasn't getting it. At least not today.

"I just wanted to, okay?" he huffed.

"Well, I appreciate it." I cut up my food and started to eat. It was your usual breakfast fare, but everything had been cooked well.

Reece stared at me intently, letting me have a taste of my own medicine. It was sweet that he was sitting there waiting for my approval.

"Good?" he asked.

"Even better because you made it for me."

AFTER I'D FINISHED MY BREAKFAST AND COATED REECE WITH enough sunscreen to protect an entire family, we made our way down to the beach.

"Are you going to be gone awhile?" I asked.

"Nah. I'm going to do a quick jog to get my heart rate up, and then we can swim."

"Okay."

He stepped closer and grabbed my waist with one hand and cupped the back of my head with the other, then pressed his lips to mine in a passionate kiss.

I was reveling in these moments. The ones where we could be out in the open without a care in the world.

"I'll see ya in a bit," he said breathlessly. His chest was already heaving, and he hadn't even started his run yet.

"See ya in a bit."

Reece walked toward the water, down to the soft, shell-free sand where the waves met the shore. He gave me a little wave, then jogged off down the beach. With each of his footfalls, his muscles bulged and flexed, propelling him across the sand like it was nothing.

I imagine this was how he felt when he watched me swim.

I settled into the sand and pulled my pencils and sketchbook out of my bag. What started out as a warm-up sketch of my muse quickly evolved into a series of vignettes that covered entire pages. Reece's sleeping face with each delicate eyelash fanning out over his cheeks. The broad expanse of his back as he stretched. His head tipped back with a genuine laugh, and another with his grumpy walrus scowl.

The crash of the waves and the seagull squawks off in the distance were the perfect ambient soundtrack while I lost myself in the task at hand.

"What're you working on?"

I jumped and clutched the sketchpad against my chest. *Definitely not obvious at all.* "Uh, just some ocean scenes. Sandpipers. Seashells." I was just listing off shit I'd noticed at the Airbnb.

Reece was staring down at me with his hands on his hips, his wide frame blocking the sun and casting me in a shadow. He was slightly out of breath from his run, and a slick sheen of sweat coated his flushed skin. "Well, are you going to let me see?"

It was a brand-new sketchbook, so there wasn't anything else I could show him.

"You don't want to see this. It's just a messy warm-up."

Reece reached for the sketchbook, but I lunged to the side, making him topple to the ground. He scrambled across the sand toward me on all fours.

"Let me see."

"No," I hissed, holding him off with my tentacles.

When I felt him relax, I let my tentacles slither away—only for the little shit to catch me off guard and launch himself at me again. This time it was a full-on wrestling match in the sand. Obviously, I was stronger, but Reece was giving it his all, bucking and thrashing against my tentacles. At some point during our scuffle, the sketchbook slipped out of my hand. When I reached for it with my tentacles, Reece took the opportunity to wriggle out of my grip. Before I could catch him, he snatched the sketchbook and shot to his feet.

"Please just let me see," he panted, holding the closed book in his hands.

He could have looked immediately, but instead he was asking for my consent.

"Fine," I relented.

He flipped the sketchbook open, and from where I was on the ground, I couldn't see his face to gauge his reaction.

"Cyrus, these are . . ." I held my breath, waiting for him to tell me how much of a creep I was. After a few tense moments, he said, "They're beautiful." He lowered the sketchpad and showed me the drawing of him smiling. "Can I keep it?"

"You want to keep it?" I asked, my voice pitching up.

"Yeah."

"Of course you can."

"You'll have to come over and we can find a place to hang it. It's not weird to have a portrait of yourself hanging in your—" He paused, the weight of reality crashing into us like a tidal wave.

I forced a smile. "Yeah . . ."

Reece sat on the sand next to me, so close that our bodies were pressed shoulder to shoulder. "Let's not talk about it right now. I want to keep living like this. Pretending like this is normal."

"Me, too." And hopefully one day it would be.

He grabbed my hand and gave it a soft squeeze. "Do you want to go for a swim?"

I knew he was suggesting it to cheer me up. It was sweet.

"I'd love to."

Reece held my hand as we waded through the shallows, down to where the sand dropped off and the water got deep.

"Don't feel like you need to entertain me," Reece said. He was bobbing up and down, riding the waves as they rolled past us onto the shore. "I want you to enjoy yourself."

He didn't have to tell me twice.

I dove underwater, jetting around him a few times until I created a tiny whirlpool of bubbles. I could just barely make out his muffled laughter.

The salt water was invigorating and made me feel more alive than I had in years. I let my body drift and allowed the soothing motion of the ocean rock me back and forth along the seabed.

This was pure bliss, and it was all because of Reece. One off-hand comment I'd made that stuck with him enough to go out of his way to do this for me.

I shot out of the water and wrapped my arms around Reece, then hoisted him into the air.

"Cyrus," he screeched, wriggling in my grip. Gods, I adored him.

I spun in a circle, watching the water slosh against his body and his face break out in a smile. Very much a contradiction to his reaction moments ago.

"I love seeing you like this," he said, circling his arms around my neck.

My hearts swelled. He didn't say he loved me, but he might as well have.

I swallowed hard, quietly forcing out, "Like what?"

His thumb gently stroked the back of my neck, and he stared into my eyes. "Happy. In your element."

"This wouldn't have been possible without you." I don't know why I'd avoided the sea for so long, but it almost felt like it was meant to be, like I was waiting for this exact moment with this exact person.

With my mate.

"You're right. It wouldn't have." He said it matter-of-factly, puffing his chest out.

"Oh, fuck you." I tightened my grip on him and yanked him down, like I was going to pull him underwater with me, but I stopped just before his chin touched the surface.

He laughed before dipping his mouth in the water, blowing a spray of salt water in my face.

"Thanks for that," I said, wiping my hand over my face.

"You're welcome."

I held on to him and we bobbed in the water, riding the ebb and flow of the waves, simply enjoying each other's company.

"So, what's on the agenda for this evening?" I asked. I knew Reece had taken care to plan this trip, and I didn't want to steamroll anything he had in mind.

"I was thinking we could go down to the boardwalk. Do a little sightseeing. Some people watching."

"Oh, that sounds lovely."

"Maybe grab a funnel cake and a lemonade," he added.

"Next you're going to tell me you want to get matching airbrushed T-shirts."

He hummed. "I was thinking more along the lines of a hair wrap, but that doesn't really work for you."

"I was thinking we could get each other's names on a grain of rice."

"We can do whatever you want, Cy. This weekend is for you."

"Well, the first thing I want to do is make you breakfast. You have to be starving."

"I won't say no to that."

Twenty-Six

CYRUS

REECE AND I PULLED INTO THE BOARDWALK PARKING LOT just as the sun was setting. The place was packed, and after driving around for what felt like ages, we finally managed to find an open spot.

"Ready?" Reece said when we got out of the car.

He held out his hand, and I paused, staring at his outstretched fingers.

Was he asking what I thought he was asking?

I stood there, frozen.

He snapped his hand back, rubbing it along the back of his neck. "Uh, sorry about that. I thought, you know, because we're here, we could do the whole out-in-the-open thing."

"No," I blurted, feeling absolutely awful that he'd misinterpreted things. "I want to hold hands."

I shuffled over to him and slid my hand over his biceps and down his arm, then pressed our palms together.

He brought our joined hands up to his lips and gave them a little squeeze as he kissed my knuckles.

"Good, because I want to hold hands, too," he said. "I want everyone to see us together."

My momentary bliss shattered then because, fuck, what were people going to think when they saw us together?

I was a spectacle in my own right, but when you put me next to an Adonis like Reece—in a romantic way with someone like him?

"Cyrus, it's fine," he said calmly.

It felt like my hearts were stuck in my throat. A tight nod was all I could manage.

These were my issues, not Reece's.

He gave me a sweet, sincere smile, the last rays of the sun catching on his windswept hair, looking every bit the muse I knew him to be, and rather than adding to my anxiety, it eased it. He made me feel seen, appreciated for who I was, and as long as we were together, that was all I needed.

We walked hand in hand to the beginning of the boardwalk. The wide wooden path stretched the length of the beach, with shops on one side and the ocean on the other. The rich aroma of greasy food was heavy in the air, the murmured conversations drowned out by the sounds of carnival games and the steady thumping of footsteps over the wooden planks.

There were so many sights and sounds, I didn't know where to look, but it also meant that everyone else was so preoccupied with everything going on around us that they didn't give Reece and me a second glance.

"So, what do you want to do first?" Reece asked.

I stared down the long boardwalk. "There's so much to do."

"I mean, we don't have to do anything if you don't want to. We can just walk. Enjoy the evening."

"Why don't we do that, and if anything catches our eye, we'll stop?"

"Sounds like a plan."

There were all the usual touristy shops that we'd poked fun at: airbrushed T-shirts, names on rice, hair wraps, and more cheap sundry shops than any town needed.

But there was one shop in particular that caught my attention. The sign read OLD-TIME PHOTOS in a retro Western font, and two mannequins dressed in American frontier period clothing were positioned out front.

It would be an interesting way to commemorate our first trip together. What I hoped was the first of many.

I stopped and Reece stopped with me, staring up at the sign.

"You want to get an old-timey photo together?" he asked, obviously judging my choice of activity.

"Well, I did," I huffed. "But not anymore."

I started to shuffle off, but Reece stayed rooted to the spot, tightening his grip on my hand.

"If you want old-timey photos, we're getting old-timey photos."

Before I could argue with him, he was already dragging me inside.

Several families and couples were dressed in fancy period clothing. Sepia-toned photos lined the walls, showcasing the props and costumes.

"Can I help you?" an orc asked. She was dressed like a 1920s flapper, with a tasseled red dress and a feathered headband wrapped around her forehead. As a creature who was alive then, I was impressed with the historical accuracy.

"We'd like to get our photo taken," Reece announced.

She tipped her head toward the counter. "You can look through those books, and when you find a scene you like, we'll get you costumed and set up. Okay?"

We nodded and made our way over to the binders lining the counter.

I picked one labeled HISTORICAL to flip through while Reece flipped through another.

In every single photo, the humans and monsters were fully dressed in period-specific costumes, really adding to the effect of the photo. The best I could do was a hat and a jacket.

"I didn't factor the costumes into the equation," I murmured.

"Don't worry," Reece reassured me. "We'll figure something out."

I continued to thumb through the binder. There were couples dressed as mobsters, dandies, and sailors. There was nothing that really worked for Reece and me.

Just when I was about to lose hope, Reece said, "What about this one?" and held his binder open for me to see.

It was a Western scene of a cowboy and a saloon girl in a bathtub together—seemingly naked except for the cowboy hats and bandanas. The saloon girl was slumped against his chest, holding a bottle of whiskey over the edge of the tub like they'd just polished it off.

"This is what you want to get?" I asked with a laugh.

It was cute, but it was quite *couply*.

"What's wrong with it?" he asked, his brows knitting together like I'd offended him.

"It's just quite the couple's scene, isn't it?" I teased.

"Okay? What's wrong with that?" he huffed.

Who was this man? And how had the goddess blessed me to be his mate? Each day he surprised me. We were growing closer, and as excited as that made me, I was still so scared of losing him once he found out the truth.

Reece put the binder down on the counter and waved the orc over. "We're ready. We want to do this one," he said, pointing to the bathtub scene.

"Sure thing," she said without batting an eye. "Give me a few minutes to get everything set up."

"We don't have to do this, you know," I grumbled as we watched her drag a galvanized steel bathtub in front of a saloon backdrop.

"Of course we do. We need something to memorialize our first trip together." He leaned into me and placed a soft, unexpected kiss on my temple.

I reared back to gape at him. "Who are you and what have you done with Reece Rollins?"

He chuckled. "I'm not always an asshole. At least not to you."

When she was finished setting up, she came back over to Reece and me.

"All right. Take your shirt off," she told Reece bluntly.

Without a second thought, he slipped his T-shirt over his head, revealing his slightly sunburnt shoulders, defined abs, and delicious happy trail. I swear it was like the shop went quiet, and every eye in the place was immediately on us. Well, on Reece. I was both annoyed and honored that my mate's body garnered so much attention.

"And you," she said, looking me up and down, "are perfect just like that."

She passed Reece a worn cowboy hat and a red bandana.

"Do we really need to wear bandanas in the bath?" I asked. It was part of the example photo, but it seemed quite impractical.

"Shh," Reece hushed me. "It's for dramatic effect."

I broke out into laughter. For someone who was skeptical about doing this in the first place, he was really getting into it.

"Will a bandana work with your fins?" the woman assisting us asked.

"Yes, I can just tie it right underneath them."

She handed me a hat and a bandana, but before I could put the bandana on, Reece plucked it from my hand.

"Allow me."

He came up behind me, carefully tying the bandana just under my fins like I'd mentioned. I could feel each of his hot breaths against my neck. Smell his woodsy aftershave.

"Th-thank you," I stammered when he stepped away from me.

He smirked, obviously aware of the effect he had on me.

"Looking good," the orc said. "Now hop in the tub."

Gods, she cut right to business. I guess you had to at a place like this.

"Let me get behind you," Reece said, already climbing into the tub.

"You? Behind me?" I teased.

He tsked, rolling his eyes. "I know that's not our usual position, but humor me just this once."

I let Reece get comfortable in the back of the tub before I settled myself in front of him. With the two of us in there, it was quite cramped.

"Okay, now lay back against him for me," the orc instructed.

Every time I tried to lean back, my cowboy hat got in the way, hitting Reece in the face or tipping off my head completely.

The orc stepped out from behind the camera, staring at the two of us with her hands on her hips. "Let's see . . . Can you hang some of your tentacles over the edge of the tub?"

I readjusted, and let a few of them casually drape over the side.

"Now, take this," she said, holding my hat out to one of my tentacles, "and this." She passed me the whiskey bottle before she stepped back to look at us. "Perfect!"

She took her place behind the camera and told us to smile as the shutter clicked and the flash hummed.

"You two are a cute couple," she said as she snapped away with the camera.

I tensed up, unsure of how to react to that statement.

"You hear that, Cy?" Reece asked. "She thinks we're cute." We were posing for a picture, but I could still hear his smile—his happiness—in his voice.

It didn't bother him in the slightest.

I relaxed and settled against Reece's warm chest. "I think we're quite cute, too."

The photographer continued snapping away, stopping every few seconds to make tiny adjustments to our pose until she was happy with it.

"All right," she said, finally stepping away from the camera. "You can get dressed and meet me back up at the counter."

We took off our bandanas and hung up our hats, and when Reece slipped his shirt back on, I could have sworn there was a collective "Awww" that echoed through the shop.

The orc motioned us over to the counter. She passed us a tablet with an album of photos displayed on the screen and explained the different packages they offered.

Reece and I agreed that one printed photo for each of us would suffice, but then it was time to pick the photo we liked best.

"Fuck, this is hard," Reece said as we scrolled.

"It is." There were so many good ones.

"I really like your smile in this one," Reece said.

In the photo, I was genuinely smiling, tipping my head back against Reece while he grinned. We looked adorable. Happy. It made me wonder if that was the photo she took right after she told us we were a cute couple.

"I like that one, too."

"Um, excuse me," he called out to the girl assisting us. "Can we get two copies of number four printed and get the digital album?"

She nodded. "You've got it."

A few moments later, she slid a bag across the counter toward us.

"All right, two eight-by-tens and a digital album. That will be eighty dollars," she said, holding the tablet out to us.

I pulled up my tap-to-pay on my phone, but Reece already had his bank card out of his wallet.

"Will you let me?" I protested.

He shook his head and tapped his card against the tablet. "You can get me my funnel cake and my lemonade."

I snorted. Him and that damn funnel cake. "Fine."

Twenty-Seven

REECE

"THAT LOOKS LIKE THE RECIPE FOR DIABETES," CYRUS SAID, eyeing my funnel cake and large lemonade.

"You should have gotten something," I said before taking a sip of my lemonade. It was perfect. Tangy, sweet, and totally worth the ten dollars Cyrus had paid for it.

"I'm still full from dinner, thanks."

"Let me know if you change your mind. I'm happy to share."

"Do you want to sit so you can eat that?" Cyrus asked, tipping his head toward my funnel cake.

"Sure."

All the benches near us were occupied, so we sat on the concrete retaining wall that separated the boardwalk from the beach. A cool breeze blew off the water and ruffled my hair.

"This is really lovely," Cyrus said, staring at the photo of us while I tore into my funnel cake.

"It is. I'm glad we got those photos taken"

"Me, too." He looked up from the photo, busting into laughter when he stared at me.

"What?" I asked.

"You look like you've been on a coke binge."

I glanced down and noticed the powdered sugar sprinkled all over the front of my black T-shirt.

"Oops," I said, swiping it off.

"No," Cyrus laughed. "It's all over your mustache." He cupped my face, and slid his gaze down to my lips before gently swiping his thumbs over my mustache. "There," he said, sounding almost breathless.

Before he could let me go, I was bringing my face to his, pressing our lips together, making out with him on the boardwalk like we were teenagers closing out the end of our first date.

In a way, I guess that's what this was: our first date out in the world, where we could be seen and heard and proud, and as happy as I was, I honestly felt so fucked because we were going to have to go back home tomorrow and slip into our "normal." Back to our life of secrecy and lies.

And fuck, it sucked.

In this moment things were so real, so tangible. I never wanted this kiss to end.

Until a giant boom sounded in the distance.

My eyes snapped open, noticing Cyrus bathed in colorful light. *Fireworks.*

There were fireworks. I wasn't sure if this was a weekly occurrence during the summer or if this was some end-of-the season celebration, but I wanted to think that it was special. That the fireworks were just for us.

We pulled away, both grinning.

"I'm going to be honest, that scared the daylights out of me," Cyrus said.

The joy on his face, his laughter, it made me feel like fireworks were exploding in my chest.

"It scared me, too. Come here," I said, reaching to wrap my arm around his shoulders.

He snuggled closer and rested his head on me while we watched fireworks dance in the sky.

AFTER WE GOT BACK FROM THE BOARDWALK, I TOOK A shower to clean myself up. Last night I'd fallen asleep, so we didn't get a chance to have sex, but there was a sort of unspoken agreement between Cyrus and me that it was happening tonight.

The very thought of him filling me up with his tentacles made my cock throb.

I wrapped a towel around my waist, covering my now semi-hard cock, before I stepped out of the bathroom.

Cyrus lay in bed on top of the covers, scrolling on his phone under the warm glow of his bedside lamp. He glanced up at me, his gaze raking down my wet body appreciatively. When his eyes focused on the swell of my cock under my towel, I let it drop to the floor.

"Fuck," he breathed, scrambling to set his phone on the nightstand.

Before he could make his way over to me, I was climbing up the bed toward him.

He bunched his tentacles together, giving me room to straddle his lap.

"How did I get so lucky?" he asked. He ran his palms along my thighs, the soft touch making me shudder.

"I'm the lucky one." It was strange because I meant it. He'd changed something in me, awakened feelings I didn't know someone like me was capable of. Even if things between us got off to a bad start, we were here now.

Together.

I grabbed his hands, pinning them over his head while I leaned over him. His breath hitched, his body tensing underneath me.

I cupped his face, pressing my nose against his and staring into his wide blue eyes. They were as deep as the ocean, as mesmerizing as a swirling sea. When we first met, I didn't appreciate them, but now they were one of my favorite features of his.

Cyrus swallowed hard and tried to turn away, but I held his face in place.

"Hey," I whispered. "Look at me."

He shook his head. "I can't. You're too handsome. You're—"

"Shh," I said with my mouth hovering right above his. I could feel his heavy breaths tickling my lips. "You're handsome, too. You deserve this." I dropped my voice even lower. "It's our last day. I want to savor it."

"Reece." My name came out strangled. Needy.

I leaned forward to kiss him and pressed my cock against his abdomen, lightly thrusting my hips to the slow, sensual rhythm of our tongues.

One of his tentacles snaked between us, making me groan against his lips when it roughly stroked my cock.

"Fuck, that feels so good," I said. Each word was punctuated by my gasps and kisses and tiny nibbles on his thin lips.

Cyrus slid his hands down my sides, past my hips to cup my ass. He tightened his grip, burying his fingers in my cheeks and taking control of my thrusts, really grinding me against him while his tentacle stroked me. It felt amazing. Almost too amazing.

"I need you inside me," I panted.

He chuckled and gave me a little swat on the ass before he moved his hands and his tentacle away.

I climbed off him and started to get into position with my ass in the air.

"Reece." He gripped my chin, forcing me to look at him. "I

was hoping we could do something different." He bit his lip, lowering his voice to a sexy, raspy whisper when he said, "I want to see that handsome face of yours while I fuck you."

"Oh." It was my turn to swallow hard. "Okay."

I lay on my back, letting my legs fall open so Cyrus could settle between them. His tentacles wrapped around my legs. One on each thigh and one on each ankle. Spreading me open for him, showing him everything while I looked down at him. Made eye contact with him.

I wasn't used to this position. It made me feel vulnerable. Exposed.

My expression must have given me away.

"Is it okay?" One of his mating tentacles trailed over my inner thigh, then wrapped around my cock, making me gasp. "Like this?"

I nodded.

"Words, Reece."

"Yeah," I gritted out, thrusting my hips, fucking his tentacle.

Our sex was usually feral—but this? This was passionate. It was slow and intentional with sustained eye contact.

Even when I felt shy or embarrassed by the sounds I was making, I kept my eyes on Cyrus, taking pleasure in the fact that he was taking pleasure in me. I'd never been with someone so attentive. So determined to get me off.

This felt even more intentional.

He spread me wider, staring down at my hole as his other mating tentacle swirled against the entrance. I sucked in a tight breath and the tentacles holding my legs gripped me tighter, the gentle pressure drawing me out of my head.

How was it that Cyrus always knew what I needed? That in this moment of feeling so utterly exposed, I needed a comforting touch, his reassuring presence?

I'd always considered myself the dominant one, but with Cyrus, I could let that slip away, feeling totally at ease when he took the lead.

His eyes darted up to look at my face. "You okay?" he asked.

"More than okay." I was ready.

He gave me a soft smile, a gentle nod, before he turned his attention back to my ass.

The tip of his tentacle slowly pushed inside, stretching me, then worked its way out, giving me time to acclimate to the sensation. When the full thickness of his tentacle breached me, those suckers popping in one after another, Cyrus and I both groaned.

"Fuck, you feel like heaven," he rasped, rubbing his lips along my calf.

"So do you."

His tentacle slid in and out, slow and shallow at first, then deeper as I relaxed.

My legs fell open, my eyes fluttering closed as I leaned into the pleasant sensation.

"Reece," Cyrus purred. "Look at me."

"I'm trying," I whined, forcing my eyes open. "It's hard."

With his tentacles still holding my legs, Cyrus leaned over me and placed his hands on either side of my head, staring down at me as his tentacle fucked my ass. I felt every movement of his tentacles, the soft glide inside me, the push and pull as he stroked my cock.

"That's it," he said, "let me see those pretty eyes widen as I fuck your ass."

I reached for him and slid my hands up his chest, over the delicate fins lining his neck, up to the angular planes of his face to smooth my thumbs across his cheeks.

I forced myself to keep my eyes on him, watching his lips part with each heavy breath, pleasure making his features tense, then relax. We were so connected in this moment, baring our souls to each other because we felt safe enough to do so.

My breathing ramped up and my balls tightened. Desperate moans worked their way out of my throat, and I bore down, forcing him even deeper. It was good. So fucking good. Just like it was every time with Cyrus.

"Fuck," I whimpered. "I'm gonna come."

"Yes, Reece. Come for me." His tone was almost desperate, like he was as close as I was. Like he needed this as badly as I did.

The thrusts of the tentacle inside me grew more frantic, those suckers popping in and out and sending little sparks of pleasure across my skin.

"Oh, fuck. Fuck!" I cried out as the tension building inside me snapped, sending warmth spreading down my spine, making me come with a loud groan.

The area between us was hot and slick, my cum covering Cyrus and me while he stroked me through my orgasm. His breathing picked up and so did the speed of his tentacles. A few more deep surges and Cyrus was coming, too, filling my ass as his body jolted. His other mating tentacle was still wrapped around my shaft, and it spasmed, mixing his cum with mine between us.

"Reece," he grunted in my ear.

I clung to him desperately, bearing down, keeping him inside me, not wanting to lose this connection. Not wanting this—whatever it was between us—to ever end.

He moved to get off me, but I tightened my grip.

"No," I whispered. "Stay like this." I quickly tacked on "Please."

Cyrus stared down at me and gave me a soft kiss to murmur against my lips. "Okay."

He let his body fall against mine and buried his face in the crook of my neck, keeping his tentacle buried inside me.

I wrapped my arm around him and traced my fingers up and down his spine.

I was so at ease, so calm and comfortable, and whatever this fluttering feeling was in my chest, it wasn't because of sex. It was something deeper. Something I needed to acknowledge at one point or another.

"Cyrus, I . . ." I couldn't find the words, but I didn't need to.

He grabbed my hand and brought my knuckles to his lips. "I know."

Emotion crashed into me like a tidal wave, making tears well up in my eyes.

We'd just had sex, but why did I feel like this was more? That we'd made love?

As much as admitting that scared me, this felt right. Cyrus was right for me.

I wasn't a crier. My dad had killed that part of me a long time ago, but Cyrus always brought out that sensitive, damaged part of me. The broken bits and pieces I'd kept hidden for so long. The floodgates opened, the overwhelming emotion flowing out of me in the form of fat tears.

"It's okay," Cyrus said, rubbing comforting circles over my chest. "I'm not going anywhere."

"I don't want to go home," I admitted.

"I don't, either, but this is all temporary, darling. After the triathlon, we can take things wherever you want them to go."

I gripped him tighter, feeling his soft skin underneath my fingertips and each of his heavy breaths, savoring these fleeting moments of normalcy, and hoping like hell I'd never have to let him go.

Twenty-Eight

CYRUS

THINGS CHANGED FOR US AFTER THE BEACH TRIP. NOW THAT we'd had a taste of what it was like to be in a normal relationship, there was this sense of longing that seemed to work its way into every single interaction. We'd hug a little longer, drag out our kisses, and hold on to our goodbyes until the last possible second. It was torture, but with just a few weeks left until the triathlon, I tried to remind myself it was only temporary.

Today Reece was doing another open-water swim. After nearly drowning the last time he'd attempted it, I knew he'd be nervous, but I had something up my sleeve that would help.

When I pulled up to his house, he was already sprinting down the driveway toward my car.

"Good morning," he said with a smile as he slid into the passenger seat. He leaned over the center console and kissed me, the wiry hairs of his beard and mustache tickling my face.

"Good morning, indeed," I said as he fastened his seat belt. "How are we feeling about today?" I asked, putting the car in drive and starting off toward the lake.

"I'm not gonna lie. I'm nervous. But I watched some videos on ankle flexion, doubled up on my electrolytes, and I've been exclusively taking cold showers, so I should be set."

"Confident and relaxed. Love to see it."

Reece slid his free hand into mine as he scrolled through his phone with the other. "So, you'll be at dinner tomorrow, right?"

A few of us had been invited to Atlas and Tegan's for what we assumed was some sort of wedding party formation. Reece and Tegan had been getting along better as of late, but he was still wary about the strength of their relationship.

Gods, he was fucking cute.

Underneath that tough exterior, he was a sensitive teddy bear, especially when it came to his younger sister.

I smiled and shook my head, using one of my tentacles to nudge his leg. "Yes, I've told you how many times already? I'll be there. I was thinking that maybe after, you could spend the night at my place? Fallon mentioned he and Jimenez are going to the club. We'll have the apartment all to ourselves."

It was brazen. Stretching our secrecy to its very limits, but I missed falling asleep next to him. Waking up and hearing his grumpy, gravelly voice first thing in the morning.

I held my breath, hoping I didn't push him too far with my request.

"I'd love to," he said without missing a beat. I glanced over at him and smiled, and he quietly added, "You better fuck me in that tub."

I lowered my voice to a soft, sensual purr, the one that drove him wild. "I'll fuck you anywhere you want, darling. Just say the word."

"Darling," he said, and leaned his head against the window, refusing to look at me. "I like it when you call me that."

I'd bet money his cheeks were flaming.

"Good, because I don't intend to stop."

I pulled the car into the empty parking lot at the lake, and we both got out.

"Gods, this was a poor choice," Reece hissed as he pulled his hoodie up around his neck. "I'm never doing a tri in the fall again."

I laughed and popped open my trunk, pulled out a garment bag, and held it up for Reece to see. "Well, that's a shame, considering you have one of these now."

Reece smiled wide and eagerly unzipped the bag. "You didn't. A wet suit. Cy, these things aren't fucking cheap."

"I know you were planning to buy one closer to the race, but I wanted you to have it. Consider it a gift from trainer to student. I guessed on the size a bit, but I wanted it to be a surprise. Hopefully it fits."

Reece launched himself at me, threw his arms around my neck, and smacked his lips against mine. If it weren't for my tentacles catching us, we would have toppled over onto the asphalt.

"I'll have to give you gifts more often. Speaking of, have you used your present yet?" I wiggled my eyebrows at him. Well, as best as I could wiggle the bumpy crests above my eyes.

He bit his lip and shook his head.

"When you do, I want you to video-call me. I want to see your face while you fuck it and think of me. Will you do that for me?" I purred against his throat.

"Y-yes. Whatever you want." His voice was practically a whine.

I loved teasing him, loved knowing that my mate yearned for me and wanted to please me.

"That's my good boy. Now, let's see if we can get this thing on. Oh, wait. I almost forgot." I pulled a plastic bag from the trunk and handed it to Reece.

With a confused look, he pulled a spray canister out of the bag. "Is this cooking spray?"

"No," I snorted. "It's some fancy spray lube. It prevents chafing and it's supposed to help with getting your wet suit on."

He grinned at me and my hearts raced.

"Thank you, Cy. I don't know what I would do without you."

My tentacles clenched tight to my arms, and I could feel my face flushing a darker blue. "I want you to do well and I know this is important to you."

Reece and I walked side by side over to the changing stalls at the entrance to the beach. They were all empty because, as usual, we were the only ones here at the lake on a cool morning.

We crammed inside the stall and Reece immediately began to undress.

"Motherfucker," he groaned as he pulled his hoodie over his head. His light pink nipples pebbled in the cool morning air, and I had to suppress the urge to pop one into my mouth.

We were here with a purpose, and that purpose wasn't to fuck in a confined space.

We did that enough at the gym.

"All right, then," I said when Reece was undressed down to his jammers. "Let me lube you up."

He put his hands on his hips and laughed. "Can you not say that? The last thing I need is to get a boner while we're trying to get this on."

"What?" I said as I sprayed his ankles and calves with the lube. "It isn't my fault you find me irresistible. Legs up."

Reece wriggled one foot into the wet suit and then the other.

"Okay, not too bad." I used my tentacles to pull the tight neoprene over his calves. "Your thighs are going to be the real challenge, though. You could crush a watermelon with these things."

Reece chuckled and wiggled his hips as we worked the material over his legs with slow tugs.

"Goddess, is this thing fucking tight." I dramatically wiped my brow with one of my tentacles.

"Will you stop fucking making me laugh?" His body shook with laughter as I continued to wrench the wet suit over it. "We're trying to do something serious and suddenly you turn into a fucking comedian."

I reached the bulge at Reece's crotch and absolutely lost it, bursting into a fit of laughter that had my fins vibrating along my neck.

"Reece!" I huffed. "Control yourself. And here you are giving me shit."

He blushed and held out his hands. "You were rubbing all over me! I'm sorry. It happens."

This was the Reece Rollins I loved. The Reece Rollins so few people got to see.

"Come on, we're almost there." I sprayed lube around his wrists and neck.

"Wait." Reece held his hand out. "Let me see that."

I passed him the lube and he sprayed both of his nipples until the pointed tips glistened.

"Don't want any chafing."

"Oh, good thinking, darling. I knew you were more than just a pretty face."

"Will you stop fucking around and help me," he said as he shimmied his arms into the wet suit.

"All right, all right." I rose on my tentacles and gripped the back of the suit, tugging it over the broad expanse of his back. "How's that?" I asked when I finished pulling up the zipper.

I stepped back, giving Reece space while he flexed his arms and shook out his legs.

"I think it's perfect. You got the sizing spot-on."

I stared at his crotch, squinting as I leaned closer. "I don't know. I think you could have used a bigger size here. I wonder if there's a cut for men with big dicks."

"You're such a horny fuck, you know that?" he said as he stepped past me and out of the changing stall.

"Oh, I know, and you love every minute of it."

"Pfft," he huffed as he stomped toward the beach. Even with his back turned to me, I knew he was smiling.

I was definitely a horny fuck, because I followed behind him just far enough away that I could watch the cheeks of his ass flex underneath the wet suit.

Gods, I couldn't wait to fuck him later.

He put on his swim cap and goggles, and I watched as he did his stretches. When he was finally warmed up, he walked over to me.

"For good luck." Reece pressed his lips against mine in a quick kiss.

I snaked one of my tentacles around his waist and pulled him closer so we were pressed chest to chest.

"You're going to do great. I know it." My tentacle gave his ass a light swat. "Now get in the water."

He pulled away from me, rushed toward the lake, and dove underneath the water the moment it was deep enough. I tapped my phone and started the timer, watching as Reece began to swim with powerful strokes.

I was nervous, and though I'd offered to join him in the water, he'd insisted on doing this on his own, driving home the fact that on race day I'd have to watch him from the shore.

His form was perfect. Not only was the wet suit keeping him warm, but it was helping with drag and buoyancy. I looked down at my phone as he reached the halfway mark and was shocked.

This was his best time yet—and in an open-water swim.

"Yes, Reece!" I shouted from the beach as he switched directions at the far buoy. I wasn't sure if he could hear me, but I wasn't going to speak to him in his head and potentially distract him.

As he got closer to the shore, I scuttled out into the shallow water, ready to congratulate my mate.

"How did I do?" he asked as he rose out of the water, trudging toward me with heavy breaths.

I stopped the timer and rushed forward, almost tackling him as I wrapped my arms around him.

"That was your best time yet."

"Are you shitting me?" He smiled wide as water dripped down his face and collected in his beard.

"No, look."

He pulled his goggles up onto his head and I held my phone out for him to see.

"Yes!" he whooped, and gripped me in another tight hug.

"You've got this in the bag. I am so proud of you."

Reece buried his face against my neck. "Thank you, Cy. Thank you for everything," he mumbled, his cool lips brushing against my skin with each word. "I couldn't have done this without you."

"You could have. Your time just wouldn't have been as good."

"Fuck you," he said with a laugh, and nuzzled against me.

But I knew what he was really trying to say, because I felt it, too.

Twenty-Nine

REECE

I FLIPPED DOWN MY VISOR AND LOOKED IN THE MIRROR, brushed my hands over my beard, and smoothed back my hair. It was bordering on too long, but I knew Cyrus liked it. I guess when you had zero hair to speak of, it was fascinating being with someone who did. I was even contemplating growing out my chest hair for him.

The things he could get me to do.

My phone vibrated in my cupholder.

**Cyrus: Are you going to come inside
or are you going to sit there checking
yourself out for another 15 minutes?**

I glanced out the window, and sure enough, there was Cyrus watching me from inside my sister's cottage. Atlas and Tegan were hosting all of us—their closest friends and family—tonight for dinner. I was sure it had something to do with their wedding party. Tegan and I had been getting along great, but was she going to ask me to walk her down the aisle? I hadn't realized how much I wanted that honor.

Reece: Fucking creep. I'm coming.

My phone vibrated again.

Cyrus: No, that's later 😉

Cyrus always had this way of making me feel at ease, of breaking any tension I was feeling. Whether it was with humor or a soft touch, it was one of the things I appreciated most about him. He knew how to reach parts of me that no one else could.

That applied to the tentacles, too.

There was a knock on the window and I almost jumped out of my skin.

"Honey, what are you doing just sitting out here?" my mother asked from outside the car.

Goddess, help me.

"Hey, Ma," I said as I stepped out of the car. "I was just catching up on a few emails real quick."

I leaned over and wrapped her in a tight hug before pulling away.

She looked me up and down. "Well, don't you look handsome."

I could feel my cheeks turning red, so I stared down at my outfit.

Yeah, I wanted to look nice for whatever wedding formality this was, but I *really* wanted to look nice for Cyrus and our plans later.

"Do you need help bringing anything inside?" I asked.

"Nope, Atlas and Tegan insisted I didn't need to bring anything. You know how stubborn your sister can be." She threw her arms in the air and shrugged, and we walked to the front door.

Of course I knew how stubborn my sister could be, because I was the same fucking way.

Before we could knock on the front door, it swung open and Atlas greeted us with a sharp-toothed smile.

"Hey there, Mrs. Rollins." He bent over to hug my mom. The two of them were comical together since she was even smaller than my sister.

"Atlas!" She swatted his chest playfully. "What did I tell you about that? It's either Mom or Pam. None of that Mrs. Rollins nonsense."

Good luck with that, Mom.

"Reece." Atlas held out his arms and I braced myself for impact.

Yep, he was still a strong motherfucker.

We stepped inside the cottage to find everyone relaxing in the living area.

"Hey!" Tegan beamed as she stepped out from behind the kitchen island and made her way over to us. She hugged our mother, then turned to me.

"Hi, big brother," she said as she wrapped her arms around me. "You look nice." She took a deep inhale against my chest. "And you smell nice, too. What is that, cologne?"

Damn. Did she really have to call me out like that? From the corner of my eye, I could see Cyrus sitting on the sofa biting back a smile. *Smug fucker.*

I rubbed my hand along the back of my neck and shrugged. "Figured it was a special occasion, might as well."

"Special occasion, indeed," Cyrus said.

Declan and Selene sat on either side of him, but Fallon and Javier were both missing.

"Where are Jimenez—I mean Javier—and Fallon?" I asked as I took a seat at the kitchen island next to my mother.

"Fallon said Javier was picking him up because they're going out later. They're probably just running a bit late. Let me send Fallon a text," Cyrus said, picking up his phone.

"Figures." Selene sighed and rubbed her temples.

"Well, uh, while we wait for them, you guys can have some appetizers. Reece, would you mind helping me set the table on the deck?" Tegan asked. "I thought that since the weather's so nice, we could eat outside." She stared at me with expectant green eyes that were identical to my own.

"Y-yeah, of course." I glanced over at Cyrus and he gave me a reassuring nod.

"Thanks." Tegan passed me a heavy stack of plates topped with rolls of silverware.

"Honey, do you need help—" our mother started as we headed toward the slider that led to the deck.

"We've got it, Mom," Tegan said as she closed the door behind us.

I set the plates on the table and quietly prepped the place settings while Tegan stared at me with her hands on her hips.

"Reece, um, I was hoping we could talk for a bit. Just the two of us."

"Yeah, uh, sure. You wanna go somewhere, or . . . ?"

"I have some lawn chairs set up in the yard. Let's go out there."

I followed behind her as she led us to a pair of chairs placed right along the tree line. We both sat, and for a while we were quiet, the silence filled by the sounds of swaying leaves and the last songs of the summer crickets.

Tegan shifted in her seat, tucking a few stray hairs from her bun behind her ear before she finally asked, "You probably know why everyone is here, right?"

I shrugged. "I mean, I figured it has something to do with the wedding party."

She nodded. "It does. But—I wanted to ask you something. You specifically."

Tegan turned toward me, her face scrunched up with a squint due to the afternoon sun. It reminded me of how she'd look up at me when we were kids, when we were still close.

"Since Dad's gone, I wanted to know if you'd walk me down the aisle and give me away." She reached over and held my hand for the first time in who knew how long. "I know you've been working on yourself, and it shows in the way you interact with Atlas and his friends. And the way you act with me. Honestly, Reece, you seem different. Lighter. Happier. I don't know how to explain it, but a few people have noticed it. I'm proud of how much you've grown, and I love you. This is going to be a special day for me, and I want you to be a part of it."

Pride welled up inside me and tightened my chest. I felt like I was going to cry.

I mean, I wouldn't, at least not right now, but I was touched.

"I love you, and I couldn't have picked a more perfect mate for you than Atlas. I'd be honored to walk you down the aisle and give you away."

I meant it, too. Every single word.

Tegan sprang up to hug me, nearly falling out of her chair in the process.

"Thank you for asking me," I mumbled against her hair as she held me tight.

"Of course. You're the only one it could have been. I just didn't want to put you on the spot in front of everyone." She pulled away and wiped underneath her eyes.

Was she crying?

I guess Tegan had missed me just as much as I'd missed her.

"Hey." I rose from my seat and rubbed her arm. "None of that. This is a happy day. I'm assuming everyone else in there is a part of the wedding, too?" She nodded. "I can't have them thinking I made you upset," I said with a smile, and Tegan laughed.

"They're happy tears, Reecie."

I put my arm over her shoulders and gave her a little squeeze. "Come on. Let's get this table set so we can eat. I'm starving."

After we had finished setting the table, Atlas carried out big trays of salad and baked ziti.

"Oh, let me grab the serving spoons," Tegan said.

She went back inside, leaving Atlas and me alone on the deck.

"She seems happy. You said yes?" he asked as he peeled back the aluminum foil covering the trays.

"Of course I did."

Atlas smiled wide and gripped my shoulder with one of his massive paws. "I knew you would. You're a good guy, Reece. I'm happy you're going to be my brother-in-law."

"I'm happy you're going to be my brother-in-law, too, but we need to talk about the hugs." I rubbed my chest dramatically and Atlas barked a laugh.

"I'll work on it." He lowered his voice to a gravelly whisper. "Speaking of hugs, are you, uh, seeing anyone?" Atlas stared through the slider to where the rest of the group was gathered.

"N-no," I stammered.

Fuck, I'm bad at this.

Atlas didn't drop it, though. "I was going for a run the other morning and I could have sworn I saw you with someone down by the lake."

"It was probably just me and Cyrus training," I said, trying to sound casual. Internally, I was shaking like a leaf.

He tilted his head to stare at me, his tail swaying back and forth slightly. "Mmm, I'm pretty sure this was more than just training."

My stomach dropped and my thoughts raced, trying to find a way to explain things.

"Hey." Atlas gripped my shoulders, forcing me to look at him. His expression was soft, happy even. "It's okay. Everything's fine. You're consenting adults. I was just asking because Cyrus seems to be doing a lot better. Before he started training you, Fallon and I were a little worried about him. I don't want to put his business out there, but he was pretty depressed."

It took a moment for what he said to register.

"Cyrus was depressed before he met me?"

"Mm-hmm." Atlas nodded.

I knew Cyrus had his own insecurities, but I never would have guessed he was depressed. He hid it so well. Maybe he needed me just as much as I needed him.

"Does anyone else know?" By *anyone else*, I meant my sister.

"Do you really think I'd do that to one of my best friends and my future brother-in-law? As much as I hate keeping things from your sister, I haven't said a word. And I won't. It's not my place to announce your relationship. If—when—you guys are ready to go public with things, you one hundred percent have my support."

I shifted my weight, stared at my feet, and bit my lip. "I hate putting you in that position, but I appreciate it. I just want to give Tegan a little more time to warm up to me before we put this out there." We were finally on the right track, and I didn't want to push it.

Our conversation was cut short when the sliding door to the deck flew open and Fallon rushed outside.

"Atlas, I need to talk to you about something!" Fallon chirped. His feathers were ruffled up around his neck, and his tail whipped back and forth. The guy was obviously shaken up about some-thing.

"Can it wait until after dinner?" Atlas asked.

"I don't know, man. I'm having a crisis here." Fallon closed his beady eyes and threw back his head, taking a deep breath.

That was my cue. Whatever was happening here was none of my business.

"I'll, uh, leave you two to it, then," I said, and slipped back inside.

"Ey, boss man!" Jimenez's voice tore through the living area the moment I stepped into the house. "I heard you're going to be walking your sister down the aisle."

I smiled. "Yep, and I'm damn proud of it."

"I can't believe my baby is getting married." My mom wrapped her arm around Tegan, putting her head on my sister's shoulder.

"She's going to be the most beautiful bride, Mrs. R." Declan raised his wineglass and took a long drink.

I wondered how long it would take for dinner to devolve into all the single parties heading out to the bar or the club. Hopefully not too long, because I was dying to have Cyrus's place all to our-selves.

Atlas popped his head through the sliding door. "We're all ready out here!"

"I wasn't finished yet," Fallon squawked.

"Shh," Atlas growled, shutting him up.

"Well"—Tegan rose to her feet—"let's eat."

We headed outside and joined Atlas and Fallon at the table.

Everyone slipped into their chairs, with Selene sitting as far away from Fallon as possible.

"This seat taken?" I asked, standing next to where Cyrus sat.

"Nope. Have a seat." Cyrus's accent combined with his soft smirk almost put me over the edge.

I needed to get myself under control. Atlas was already onto us, and I wasn't ready for anyone else to know yet.

Atlas cleared his throat from where he sat at the head of the table. "Tegan and I appreciate all of you joining us today. As you've probably already guessed, we'd like to ask each of you to play a part in our special day."

Tegan reached over and gripped Atlas's massive hand. "You've all heard that Reece has agreed to give me away at the ceremony." Cheers came from around the table and Tegan smiled sweetly at Selene. "Selene, I was wondering if you'd be my maid of honor?"

Selene grinned at Tegan. "It would be my pleasure."

"Dec." Tegan looked across the table at Declan. "Will you be my bridesman?"

"Teg, I will be whatever you need me to be."

"And, of course, you'll be the matron of honor, Mom," Tegan added.

Mom fanned her eyes, on the verge of tears. "Oh, honey. I can't wait."

Atlas looked at Fallon, giving the griffin a knowing smile. "While I do love my brothers, they live across the country. They'll be coming to the wedding, but it just didn't feel right asking one of them to be my best man. Fal, you're my oldest friend. Would you do me the honor of being my best man?"

"A-man, I'd love to. I'm going to throw you a killer bachelor party," Fallon chuffed.

"Cy, you're my second oldest friend, and I'll need someone to keep Fallon in check. Will you be one of my groomsmen?" Atlas stared down the table at Cyrus.

Cyrus nodded. "I'd be honored to. I'll do my best with Fallon, but no promises."

The three of them had such a tight friendship, and despite the fact that I was originally an asshole, they'd accepted me into their circle with open arms. They were good guys.

"Uh, what about Jimen—I mean, Javier?" I asked, realizing his role in the wedding hadn't been established.

"Oh, Tegan asked me to be the officiant. I got a certificate on-line." Jimenez raised his chin at me and smirked.

"Well, with that settled, let's eat." Atlas scooped a generous serving of ziti onto his plate.

While everyone talked and ate, I slid my foot over until it tapped Cyrus's tentacles. One of the long appendages coiled around my ankle and gripped it softly while he continued his conversation with Jimenez. I had to shovel my food into my mouth to keep myself from grinning like a fool.

There I was, sharing a meal with my family and friends—both old and new—celebrating my sister's upcoming wedding.

I cared about everyone at this table, but the person sitting next to me was the most important one of all.

Thirty

CYRUS

MY TENTACLES SHUFFLED OVER THE CARPET, PROPELLING ME down the hallway and back again.

Why was I so nervous?

It wasn't like this was the first time Reece had been over to my place. It was just the first time the two of us would be here alone, in my apartment.

We were free to do as we pleased, wherever we pleased.

A gentle knock echoed down the hall, and I did my best not to bolt toward the door. Well, I couldn't exactly bolt, so I did my best not to rush to the door, which would indicate I'd been impatiently waiting in the hallway for Reece to arrive.

"Hi," Reece said.

"Hi."

We stood there for a second just staring at each other when I grabbed him with my tentacles and pulled him inside.

"Fuck," he groaned as I pinned him against the wall. "I have been dying to touch you all night."

I laughed and slid my lips over his neck while I rolled my hips against his. "It was torture. And when you sat down next to me, what was that about?"

"You're not the only one who's a tease."

His breath hitched as one of my mating tentacles unraveled and massaged his cock. "Mmm, my sexy little tease. Already so hard for me. What do you want to do first? If you're hungry, we can—"

"Cyrus, I swear if you don't get inside me soon, I'm going to come in my pants. Tonight was nonstop edging."

I gave him a quick kiss and pulled away. "All right. Hold your horses. I'll get you off. Do you want to take a bath together first?"

Ever since I'd sent Reece a series of photos of me taking a bath, he'd been obsessed with the idea of us fucking in my soaking tub.

"Fuck yeah, I do," he blurted and immediately started kicking off his shoes.

"Control yourself, darling. We have all night. Grab your shoes and undress in my room. I don't want your clothes all over the place when Fallon comes home. And where did you park your car?"

I was hopeful that Fallon would spend the night with one of his conquests or end up passed out at Javier's house, but on the off chance he did come home, I wanted it to appear like I was alone. Reece could quietly slip out in the morning and all would be well in the world.

"Don't worry, I hid it around the block. And it's Fallon we're talking about—do you really think he'd notice my car in the parking lot?"

I shrugged and started down the hallway, with Reece following behind me. "You never know. I'm just trying to keep this as quiet for you as I can."

We walked into the bathroom and Reece was silent as I

grabbed fresh towels, no longer showing the enthusiasm he'd had out in the hall.

"Is something wrong?" I asked and scuttled toward him, my tentacles popping along the tile as I went.

His face flamed red and he rubbed his hand along the back of his neck. "At the party. Atlas, um, he stopped me outside. He knows about us. He saw us together down at the lake."

Reece leaned against the vanity and I stood beside him. I reached over and took his hand while my tentacle wrapped around his arm.

"Did he tell anyone?" I asked, keeping my voice calm and quiet.

Reece shook his head.

"How do you feel about that? I know you wanted to tell everyone on your own terms and I respect that."

He scrubbed his free hand over the wiry red strands of his beard. "I mean, I guess out of all the people to find out, Atlas is the best one. Better him than Fallon. But I thought for sure we were being careful. I'm going to tell Tegan after the triathlon, but I just—"

"Hey." I stepped in front of him. "It's okay to be upset about this. You're allowed to feel that way." I grabbed his other hand and pressed my forehead against his. "And I know you'd never keep us a secret forever, but you're allowed to take as long as you need to process things. Atlas is as loyal and trustworthy as they come. When you're ready, he'll be there to support us. He won't say a single thing to Tegan before then."

Reece tightened his grip on my hands. "You're right. I'm so happy, but I'm afraid of ruining it."

Knowing my mate was happy had me practically bursting with pride. "Reece, nothing could ever ruin this."

There was a small part of me that had my doubts, though. I had this lingering fear that as soon as we went public with our relationship or as soon as I told Reece about the mate bond, he'd backslide and regret everything between us.

I'd be crushed.

That was a worry for another day, though.

Tonight, I wanted to enjoy him, to enjoy us.

I dipped my head, pressed my lips to his, and with a low groan, I slid the soft pads of my tongues into his mouth, swirling and teasing until Reece lightly bucked his hips into mine, searching for friction.

I released his hands and pulled away, slipping down his body until the bulge in his pants was level with my mouth.

"How many times do you think I can make you come tonight?" I asked, tilting my head back to stare into his eyes as I slowly undid his belt.

"Over and over, until I pass out, preferably." He reached for his waistband, but I caught his hands with my tentacles and re-strained them behind his back.

"Someone's impatient," I said with a smirk. "You stay put, darling. I'll give you what you need."

With steady hands, I started to pull his shorts down.

"What. Is. This?" I gasped at the sight of the thin black lace that strained against the impressive length of Reece's cock. Skinny straps on the sides dug into his hips just slightly before disappearing between the cheeks of his ass.

I knew full well what it was, but I wanted my mate to say it.

His cheeks flushed beet red. "It—it's a thong. This was part of a dream I had. A dream about you," he mumbled under his breath.

"Mmm," I purred and nuzzled my face against the material. Against Reece's cock. "If this is part of the dream, you'll have to fill me in on the rest of it."

It turned out my straitlaced mate was kinkier than I'd thought. I wanted to please him, to live out every fantasy his deliciously dirty mind could come up with.

"In fact," I said as I pulled the thong to the side, allowing Reece's cock to drop free. "Why don't you tell me the details of this dream while I suck you off? Hmm?"

I placed a delicate kiss on the tip of his head, smearing the bead of precum that had collected there over my lips. My tongues darted out to lick my mouth, and I hummed with satisfaction at the flavor.

Reece swallowed hard, his breath coming out as harsh pants while he stared down at me.

I was a hair's breadth away from his cock. It would take nothing to open my mouth and slip him inside, but I wanted him to answer me first.

I wanted him to tell me about the dream.

Just when I started to pull back, Reece spoke. "You were degrading me. You were asking me how much I liked it. You said it was the tentacles. That it's always the tentacles . . ."

I parted my lips and slid the smooth head of Reece's cock into my mouth.

"Shit," he hissed through clenched teeth, his hips thrusting slightly and his arms straining against my tentacles. Reece was strong, but my mate was no match for the restraints.

Go on, I told him using my telepathic abilities while I held his cock still in my mouth, refusing to take him deeper until he told me more of the dream.

"One of your tentacles slid around my throat and choked me. Not too hard, just a little bit. Just enough to make breathing tough."

Oh? Do you like that sort of thing?

My eyes were fixed on Reece's fevered expression as I bobbed my head, using my tongues to caress the wide vein running along the underside of his cock.

"Y-yes. I think so." He groaned through parted lips and threw his head back. "I—I've never done it before."

Would you like to try it?

Consent was key, and I never wanted to do anything to Reece that made him feel uncomfortable. Especially something like breath play. You had to have trust.

I moved my head faster, taking the tip of his cock into the back of my throat while my tongues coiled around the shaft.

"Fuck. Yes. Please," he said through gritted teeth.

My tentacle traced up his body before wrapping around his neck, slowly increasing the pressure along the sides of his throat.

How's that?

"Amazing," he rasped against the soft squeeze.

Good.

He gasped as I plunged the full length of his cock into my mouth.

Unlike humans, I didn't have a gag reflex. I could take his cock into my throat as far as it would go.

And I did.

Over and over again.

"Holy shit, Cyrus," Reece huffed, thrusting his hips to meet my mouth.

What else happened in the dream?

"I—I begged you to fuck me. You gave me your suckers. You played with my prostate. We both came hard. And you told me how well I did." He was trying to focus but his words came out in a rushed string.

It appeared that my mate—the musclehead parks worker triathlete—was into lace thongs, praise, and degradation.

How did I get so lucky?

"Cyrus," he panted. "Gonna come."

Give it to me, darling. Come in the back of my throat. Let me taste you.

I forced him deeper, his hips slamming against my face as he filled my mouth with his cum. The salty flavor was exquisite, and I used my tongues to work every last drop out of his cock.

"Motherfucker," he groaned as his body convulsed against the restraints.

I pulled away just slightly, allowing my tongues to swirl over his shaft several times before I popped off his cock.

"Was it good?" I asked, staring up at him expectantly.

I knew the answer was yes, but again, I needed my mate to say it. I needed verbal confirmation that my dual-tongued blow jobs were the most superior in all the land.

His eyes were hooded and his chest heaved as he looked down at me. "You are the king of blow jobs, Cy."

"Damn right, I am."

My tentacles released him, and I rose to a standing position.

"How about that bath now, hmm?" I asked, skating my hands under his shirt, along his cut six-pack.

"Please." Reece circled his arms around my neck and pulled me in for a kiss.

He slipped his tongue past my lips and claimed my mouth with possessive strokes. Apparently, it didn't bother him that he'd just filled it with his cum.

"I love how fucking filthy you are," I mumbled.

He laughed as I pulled away. "There are worse things than tasting my own cum."

I shuffled over to the tub, starting the tap while Reece undressed. Since he'd be joining me, I didn't add my usual salt crystals, opting for a lightly scented bubble bath instead.

As I was bent over the tub, using my tentacles to agitate the water, I felt the warmth of Reece's nude body press up against me. Strong hands wrapped around my chest, and he nestled his face against my fins.

"I just can't get enough of you," he whispered. "You look so handsome. So focused. I had to touch you."

Months ago, Reece would have shied away from touching me; now he actively sought me out.

A wide smile spread over my face, and I ran the backside of my hand along his beard, right where the stubble ended and the smooth column of his neck began.

How was it that someone ripped from the pages of *Men's Health* magazine found me attractive?

It had to be because of the mate bond. That was the only explanation. There was no way I could pull a guy like Reece otherwise.

"Everything okay?" he asked when I didn't respond to his compliment.

"Everything's fine. Better than fine, actually." I looked down at the bubbling waterline of the tub. "We can get in now if you'd like. It can fill up the rest of the way with us in there."

He nodded, releasing me so that I could slide over the side and into the bath.

I hummed as the warm water blanketed my body, and I held my hand out to help Reece. He stepped in and settled himself next to me in our bubble fortress.

"This is really nice," he said, collecting a mound of bubbles in his hand, then blowing them into the tub.

While I called it a soaking tub, it was more like a Jacuzzi or hot tub, with ample room for two grown men to lie comfortably.

"Come here." I braced myself against the side of the tub and used my tentacles to pull Reece against me. "It's like our cowboy photo shoot but reversed."

"This is even better," he mumbled, snuggling closer and pressing his ear to my chest.

We sat like that for a few moments, enjoying the closeness of each other as the tub filled.

"Cy," Reece said the moment I shut off the tap.

"Yes, darling?"

"Your heartbeat. It's sort of weird." He rubbed his hand over my chest, feeling my thumping hearts underneath.

"That's because I have three hearts."

And they all beat for you.

He stared up at me, a light coating of bubbles stuck to his beard. "Really?"

"Really."

"Wild."

Reece wiggled against me, and I could feel his hardening cock poking my tentacles.

"Already?" I asked with a laugh.

The needy thing had just gotten off.

"I can't help it." He rubbed his hands over my chest, continuing upward until his fingertips trailed over my fins. "You turn me on. And you did promise me you'd fuck me in this bathtub."

"Well, I can't break a promise. Sit up for me."

Reece sat sideways in my lap, his back braced against the tub wall and his feet propped against the opposite ledge. He sat just high enough that the head of his cock jutted out from the water's surface, giving me the perfect view.

"You're going to stay still for me." I coiled my tentacles around Reece's arms and pinned them behind his back.

"Fuck," he murmured as I curled one of my tentacles around the base of his cock.

"Spread your legs," I instructed, my voice flat.

He complied but didn't move his legs nearly as far apart as I wanted them.

With one hand, I gripped his thigh and forced his legs wider, sending water sloshing over the edge of the tub.

"Shit, Cy," he panted.

Apparently, Reece liked it rough.

My mating tentacles uncoiled from my arms, the tips already coated in a light sheen of lubricant.

"Open your mouth," I commanded.

If he wanted breath play, I'd give it to him—and get myself off at the same time.

Reece parted his full lips and I slid a mating tentacle into his mouth. With quick thrusts, I worked the slick tendril into the back of his throat as he gagged around it.

"Take it, my needy boy. I'm going to fill all of your holes. Leave you dripping with my cum like the little cum slut you are."

Degradation wasn't normally my thing, but if Reece was into it, I was willing to do a bit of role-playing.

Beneath the water, I slid my other mating tentacle over his ass and circled his entrance, coating the area with lube. This was one of the perks of being a kraken, I was designed for sex in the water.

"Are you ready, darling? Ready to be stuffed with my tentacles?" I asked.

He let out a muffled groan as I slowly pushed the tip inside, giving his body time to adjust to the stretch.

I stared at him and smirked, reveling in the fact that I could reduce this hypermasculine man into a desperate whimpering mess.

He was so damn pretty like this.

Saliva dripped down his chin, his eyes watering as I continued fucking his mouth. My tentacle stroked his cock, gripping and twisting his shaft, distracting him as the tentacle in his ass burrowed deeper.

It wasn't enough, though.

I knew my mate.

He needed more.

Another one of my tentacles slid out of the water, over his stomach, and up his chest, coming to a stop at one of his nipples.

"These sexy pecs," I growled.

The tip of my tentacle curled around his nipple, giving it a sharp pinch.

"*Fuh*," Reece mumbled against my tentacle, his body jolting against the restraints.

"Do you want to come?" I asked.

He gave me a slow nod.

I forced the mating tentacle in his ass deeper, pushing the rows of suckers past the tight ring of muscle.

"Gods, Reece," I groaned, enjoying the sensation just as much as he did.

With both of my mating tentacles being stimulated, I was close to coming myself.

The suckers coating the underside of my tentacle found his prostate, massaging the gland with rapid passes before attaching.

"*Cy*," he moaned around my tentacle, his body quivering as he came.

"Yes, yes," I rasped, my gaze focused on his cock as thick spurts of cum coated his chest.

Warmth spread along my mating tentacles as I found my own release, flooding Reece's mouth and tight channel with my cum. His Adam's apple bobbed with each of his desperate swallows, and a small stream of my cum trickled out of the corner of his mouth.

Slowly, I pulled out of him, savoring his contented expression as I wiped the cum off his face.

"You did so well, taking all of my cum like that," I praised.

Reece groaned and threw his head back. "You fucking wrecked me, Cy."

I laughed and used my tentacle to pull the stopper, draining the bath. "You said you wanted me to fuck you in the tub. I wanted the first time to be memorable."

"Oh, it's fucking memorable all right. I'm gonna be walking funny tomorrow."

"Shut up," I said, pulling him closer and pressing my lips to his.

"Maybe not, but my nipple is going to be sore for sure."

"Well, I guess I'll just have to kiss it better, then, won't I?" I smirked before rising up on my tentacles. "Come on, let's rinse off in the shower and get to bed."

Thirty-One

REECE

"WHAT'S WRONG?" CYRUS ASKED AS I ROLLED OVER FOR what felt like the hundredth time.

His bed was comfortable, and obviously I enjoyed his company, but even after back-to-back orgasms, I just couldn't get my thoughts to stop racing.

"I'm just—feeling a little anxious."

Cyrus shimmied next to me so that my back was pressed against his chest, and he wrapped one of his arms around me. "Talk to me, darling," he whispered.

"I just have a lot on my mind. The triathlon is coming up. The fact that Atlas saw us. My sister asking me to give her away."

"Well," he said, rubbing his thumb over my stomach with slow strokes, "you've been busting your ass in training and you're going to do amazing in the triathlon. While there are worse things than Atlas finding out, it's okay to be upset that it wasn't on your terms. And your sister asking you to give her away—that's such a huge step forward in your relationship. You've come so far in the last three months, Reece. It's normal to have mixed feelings about that or worry that you're going to do something to screw it all up. But you're doing wonderful, darling. Sure, there might be setbacks, you might not place as well as you want to, and you might piss your sister off again at some point. No, not *might*, *will*. But you're out here giving it your all, regardless of what the final outcome is. I'm proud of you for that."

Cyrus was right. This was all part of change, of growth. It was going to be uncomfortable. I was going to have moments when I doubted myself or doubted the process, but I was giving it my all. That's what mattered.

And the fact that Cyrus was proud of me, that was an added bonus.

Cyrus pulled away from me and sat up. "Lie on your back. I want to try something."

I snorted and rolled over. "Gods, Cy. You really want to fuck again? I don't know if my ass can take any more."

He laughed and pulled the sheet from my waist, revealing my soft cock. "No more fucking, at least not yet. Have you ever heard of cock warming?"

"I mean, yeah. I've heard of it. I've never done it or had it done to me."

"Would you want to try it? I think it might help you relax a little bit. Just until you fall asleep, and you can still talk to me while I do it. If you don't like it, we can stop."

Having a—*friend*—with telepathic abilities had its advantages, and I did enjoy intimate touches when it came to Cyrus.

"Sure." I put my arms behind my head. "But I swear if you fall asleep and chomp off my cock with those piranha teeth, I will be pissed."

He laughed and slid down my body before slipping my cock between his soft lips. There wasn't any head bobbing or lip and tongue action; he laid his head against my pelvis and held my limp cock in his mouth.

And it felt amazing.

Like a warm hug for my dick.

For the record, I'd never chomp off this absolute piece of perfection. Do you like it?

His sexy British accent echoed inside my head and I couldn't help but smile. "Yeah. It's different, but it feels good."

I knew you'd like it. You're always content when I'm touching your cock.

"Not just when you're touching my cock," I huffed. "I like it when you touch me in general."

That makes me laugh, considering your reaction the first time I touched you.

"Well, I was an asshole."

Was?

"Shut up," I mumbled, and for a few minutes we were quiet before I spoke again. "Cy, can I touch you?"

Please. You never have to ask.

I pulled my hands from behind my head and let them rest on either side of Cyrus's face.

"You're fucking handsome, you know that?" I rubbed my fingertips over his fins.

Cyrus laughed around my cock, almost spitting it out.

I am not.

"You are. I stare at your stripes constantly. And that body. You're fucking ripped. Even if you don't see it, you're sexy to me."

I meant every word. I could look at the patterns covering Cyrus's body for hours, and watching him jet through the water was hypnotic. He was a generous lover and a loyal friend. Him coming into my life had changed everything. Had changed me.

I'm glad you think so, darling.

My cheeks warmed like they did every time he called me that. I never wanted him to stop. I never wanted what this was between us to stop.

"I really care about you, Cy," I said, fighting back a yawn. My eyelids felt heavy, and my fingers started to slow down.

I care about you, too, Reece. More than you could possibly fathom.

I didn't need him to tell me, though. He showed me with his actions every day.

"CYRUS, I BROUGHT BEIGNETS!"

The bedroom door flew open, and Cyrus and I bolted upright.

Fallon was standing in the doorway staring at the two of us in bed together.

"Oh, holy gods!" Fallon screeched as I scrambled to cover my naked body with a blanket.

My heart raced and my chest felt so tight, I had to force myself to breathe.

Fallon had caught us.

The biggest loudmouth around knew that Cyrus and I were hooking up.

"Do you not knock anymore?" Cyrus hissed, his color shifting to a deep blue. "Get out."

Fallon opened his mouth to protest but ultimately turned around and slammed the door shut behind him.

"Fuck!" I shouted, running my fingers through my hair.

"Reece, I am *so* sorry," Cyrus said quietly. "He normally parties so hard that he's hungover the next day. I didn't think he'd make it back home, and he doesn't typically barge in like this."

Cyrus reached for me, but I pulled away. I couldn't handle being touched right now. All of this was too much.

Without saying a word, I got out of bed and walked into the

bathroom. I locked the door behind me and collapsed on the cool tile floor.

This wasn't Cyrus's fault. I knew that. But I was angry and upset. I needed a few moments to process what had just happened.

"Reece," Cyrus whispered from the other side of the door. "Please talk to me. Don't shut me out."

I brought my knees to my chest, wrapped my arms around them, and curled into a tight ball. "We should have just told everyone. Now they're going to hear it from Fallon."

"You don't know that. He would never intentionally do something to hurt me, and now that extends to you. We should go talk to him. And I know you love beignets."

I sat there for a few minutes, taking deep breaths and getting my emotions in check. The old me would have stormed off or threatened Fallon with bodily harm if he muttered even one word of this to anyone else.

But I didn't want to be that person anymore.

And I did love beignets.

"Okay," I huffed and rose to my feet.

When I opened the door, Cyrus was standing there with my clothes in his hands. His color was back to normal, but I could see the hurt in his eyes.

I'd pulled away from him, just like I did at the party. I hurt him, but he was still here, still waiting for me, just as kind and steady as always.

I stepped closer, threw my arms around him, and pulled him in for a tight hug. His heartbeats reverberated out of his chest and into mine, calming me with their steady rhythm.

"I'm sorry," I murmured against his skin.

"It's okay." He ran his hands over my back, the soft touch making me shudder. "You're still naked."

"I am."

We both vibrated with laughter, the tension of what just happened slipping away.

Cyrus waited patiently while I dressed, and once I was ready, we walked down the hall to the living area.

The box of beignets sat on the counter and the sliding door to the terrace was open.

"I am so, so sorry," Fallon chirped the moment Cyrus and I joined him on the outdoor sofa. "I'm not used to you having anyone over, and gods, Reece was the last person I expected. I knew you guys were getting close, but I didn't know it was like this." The words rushed out. It was obvious he was just as flustered as we were.

I worried my lip a second before reaching over and grabbing Cyrus's hand. "We, uh, we've been seeing each other for a few months now. We—I was waiting for the right time to go public with our relationship."

Fallon fluffed his feathers and nodded. "I respect that, man."

"We'd appreciate it if you kept this quiet for now. Just until Reece is ready." Cyrus gripped my hand tighter and gave me a soft smile.

"Whatever the two of you need. I freaking knew something was going on with you, Cy. All the paint—"

Cyrus cleared his throat, and Fallon clamped his beak shut.

All the paintings?

"Anyway." Cyrus rose up on his tentacles. "Why don't we dig into those beignets and I'll make us some coffee, hmm?"

"Yeah, sure." Fallon stood and started to follow Cyrus inside. "But just so you know, the image of Reece's cock is, like, burned into my brain. You're fucking hung, man," he quipped to me over his shoulder.

Cyrus whipped around and glared at Fallon, his thin lips pulled back and his sharp white teeth bared. "If you value your life, stop it right now," he hissed. His body was already darkening to that blackish-blue hue it took on when he was angry.

Fallon certainly knew how to push people to their limits.

"Hey, man. We're cool, we're cool. I was just trying to lighten the mood. It'll never happen again." He put his talons up, rearing back.

Cyrus blinked several times and took a deep breath, his color slowly fading to its familiar teal blue as he relaxed.

You would think I'd be afraid of Cyrus when he acted like that—the possessive, dominant version of himself—but it fucking turned me on. If Fallon wasn't here, I'd beg him to spread me over the island and have his way with me.

It would have to wait for another day, though.

The three of us moved inside without another word, the tension in the room heavy.

Cyrus set to work starting the coffee, and Fallon sat down on one of the stools around the island. His feathers lay flat against his body, and his tail hung limply behind him.

I patted Fallon's back and offered him some comfort before sitting down next to him at the counter. "It's all right, bud. He didn't mean it."

Cyrus turned away from what he was doing and stared at Fallon. "I'm sorry I overreacted. But in the future, please don't talk about the impressive size of Reece's"—he thought for a moment—"*equipment* in front of him like that."

My cheeks burned.

The *impressive size* of my equipment.

Holy gods.

I reached across the island and pulled the box of beignets closer to Fallon and me. "All right, then. Well, now that we've gotten that awkward conversation out of the way, let's eat."

Thirty-Two

REECE

FALL IN BRIAR GLENN WAS MY FAVORITE SEASON. THE SUBTLE chill in the air, the sweet scent of freshly fallen leaves, and the way the woods seemed to come alive with color. It was perfect. Ideal for a camping trip, really. Unfortunately, the rest of this situation was less than ideal. It was finally time for the promised camping trip where I'd have to be around my sister, the guy I was secretly fucking, and two people who knew our secret.

Jimenez was supposed to join us, but he'd canceled at the last minute. Because of course he fucking did. I was really hoping that blissfully unaware golden retriever was going to be here to serve as some sort of buffer between us all, but he'd crushed those dreams with a single text message.

For the next twenty-four or so hours, I was going to be a ball of fucking nerves.

I leaned against my car, anxiously tapping my foot while I waited at the trailhead that led to the campsite for everyone else to arrive.

Of course it was Cyrus who showed up first. Just Cyrus. No Fallon.

"What the fuck do you think you're doing?" I asked the moment he got out of his SUV.

There was no way this was happening. It couldn't just be me and him with Atlas and Tegan.

He rolled his eyes and sighed. "Do you think I'd do this on purpose?" he asked with that signature British snark of his. I hated how hot it was. "Fallon is the one who set this up. I begged him to come along, but he gave me some excuse about a last-minute VIP experience at one of the clubs he frequents."

"That's funny because Jimenez canceled, too."

"Fallon knows that we're"—his tentacles gesticulated wildly—"whatever it is we are."

Whatever it is we are . . .

It hurt to hear Cyrus refer to things between us that way, but I'd never put a label on things between us. He was probably waiting for me to make that move.

"Cy, I—" Before I could continue, Atlas and Tegan pulled into the parking lot.

My sister was smiling and waving aggressively in the passenger seat, obviously excited.

"Well, here we go," I grumbled but forced a smile.

This was fine. Everything was going to be fine.

"Hey!" Tegan said, bright, chipper, and totally unaware of the tension between Cyrus and me.

"Hey," Cyrus and I said in unison. We both sounded slightly awkward, but she didn't seem to notice.

"Fallon and Javier not here yet?" Atlas said, looking around the parking lot.

"It seems that Fallon and Javier have other plans this evening.

Ones that don't involve hot dogs and sleeping outside," Cyrus said.

"I mean, knowing the two of them, it's not entirely impossible that their night will end up the same way," Atlas joked.

"It's their loss," Tegan said. "I think it'll be a lot more fun with just the four of us anyway."

"Right?" Cyrus looked at me, his lips tipping up with a satisfied smirk. "Loads of fun."

Why did he have to bring up *loads* at a time like this? He was enjoying this a little bit too much, and we hadn't even gotten to the campsite yet.

"It'll be great," Atlas said. "Do you have all the stuff, Reece?"

I popped open my trunk. "Yep. I have a bunch of camping chairs, three tents—"

"I think two tents will be plenty. You don't mind sharing with Reece, do you, Cy?" Atlas asked.

Fuck, I swear everyone was conspiring against me to make this as awkward as possible.

Cyrus looked at me, his lips twitching with a sly smile. "I don't mind at all."

"Perfect," Tegan said. "The sooner we get the tents up, the sooner we can relax."

We unloaded the vehicles and dropped everything at the campsite. Things were winding down for the season, but with the cool, comfortable weather, there were still a fair amount of campers in the park. One of the perks of working for the Parks Department meant that I was able to snag a double campsite reservation. Technically, I was still working and was on call for any emergencies at all the parks we managed, but that was rare.

Campers checked in online and, for the most part, followed all the rules and regulations of the campground without any issues. I was hoping that would be the case today.

"All right," I said, surveying the site. There was plenty of flat ground on either side of the firepit, meaning I could set Atlas and Tegan up on one side and Cy and me on the other. As far away from them as possible.

Knowing Cyrus, there was no way we were sharing a tent and just sleeping next to each other. Even if I tried to resist, all my willpower went out the window when it came to him. And if I was really being honest with myself, the whole sneaking around thing was pretty hot.

Soon, it would be time for us to take things public. That scared me in more ways than one. It meant that my sister would find out about us, but it also meant that I'd have to confront the fact that this was my first real relationship. That what I felt for Cyrus was nothing I'd ever felt before.

"We'll take this spot over here," Atlas said from the opposite side of the campsite.

"Uh, okay," I said awkwardly. I looked at Cyrus, noting the shit-eating grin on his face. "Guess that means we're over here," I mumbled.

"Guess so," he said, smug as fuck.

"Why does the universe hate me?" I said under my breath.

"Personally, I think the universe favors you. I mean, you'll think that when I'm sucking your cock later."

"Cyrus," I hissed, throwing the tent poles on the ground. He wasn't wrong, but he didn't need to say it out loud. "Will you shut up!"

He laughed. "It is too easy with you."

"You can't talk about that sort of thing with my sister over there."

"Relax. No one can hear us. You should be more worried about them hearing us later."

I couldn't do this. I stepped away from our tent and watched Atlas and Tegan struggle with theirs across from us.

"Do you guys need a hand? I think Cyrus has everything under control over here," I offered.

"That would be great. I don't remember this being that hard when we were kids," Tegan said. Her arms were full of tent poles, and she couldn't seem to get them to connect.

I went over and plucked a pole out of her hand. "That's because Dad and I would do it while we gave you some menial task, like collecting kindling."

She dropped the rest of the poles and crossed her arms over her chest. "That's not how I remember it."

"Well, you're remembering it wrong." I gave the pole a little tug, easily snapping it together.

"Thanks for your help, Reece," Atlas said. With his giant paws, he couldn't get the poles threaded through the tent canopy.

"It's no problem at all. I've been camping enough times that I could put one of these together in my sleep."

While I finished their tent—with minimal help from Atlas, might I add—Cyrus and Tegan set up the rest of the campsite.

A plastic tablecloth pinned to the picnic table was covered with plates, utensils, and snacks. Plastic cups were stacked next to the jug of drinking water I'd brought, and the spigot hung over the edge of the table, making it easy to fill up cups or wash hands.

Four camping chairs circled the firepit, just far enough away that no one's boots, paws, or tentacles were in danger of getting burned.

"It looks so good," Tegan said, surveying camp with her hands on her hips.

"It does," Atlas agreed. "Great work, baby." He wrapped his arm around her and gave her a kiss on the cheek.

Fuck, he was a good guy. He practically worshipped the ground she walked on.

We sat around the firepit taking in the sights and sounds of nature.

"This is so nice," Tegan said, wiggling in her seat. She was so happy being out here. It made me feel good that we all came together to make it happen.

"It is," I agreed.

"What's in the cooler, Cy?" Atlas asked. He and Tegan were responsible for snacks, I brought the camping equipment, and Cyrus was assigned to the actual meals.

"I went the traditional route with burgers and hot dogs, and tomorrow morning I'll make bacon and eggs before we pack up."

"And I brought everything for s'mores," Tegan added.

Fuck, I loved s'mores. The perfect mix of melty, sweet, and crunchy.

"Perfect." I looked at the charred pieces of wood sitting in the firepit. In my rush to get everything together, I'd forgotten to grab firewood. "I have to go to the storehouse and get some firewood," I said, rising out of my chair. "The bathrooms are over that way. Anyone need to go?" The image of Cyrus kissing me while he pinned me to a tree flashed in my head, and I selfishly hoped that Atlas and Tegan would say no and Cyrus would say yes.

That little fantasy was crushed when Tegan hopped out of her chair and said, "Oh, I do."

Atlas and Cyrus looked at each other. Tegan didn't clock it, but to me, it was obvious that Cyrus was speaking to Atlas telepathically.

Atlas smiled at my sister. "Nope. I'm good."

"Me, too," Cyrus added.

For the second—or was it the third?—time today, I'd been set up.

"All right, suit yourselves." I shrugged. "I don't want to hear any complaining when you have to find it in the dark later."

Atlas chuckled. "I think we'll be just fine."

I started down the path that led to the storehouse and bathrooms with Tegan following behind me. One of the first projects I'd petitioned for when I took over the Parks Department were clearly marked paths to the park's amenities. I wasn't going to have anyone else go through the childhood trauma I'd experienced traipsing through the woods by myself.

Other than our crunchy footfalls over the fallen leaves, the forest was silent. The last rays of the setting sun filtered through the trees, casting shimmering shadows as the breeze shook their leaves.

Even though I spent every day outdoors, I never got tired of Briar Glenn's beauty: The fresh air. The lake. The thick forests and wide, sprawling fields. I couldn't think of anywhere else I'd rather be. As long as it meant that Cyrus was here with me.

The thought stopped me dead in my tracks, and Tegan nearly crashed into my back.

"What's wrong?" she asked, giving my sleeve a little tug.

I swallowed hard and shook my head, feeling the guilt churn my stomach. "Nothing," I forced out. "Everything's fine."

Tegan put her hand on her chest and puffed out a heavy breath. "I was worried there was a bear or something."

While there were a lot of black bears in this part of the Northeast, I'd only ever seen three the entire time I'd lived here.

"I think Briar Glenn is a little too busy these days for that," I said with a smile. That and the fact that a massive wolven prowled the woods every full moon. I'm sure one whiff of Atlas's scent was enough to scare away any predators.

"As much as I appreciate the growth, I miss the times when it was quieter. I think that's why I wanted to come out here so bad. Even if it's just for a night."

"I would have asked you to go camping sooner if I knew you wanted to go that bad."

"How were you supposed to know if I didn't tell you . . . ?" She trailed off like it bothered her that we didn't talk that much, just as much as it bothered me. "I'm really happy we could do this. When you and Dad would go on your camping trips, I always hoped he'd take me with you."

"You went camping with us every summer."

"Yeah, but you and Dad went every month."

I let out a dry laugh. "Tegs, our monthly camping trip was nothing like when we went as a family. I would have much rather stayed home with you and Mom."

"Why?" she asked quietly. She knew things between my dad and me were different from how he was with her, but did I really want to tarnish the image of him she had in her head? Maybe I had to in order to explain some of the resentment I felt toward her, the reason why the old man's passing made me breathe a giant sigh of relief.

"Dad would just drink the entire time and remind me what a mistake I was," I said, coming right out with it.

Hurt flashed over her face. Genuine hurt. And fuck, did it make me feel bad. But it was the truth.

"I'm sorry," she whispered. I hated that she was apologizing when none of this was her fault.

I forced a smile, hoping it might make her feel better. "It's okay."

She shook her head. "It isn't, though. If I would have known what you and Mom went through—"

I cut her off. "No. You had your relationship with Dad, and we had ours. It's okay. You don't have to feel bad about it."

"Easier said than done," she grumbled under her breath.

I nudged her shoulder. "I'm sorry that things between us got so twisted up. I just think I didn't know how to carry on with our relationship once Dad died." It felt good getting that off my chest.

"You mean you weren't being an overprotective prick on purpose?"

"I mean, maybe." I chuckled. "I just love you and I want the best for you. I didn't think it would happen so soon. That's all."

"When I first told Mom that Atlas and I were mates, I asked her if she thought it was too soon. She told me that when the goddess brings two people together, she's never wrong. Sometimes life throws you a mate when you're least expecting it."

"Yeah, I guess it does."

The trees parted, revealing the bathrooms and weathered storehouse at the end of the trail.

"We made it," I said, leading Tegan to the little cubby that held all the firewood.

"Do we just take it?" Tegan asked.

I shook my head, laughing at my baby sister. "No. We leave money in the box. We don't want the Parks Department coming for us."

She stared at me, her expression flat. "You're the Parks Department."

"I am, and I'm going to let it slide just this once," I said, wagging my finger.

Technically, I'd been letting it slide since childhood. Not once had I ever paid for firewood.

I grabbed a bundle from the pile and led Tegan around the building to the bathroom. Thankfully, it was an actual bathroom. With toilets that flushed and running water.

While she did her thing, I leaned against a tree and thought about how good it felt to get that off my chest. And when the time came to tell her about me and Cyrus, that was going to feel good, too, regardless of what her reaction was.

"All set?" I asked when she rounded the corner.

"Yep."

We started the walk back to the campsite, and after a few moments of silence, Tegan said, "You know, Atlas said the same thing about Dad."

"He did?" It caught me a little off guard because it meant that she and Atlas talked about our relationship.

She nodded.

"Well, he's a smart guy." I shifted my weight and rubbed my hand over the back of my head. "I, uh, I'm really glad we could work things out, Tegs. I don't know if I said that the last time we talked."

"You did, but I'm glad we could work it out, too."

Fuck. The triathlon was next weekend, but here we were, having this heartfelt, in-depth conversation. Maybe this was the right moment to tell her about me and Cyrus?

My heart rate ramped up and my throat felt tight.

"Teg, there's something I want to tell you . . ."

"What is it?" she asked, staring at me expectantly.

"I just—" Fuck, this was harder than I thought. And this really seemed like the sort of thing I should have consulted with Cy about, especially since we were going to have to sit at a campsite with Atlas and Tegan all night long.

What if she blew up on me and that was that?

No, this wasn't the right time.

"I'm just"—I paused, trying to find something, *anything* else to say—"so happy for you and Atlas. I really like him."

There was a self-assured smirk on her face. "I knew you'd come around. And I'm glad you like his friends, too. You and Cyrus seem like you've gotten close since you started training."

"Oh, do we?" I tried to sound surprised, like I didn't sneak around with Cyrus every chance I got.

"Yeah. It makes me happy because you've never really had many friends."

Well, she wasn't wrong. I hung around with some people when I was in school, but I was never really part of a group. I was always the fringe friend. The one who was an afterthought, who was begrudgingly allowed to tag along when no one else was available.

My attitude played a big part in that. The attitude I'd developed from living with my father. It was just another way he'd damaged me.

"Well, shit, Tegs. Way to make me feel like a loser."

"You're not a loser at all. I just always thought you liked being alone and that you wanted to focus on sports rather than being social. There's nothing wrong with that."

"Yeah."

"Listen, I know you're my big brother, but you don't have to keep things from me just for my sake. I want you to feel comfortable sharing with me."

My heart leapt into my throat.

Fuck. Fuck. Fuck.

Did she know? Was she trying to get me to tell her about Cyrus?

When I didn't say anything, she threaded her arm through mine, leaned her head against me, and gave me a little squeeze. "Dad might not be here for you to work things out with him, but I'm happy to listen."

I puffed out a tight breath. She meant my childhood trauma, not my relationship with Cyrus. "Thank you," I said, squeezing her back.

When we returned to camp, Atlas and Cyrus were parked in their chairs right where we'd left them.

"Got the firewood," I said, hoisting up the bundle.

"Good, because we were simply freezing here without it," Cyrus said flatly.

I had to fight the urge to give him my signature *Fuck you*. He knew what that meant, but it might have sounded a little harsh to Atlas and Tegan.

I ignored him, pulled out my pocketknife, and cut the logs free. I needed something to focus on.

Atlas watched me for a second, then got up from his chair. "Come on, baby." He held his massive hand out to my sister. "Why don't you show me those kindling-collecting skills I've heard so much about?"

She snorted. Gods, she was just like our mother. "Prepare to be impressed," she said, and they wandered off into the woods.

"How was that?" Cyrus asked as I stacked the logs in the firepit.

"Oh, you're interested because you set me up?"

"Tegan was very excited and nostalgic about this trip. We just wanted to give the two of you some space to talk."

"And we did." I went back to stacking, hoping my response got under his skin.

"Well?" he asked. *Mission accomplished.*

"We talked about my relationship with our dad. I don't think she realized quite how bad things were, but I'm glad I got it off my chest. It feels like another step in healing things, ya know?"

"That's great."

"And then, while we were having that heartfelt discussion, I thought it might be a good time to tell her about me and you."

"Oh?" he said, his bumpy eyebrows drawing back.

I nodded. "But it didn't feel right to do it without your consent. And I wasn't sure if you wanted to be there or not."

His expression softened. "Darling, consider this my consent. You tell her when you think the time is right. In my presence or not."

He was always so fucking good to me. So patient and sweet and kind, even when I didn't deserve it. Even when he was depressed and going through his own shit, he still put me first.

"I appreciate you," I whispered. I wanted to say more, to tell him exactly how I felt. I wanted to jump into his arms and kiss him and bury my head in the crook of his neck and list every single thing that made him wonderful over and over again until he believed it.

Tears welled up in my eyes, blurring my vision. Fuck, I had cried more in these last few months with Cyrus than I had in the past twenty years.

"Reece . . ." I could hear the concern in his voice, the confliction. He wanted to comfort me, but he couldn't.

"I'm fine," I said, wiping my eyes with my sleeve. I needed to get it together before Atlas and Tegan got back. "These damn fall allergies."

He didn't say anything else. He just let me sit with my emotions and stack and restack the firewood as many times as I needed to.

A few minutes later, Tegan and Atlas returned. Atlas's arms were full of tiny sticks and twigs, and my sister had a triumphant smile on her face.

"Ta-da," she said as Atlas set the pile down by the firepit.

"Whoa," I said. "Looks like all those years of practice paid off."

"It's okay to be jealous of my skills," she said.

"Do you know how to start a fire?" I asked Atlas.

He shook his head. "Nope."

"Well"—I pulled one of my homemade fire starters and a lighter out of my pocket—"you're going to learn today."

Thirty-Three

REECE

CYRUS LOOKED SO DAMN HANDSOME TONIGHT. THE FIRELIGHT flickered, lighting up the defined angles of his face and making the translucent fins along his neck shimmer in the darkness. His mating tentacles were wrapped around his arms, contracting and releasing like they were antsy. Like there were other things on his mind besides sitting next to the campfire.

He caught me staring, his lips tipping up in a subdued smile. *Soon*, his voice echoed in my head, soft and seductive.

I swallowed hard and shifted in my chair, painfully aware of how slowly time was ticking by. It was only ten, but things had been winding down for a while now.

Atlas's gaze snapped up from the fire, his golden eyes darting between me and Cyrus.

"I, uh, I think we should call it quits for tonight, baby," he said, squeezing my sister's thigh.

Did Cyrus say something to him telepathically or was he reading the room?

"Yeah." Tegan sighed. "I'm pretty tired."

"Okay," I said plainly. I couldn't even bring myself to press them about staying up longer. I wanted my alone time with Cyrus.

"Are you good with the fire and everything, Reece?" Atlas asked.

I opened my mouth to answer, but before I could, Cyrus said, "Yep. We'll take care of it."

Tegan grabbed Atlas's arm. "Perfect. Good night," she said, and started dragging him toward the tent.

"Good night," Atlas called out over his shoulder as Tegan ushered him inside.

"Night," Cyrus and I said behind them, barely getting the word out before the zipper whirred shut.

Because they were far enough away from the fire, we could hear their muffled voices but couldn't make out a single word they were saying. That meant that our tent, on the opposite side of the campsite, would give us some privacy.

Perfect.

Cyrus and I sat there staring at each other like we weren't sure how to act now that we were alone.

"Um, will the cooler be okay here?" he asked.

"Yeah, there haven't been any bear sightings in years. Not that we'd have to worry with Atlas with us."

"Yeah." He laughed awkwardly before his voice chimed in my head: *We are so bad at this.*

I nodded my agreement.

"I think I'm going to head to bed, too," Cyrus said, rising from his chair. "Do you need a hand with the fire?"

"Nope. I've got it."

"Cool. Good night." He winked. *I'll be waiting for you.*

"Night."

Cyrus shuffled off toward the tent and I took care of the fire, dousing it with water from the jug. I grabbed my lantern off the table and made my way to the tent. Excitement prickled my skin as I unzipped the door and crouched inside.

The lantern lit up the small space, revealing Cyrus lying there on top of the sleeping bags waiting for me.

He grinned before bringing one webbed finger up to his lips, urging me to stay quiet. *Lie down.*

I swallowed hard and joined him on the blankets. Sexual tension simmered between us, the anticipation so hot and heavy that I was sweating through my flannel.

You were gone for a while earlier. Did you . . . ?

I nodded aggressively so he could see me.

Oh, thank fuck, he said, climbing over the blankets and on top of me.

His tentacles reached out, gripped my wrists, and pinned them over my head. For a few beats he stared down at me, watching my chest heave, obviously aware of the stiff length of my cock pressing into the soft space under his parachute.

He rocked his hips, rubbing himself on my cock, and I had to bite my lip, holding in the moan that threatened to slip out.

In the soft glow of the lantern, I could make out the utter look of enjoyment on his face. He was teasing me, painfully so, and enjoying every second of it.

Is this what you thought about all night, my little slut? You were sitting across from your sister and your future brother-in-law thinking of all the things you wanted me to do to you?

I bit down harder and pursed my lips, because fuck, that's exactly what I'd thought about. I'd never wanted someone so badly. It was a craving, an overwhelming need to see him and touch him, taste him, and be fucked by him.

I widened my eyes and stared up at him pleadingly, hoping I could persuade him to give me what I wanted.

You look pathetic, using those doe eyes to get me to fuck you.

One of his tentacles snaked between us, squeezing my cock through the rough material of my jeans.

It pulled a strangled sound out of me, and one of his tentacles quickly slapped against my lips, silencing me.

You have got to be quiet. You don't want anyone to hear us, do you? What will they think if they hear the slutty noises you make when I'm eating your ass.

Eating. My. Ass.

Cyrus's dark chuckle swirled around the base of my skull, making my body break out in goose bumps. *You like the sound of that, don't you? I needed you nice and clean, ready to be tongue fucked. Tell me, Reece.* The tentacle rubbing my cock pressed harder, making me thrust my hips into Cyrus. *How long are you going to last?*

At this rate, not long at all.

I loved this dominant, feral side of him. He was the only person I'd felt close enough with to engage in this sort of play.

I'm going to release you, and you're going to strip for me.

Strip for him. With the—

With the lantern on, he added, like he was reading my mind.

What was wrong with him? What if Atlas and Tegan saw us from their tent?

He slithered off me and leaned back on his palms to watch me.

I sucked in a few deep breaths, willing myself to calm down. The only thing I could hear was the rapid pulsing of my heart.

I'm waiting, he said, his voice an impatient snap.

I stood up, and with shaking hands I unbuttoned my flannel and slipped it off my shoulders, then tugged my T-shirt over my head.

Cyrus's eyes roamed down my body, and I followed his gaze,

taking in the way the glow of the lantern highlighted every defined line of my abs and the V of my hips.

Before I could even reach for my belt, Cyrus was crawling over to me, his slick body gliding over the soft swishy material of the sleeping bags with ease.

Allow me, he said, staring up at me with an insatiable hunger in his eyes.

He slowly unbuckled my belt, carefully unbuttoned my jeans, then slid them down my thighs. Anticipating that I'd be sharing the tent with guys other than Cyrus, I hadn't planned any sexy underwear. Just my normal boxer briefs.

And fuck, knowing how much it drove Cyrus wild when I wore a little something, I wished I would have.

My underwear was the next thing to go, letting my cock slap against my abdomen.

Cyrus grinned, obviously amused. *It never gets old*, he said. *Such a perfect fucking cock.*

He stuck his tongues out and leaned in, licking my cock from base to tip. When he reached the head, I tried to thrust into his mouth, but he drew back.

Hands behind your head, he instructed.

Fuck.

I did as he asked, holding the back of my head while my cock hovered right in front of his lips.

He grinned, obviously pleased with my compliance. *Good boy.*

His lips parted and he took me in his mouth, those tongues swirling around my head and then down the length of my shaft as he took my cock into the back of his throat. I pursed my lips together, fighting to keep quiet.

Quiet, Cyrus said, staring up at me. *The moment you make a noise, this is over. Then you'll have to spend the rest of the night thinking about what you could have had.*

He picked up the pace, bobbing up and down on my cock, taking me so deep that his lips touched my pelvis and his spit dripped down onto my balls.

I could feel my body tensing, aching for release. Cyrus could feel it, too.

But before I could get off, he popped my cock out of his mouth and wiped his lips with the back of his hand. *Lie down.*

I cupped my cock, holding it against me while I changed positions so no one passing by could see the outline of my erection jutting out from my body.

Cyrus crept between my legs and wrapped his tentacles around the backs of my thighs, spreading me wide for him.

He leaned in and hummed low, low enough that only I could hear it, and pressed a soft kiss to my hole that made me suck in a tight breath.

It's okay, he cooed, kissing my inner thighs. *I promise I'll take good care of you. You're safe with me. It's going to feel so good.*

I took a deep breath, pushed my nerves down, and let my legs drift apart.

That's a good boy, he said, praising me. His tongues made contact with my skin, swiping over the tight ring of muscle one time, then another, making me stifle a groan. *A very good boy.*

My cock was so hard, it hurt. I needed him to touch me. Jerk it or suck it or something.

Impatiently, I reached for it, but before I could grab my shaft, Cyrus's tentacles were on me, pinning my arms down at my sides.

Ah, ah, ah.

His tongues pushed against my hole slightly, the gentle pressure replaced by the sensation of them stretching me as they worked their way inside.

"Fuck," I whispered as quietly as I could.

The soft waves of pressure changed to scorching heat as his tongues slid in and out, scissoring and stretching, working my ass until I was bearing down, forcing them deeper, burying Cyrus's face between my cheeks.

Cyrus let out a pleased hum, one I could feel in my balls.

I was already so close, and he hadn't even touched my cock yet.

Do you need more? he asked.

I nodded.

Beg.

"P-please," I stammered, my voice so tight, it almost hurt to grate out.

Two of his tentacles slithered up my thighs. One wrapped around my cock, and the other gripped my balls. His entire body worked in unison, his tongues and tentacles stroking and teasing and tasting until I was a squirming, panting mess shamelessly bucking my ass in his face.

He buried his tongues deep, sucking my hole and humming, pushing me over the edge.

I came hard, shooting my cum onto my abs while I grunted, grinding my ass against Cyrus's face, those delicious tongues pulsing in and out until the last waves of my orgasm slipped away.

I lay there, my chest heaving, as Cyrus slowly rose between my legs. He stared at me, smirking and satisfied with the work he'd done.

Before I knew what was happening, he leaned over, maintaining eye contact with me as he lapped my cum off my abs, tracing every line that had been highlighted by the lantern light earlier, cleaning up every last drop of cum.

When he was finished, he collapsed next to me.

Good? he asked.

I fumbled around for my phone and typed out a message, then

held the screen out for him to see. After the noises I was sure we were making, I didn't dare utter a single word.

How the fuck do you think it was?

He vibrated with laughter.

I set down my phone, this time reaching for his hand. I twined our fingers together as best I could with his webbing, gently yanking on his arm to pull him next to me.

This was never going to get old. Feeling his skin against mine, the slow beating of his hearts against my ear.

It was another one of those times when I wanted to say everything. I wanted to tell him that he made me feel like I could dive into the depths of the sea and swim across every ocean if it meant that he would be there waiting for me with open arms.

But I didn't have to tell him.

The way he stared into my eyes and ran his thumb along my cheek, I could tell he already knew.

Thirty-Four

CYRUS

over the phone.

The triathlon was the following morning, and we'd decided it was best if Reece slept in his own bed and kept to his usual routine. I had this annoying habit of distracting him with sex.

"Eh, I'm a little nervous." It was late in the evening, and I could hear him rustling around on his bed, getting comfortable. "But, uh, I'm looking at the race differently now."

"Differently how?"

"I think I've been going about this the wrong way. This is my first triathlon. I'm competing against people who have done this before. Realistically, I'm not going to be the best. But I can be *my* best. I'd like to finish in under ninety minutes. With my training times, it's definitely possible, as long as my transitions don't slow me down."

This was it.

It wasn't just the swim time Reece had been working on improving but also his mindset.

"I am so proud of you. It's nice to see you letting go of that 'if you're not first, you're last' mentality."

"I'm trying." His blankets rustled around again. "I'm feeling antsy. I wish you were here . . . so we could do the thing."

"The thing?" I asked, knowing full well what he meant but wanting him to say it.

"Cock warming," he mumbled under his breath, like he was embarrassed someone would hear him.

It was his latest obsession, and I loved the comfort I was able to provide him by doing it.

"Well, I'm not there right now, but I know something else you can do to work out that stress. You could use your tentacle friend."

I'd ordered Reece that tentacle dildo ages ago, and he'd yet to keep good on his end of the bargain.

"Do you think it's a good idea the night before a race?" He sounded both intrigued and hesitant.

"It isn't any bigger than my tentacles. And I believe it was Pliny the Elder who said, 'Athletes when sluggish are revitalized by lovemaking.'"

I heard Reece moving around his room. "Well, if Pine Tree says it."

"Pliny, not Pine Tree!" I laughed. "He was a Roman scholar. Why don't you get yourself set up and video-call me back?"

"All right. Did you, uh, have any special requests?"

My good boy was always so eager to please.

"You know what I like. Talk to you soon."

"Bye."

The moment the call disconnected, I grabbed my laptop, set it up on the nightstand, and tilted it toward the headboard so Reece would be able to see me. I wasn't going to have him fuck himself with his dildo without offering anything in return.

I pulled my stroker out of the nightstand, and after about ten minutes, Reece initiated the video chat.

"Can you see me okay?" he asked. His face was so close to the camera that it filled the entire screen.

"Yes, I can see you." I laughed and leaned against my headboard. "You can move back a bit now."

Reece dug his teeth into his lip before stepping away from the screen.

He was dressed in nothing but a navy blue athletic thong, the tight globes of his ass devouring the thin piece of material with each of his steps.

"Shit," I huffed.

My mate was breathtaking.

From what I could tell, he was in his bathroom with the blue-green tentacle dildo suctioned to the tile floor.

"Do you like it?" He did a few poses, flexing his muscles.

"I fucking love it." My mating tentacles were already tingling, begging to play. "Get your lube and warm yourself up a bit first. Show me how you play with yourself when I'm not there."

Reece started to slip the thong down his waist.

"No, no. Leave it on. Just push it out of the way," I instructed, my eyes focused on the strain of his thick cock against the fabric.

He snatched the lube from the counter next to him and lowered down in front of the camera. With a snap, he popped open the cap and squeezed a generous amount into his hand.

His eyes were shut, his lips parted with tiny groans as he palmed his cock using his unlubed hand.

"That's right. Pull it out for me, let me see you."

Reece shifted the material to the side, letting his dick and his balls slip loose from the confines of the thong. He spread the lube up and down his shaft with rough strokes, the wide vein on the underside bulging with each pass.

My mating tentacles throbbed with need as I recalled how he felt inside my mouth, how it felt being inside him.

"Yes," I groaned.

My eyes remained glued to the screen, taking in the beauty of my mate as my tentacle circled the entrance of my stroker.

"More?" Reece asked, his voice husky.

"Mm-hmm." I nodded aggressively. "More."

Again, the cap of the lube snapped and Reece applied it to his fingers. He adjusted his position and pulled the thong to the side to give me a better look at his entrance. With two fingers, he circled his hole, coating it with lube before easing his fingertips inside.

"Fuck." He threw his head back with a moan, then watched me with hooded eyes.

My mate liked watching me as much as I enjoyed watching him.

I pulsed in and out of my stroker. My tentacle writhing and twisting, wishing I was fucking Reece, wishing I was there to bring him the pleasure that only I could.

"Good boy. Fuck yourself with your fingers. Get ready for your toy," I said, praising him.

Reece scissored his fingers, stretching and prepping before adding a third.

"Stroke your cock with your free hand," I commanded, my voice stern.

"Dammit, Cy," he whined. "I'm going to come before I get on the dildo."

"Shh, you'll be all right. Nice and slow. Stroke that pretty cock for me, darling."

His free hand gripped his cock, jerking it with lazy strokes while he finger-fucked his ass.

"Good boy. You're so obedient. Are you ready to use your toy?"

I was getting close myself, and I knew it wouldn't take Reece long to come once he got on top of the dildo.

"Yes, gods yes." He slowly pulled out his fingers and positioned himself over the tip of the tentacle dildo.

While the color resembled mine, that was about where the similarities ended. For this, though, it would do.

"Ready?" Reece asked, those green eyes staring at me through the webcam.

"Yes, nice and easy."

Slowly, Reece began to lower himself onto the tapered tip of the tentacle, his thighs spread wide so I had a clear view as it disappeared inside him.

"Shit," he hissed, rocking slightly and taking the dildo deeper.

"How does it feel?"

"So good," he panted.

"Do you want to come?" I already knew the answer.

"Please."

I loved it when he begged.

"Bounce for me and jerk off." My eyes were glued to the screen, watching Reece's every move while my tentacle bored into the stroker.

"Cyrus," he groaned. He stroked his cock, his body pulsing on the dildo. "Gonna come."

"Come for me, darling. Give me your cum."

Reece grunted and tightly gripped his cock, his body jolting as thick streams of cum shot out onto his hand.

"Yes. Fuck, yes," I moaned, my tentacle flooding the silicone channel with cum.

"Gods damn." Reece grabbed a towel and used it to wipe his hands before rising off the dildo on stiff legs. "It's all right but not nearly as good as the real thing."

He tucked his cock back into the thong and stretched out on the floor in front of his laptop.

"Oh, thank gods. I was worried it was going to replace me."

"Nothing could ever replace you."

His heavy eyelids. The dreamy tone of his voice.

I hoped my mate actually felt that way and this wasn't just postorgasm bliss talking.

As much as I was dreading it, I'd have to tell him soon. Regardless of the possibility of rejection, he deserved to know the truth.

It would have to wait, though. With the triathlon tomorrow, he didn't need any additional stress.

"Feeling better?" I asked as I slid my tentacle out of the stroker and wriggled it against a towel.

"Much better. I still wish you were here, though." He let out a long yawn.

"I wish I was, too. But I'll see you bright and early tomorrow. You should take a shower and get some rest, darling. Three a.m. will be here before you know it."

"Thank you for helping me relax, Cy. I'll see you tomorrow."

"Good night, Reece."

"Good night." He gave me a sleepy smile and then closed his laptop, ending the chat.

I stared at the black screen, and a rush of feelings overwhelmed me.

It was a confusing mixture of giddiness, anxiety, and adoration.

Reece Rollins wasn't just my mate.

He was the love of my life.

Thirty-Five

REECE

I PULLED OUT MY PHONE AND READ HIS TEXT MESSAGE ONE
last time.

> **Cyrus:** I know you're probably
> nervous as all get out, but you're
> going to do great. I'm so proud of you
> and how far you've come. I'll be there
> in a bit to cheer you on. 😉

I'd texted him back with a stupid smile on my face. I don't
think I'd ever get tired of hearing that he was proud of me.

Gods, I wish he was here.

He was right, I was nervous.

The oatmeal I'd eaten three hours earlier sat in my stomach
like a lead weight, and I'd taken more trips to the bathroom than
I cared to admit.

Since this was my first triathlon, I'd arrived at the lake two
hours early to make sure my transition areas were properly set up.

With my improved swim time, they'd be the main setback when it came to my ninety-minute goal.

The cool fall air stung my nostrils as I spread a towel over my transition area, using my bags to keep it from blowing away. Overnight, the temperature had dropped significantly. I'd be thankful for the extra layer of insulation from my wet suit during the swim portion of the race.

The triathlon course was set up in a loop. We'd start at the beach with the swim portion, transition to our bikes, and do the 20K ride back around to the beach, then run 5K circling back to the lake.

I was just about to start my warm-up when I heard "Reecie!" ring out across the beach. The other competitors turned their heads and stared in the direction of the noise.

My support crew was here.

Atlas, Tegan, my mother, Fallon, Jimenez, and Cyrus made their way down to the shore. Over their jackets, they were wearing safety orange T-shirts emblazoned with "Team Reecie." In Cyrus's case, the shirt had been cut into a short crop top that just barely covered his chest.

My cheeks were hot with embarrassment, but it was endearing in a way. My friends and my family had all shown up to support me.

"You, uh, weren't kidding about the T-shirts," I grumbled as Atlas wrapped me in one of his rib-crushing hugs.

"I tried, bud," he mumbled before pulling away.

"We wanted you to be able to see us!" Tegan smiled and held out her arms for a hug.

"I'm assuming 'Reecie' was your contribution?" I asked, hugging my sister tightly.

"Of course it was. I came up with the idea and Mom made

them. Gotta let everyone know you aren't quite the hard-ass you act like you are."

Things between Tegan and I had really improved over the last few months, and interacting with her like this never failed to warm my heart. It made me realize how much I'd missed being a part of her life.

"Oh, look at my babies!" our mother shrieked, then joined us in our hug. "One is getting married and the other is about to race in his first triathlon!"

Jeez, Ma. Way to rub that in.

Racing in a triathlon sort of paled in comparison to marrying your fated mate.

Reluctantly, she let us go, and I walked over to greet Fallon, Jimenez, and Cyrus.

I'd felt slightly awkward around Fallon since he'd walked in on us and seen my cock, but as far as Cyrus and I could tell, he hadn't let a single word slip. He was probably scared of pissing Cyrus off.

"Thanks for showing up to support me."

Javier shook my hand and pulled me into one of those bro hugs they all loved so much. "Wouldn't miss it, boss man."

Fallon ruffled his feathers, his tail flicking back and forth. "Gotta come out and support our friend."

Cyrus gave me a warm smile.

We stared at each other for a moment before I held my hand out and welcomed him into a hug just like Jimenez had done with me a few moments before.

To everyone else, it would seem innocent enough, but I needed the comfort his touch provided me.

"You're going to crush that ninety-minute goal. I know it," he murmured before I stepped away.

"I, uh, I gotta get warmed up. I'll see you at the finish line." I scrubbed a hand over the back of my neck and smiled at my group of supporters.

"Good luck, Reecie!" Tegan beamed, and they waved me off to start my warm-up.

I LINED UP WITH THE REST OF THE COMPETITORS ON THE beach and waited for the race to start.

My heart was pounding.

A lifetime of physical fitness.

Three months of training.

It had all led up to this moment.

I didn't have time to dwell on my anxiety, though. The sound of the whistle rang out over the beach, and a sea of bodies bee-lined toward the lake.

It was organized chaos as I jumped into the water. Doing my best not to focus on everyone around me, I set my sights on the buoy and started to swim.

With steady kicks and sure strokes, I shot through the water, propelling myself forward with a speed that I wouldn't have been capable of just three months ago.

Cyrus had worked so hard for this.

I'd worked so hard for this.

Regardless of the outcome, as long as I gave it my all, that's what mattered.

That was something to be proud of.

Thirty-Six

CYRUS

I STOOD NEXT TO TEGAN IN THE SPECTATOR AREA, WATCHING with bated breath as Reece hit the buoy line and swam back toward the shore. His form and his focus were spot-on today, and even as a first-time participant, he'd broken away from the group early.

"He's doing amazing. All that training is really paying off. How's his time, Cy?" Tegan asked, her hands white-knuckling the metal partition in front of us. The anticipation and excitement on her face was endearing, and knowing it was all for her brother made my heart swell.

I grabbed my stopwatch and checked the timer I'd started the moment the whistle blew. "He's on pace to complete the swim in seventeen minutes. That's one of his better times."

My mate was doing so well.

He'd come so far over the last three months, and not just with training. His personal growth, his relationship with his sister, *our* relationship—it was awe-inspiring.

"Go, Reece!" Atlas howled, his deep voice bellowing across the lake.

Reece continued to push himself, swimming hard and fast back to the shore.

He bolted out of the water on shaky legs and headed straight for his bike in the transition area. I held my breath as I watched him struggle with the leash for his wet suit zipper.

I knew that the swim was the part of the race that would give him the most trouble. Even with as many timed drills as we'd completed, they were nothing compared to the adrenaline and fatigue of the actual race.

"Come on, Reece. Come on," I mumbled under my breath and checked the stopwatch. Every second he fought with the wet suit put him further away from his ninety-minute goal. My instincts were riding me to hop over the partition and help him, but he had to do this on his own.

His fingers finally caught the leash, and I shouted out his name.

Reece stared in our direction, spotting the bright orange T-shirts, smiling wide as he put on his bike gear.

"That damn wet suit," his mother hissed and shook her head.

"It's all right," I reassured her. Reece mounted his bike and pedaled off to start the 20K bike ride. "He'll make up for it with the bike and the run. They're his strongest events."

"Oh, for sure. He's got this in the bag," Fallon chirped and ruffled his feathers. "It'll be thirty minutes or so before they circle back around, right? I think I'm going to go grab a hot chocolate. It's freezing."

"I'm in," Javier said. "I can't handle the cold."

"I'm good, thanks." I was too on edge for a hot chocolate, or to do anything other than stand and wait for my mate.

"Tegan, Mom, do you want to check out the snack stand? We have some time." Atlas looked at them expectantly.

"That sounds lovely, Atlas. I'll treat." Reece and Tegan's mother patted his arm affectionately.

Gods, she was adorable. The hidden parts of Reece's personality reminded me a lot of her.

Tegan gave me a soft smile. "I think I'll stay here and wait with Cy if that's okay, but you can bring me back a hot chocolate if it's not too much trouble."

Atlas leaned over and nuzzled his nose against her face. "You got it, baby."

The group walked off to the concession stand, leaving Tegan and me standing alone.

We were silent, our eyes glued to the road, waiting for any signs of the competitors.

"Thank you," she said quietly.

"It was nothing, really. Your brother is an impressive athlete."

Tegan turned to face me, her freckled cheeks and nose flushed red from the cold. "No, not just for that. I don't know what's going on between the two of you, but ever since he started training with you, he's been different. It's like . . . you've fixed something that was broken inside him. This is the happiest I've seen him in a long time, and I think it has something to do with you." She threw her arms around my neck and wrapped me in a tight hug. "So, thank you."

I stood there, stiff and in shock, before belatedly hugging her back.

Obviously, I knew that Tegan's relationship with Reece had improved, but I never expected her to associate me with the changes she'd seen in him.

Atlas had sworn to Reece that he wouldn't say anything, and I trusted my friend.

But maybe Reece and I were giving away more than we thought.

She pulled away and wiped the corners of her eyes. "Sorry, I just never thought I'd see this side of my brother again."

"I'm very proud of him."

She smiled and nodded. "Me, too."

Thirty-Seven

REECE

"MOTHERFUCKER," I GROANED THROUGH A MOUTHFUL OF EN-ergy gel.

The shit was so sugary, but I needed to take it now if I wanted to have energy for the run.

I washed it down with a long drink of water, slammed my water bottle back into the holster, and pedaled like my life depended on it.

It wouldn't be long before the road curved back around to the beach, and I'd do my second transition. My wet suit had been a major pain in the ass for the first one, eating up a good bit of the progress I'd made with the swim, but it was all right.

I was still on pace to make my ninety-minute goal.

The road opened up around the bend, and I could see the bike racks and the spectator area. I could just barely make out Cyrus and Tegan standing next to each other in those obnoxious shirts.

I dismounted and locked eyes with them while I jogged my bike over to the rack.

"Go, Reecie, go!" Tegan shouted.

"Yes, Reece!" Cyrus whooped, with several of his tentacles flailing around in the air.

My muscles were screaming, but seeing them standing there together, waiting for me, supporting me, it encouraged me to keep pushing.

There were a few other competitors in the transition area as I rushed to slip on my running shoes and snap on my number belt.

Exhaustion was setting in, but this was the last leg.

I could do it.

MY CHEST BURNED WITH EACH BREATH AND MY LEGS TEE-tered beneath me.

I was twenty minutes into the run, and I was hitting a wall.

"Gods damn it," I huffed as a minotaur jogged past me.

I'd come so far, so fucking far, and I was going to shit the bed on the run, the part of the race that was arguably my strongest event.

The finish line had to be close.

The finish line where my friends and family would be waiting for me.

Where Cyrus would be waiting for me.

We'd spent three months preparing for this moment. He'd taken time out of his life to prepare me for this, to make me the best I could be.

Gods, I wanted to see him.

I wanted to hold him in my arms and tell him all the ways he made my life better.

All I had to do was get to the finish line, and he'd be right there.

I dug deep, focusing on my breathing and my running technique, willing myself to move, knowing that with each step I took, I was closer to Cyrus.

Thoughts of him flooded my mind, allowing me to tune out the chaos around me and push through the stinging ache of my muscles, which worsened each time my feet pounded against the pavement. Cyrus's smiling face, his warm laughter. The way his eyes lit up when his gaze met mine from across the room. I was lucky. Lucky my sister met Atlas. Lucky we had that terrible interaction at the engagement party. Lucky to have Cyrus in my life.

Eventually, the finish line came into view, and just as I expected, Cyrus was there.

I never thought I'd say it, but I was so fucking thankful for those awful shirts.

I started to sprint, to pump my legs and my arms, to do whatever I could to propel myself to Cyrus faster.

My toes crossed the finish line, but I didn't stop until I reached him.

"Reece! You did it!" he yelled over the commotion around us.

But my goal, the ninety minutes, it didn't matter right now.

Cyrus was all that mattered.

I stumbled forward, wrapped my arms around him, and buried my face in his neck, not caring that we were surrounded by our family and friends.

Everything in the background seemed to fade away, until it was just me and Cyrus standing there.

"Are you all right?" he whispered against my temple. "Everyone is staring at us."

I looked up at him, my chest heaving as I caught my breath. "Let them stare."

I was so fucking tired of hiding our relationship and letting my fears control me.

So, without a second thought, I kissed him.

Cyrus groaned into my mouth, his hands tangling in my hair as his lips parted for me, our tongues brushing against one another with slow strokes.

It wasn't our usual frantic kissing. It was more sensual, more romantic.

But we were brought out of the moment fairly quickly.

"I knew it!" Tegan shouted with an excited smile on her face.

"You knew?" I said quietly.

She nodded.

"Tegan, I wanted to tell you, but things were going so well between us, and with my previous dating history, I didn't want you to be mad—"

"Reece. I'm you're sister. I love you and I just want you to be happy. I was trying to get you to tell me during the camping trip, but then you clammed up and I worried I was pushing you too hard."

"How did you know?"

"I mean, you made it pretty obvious. I've never seen you look at someone the way you look at Cyrus. It's like he's your whole world."

"He is my whole world." I grabbed Cyrus's hand and looked at everyone gathered around us. "It's about time we tell the rest of you that Cyrus and I are in a relationship. We've been seeing each other for a while now."

"Thank gods," Atlas and Fallon said in unison.

Tegan stared at Atlas, her mouth hanging open. "You knew and didn't tell me?"

"I'm so sorry, sweet thing," Atlas said, his ears drooping, "but I promised I wouldn't say anything until Reece was ready." That was enough to pacify my sister.

Fallon held his head high, his tail happily swaying in the air behind him. "I didn't say anything, either, but damn, am I glad the cat is out of the bag. I suck at secrets."

Cyrus laughed. "We know."

"Oh, this is so wonderful. Come here, honey." My mom stepped forward and pulled Cyrus and me into a tight hug.

She was almost as bad as Atlas, *almost*.

A breeze whipped past and goose bumps popped up along my bare arms, reminding me that I was still post-race and dressed in nothing but my tri suit.

"Come on, let's get you changed before you catch a cold," Cyrus said, eyeing the goose bumps with concern.

"Yeah, you go with Cyrus and we'll get your gear packed up." Atlas was always so fucking kind. He really was the perfect mate and husband for my sister.

"Are you sure? But I need my ba—"

"I have it right here." Tegan unclipped my keys and handed them to Atlas before passing me my bag. "Now go."

Cyrus gripped my hand tight and led the way over to the changing stalls. "Well, that was certainly an impressive finish."

"I'm so sorry. I was hitting a wall and the only thing that pushed me through was thinking about you, and then when I saw you . . ."

He looked over at me and smiled, those piranha teeth gleaming in the morning sun. "I'm really what pushed you through?"

"You were the only thing that mattered. Not the race, not the ninety minutes, just *you*."

Cyrus slipped inside the changing stall and pulled me inside with him.

"Really, Cy? I mean, the crop top is absolutely doing it for me, but right after the race?" I asked with a laugh.

"Shh," he mumbled, pulling me tightly to him. "I just wanted to do this."

Cyrus pressed his lips to mine and gave me another tender kiss before he slowly pulled away. "Okay, now you can get dressed."

I shimmied out of my tri suit and Cy whistled once I was fully undressed.

"Are you still coming over today?" he asked.

I pulled up my sweats with shaking hands. My muscles were already feeling tense. "Yeah. I'm going to run home and drop my stuff off and then I'll be over."

"Perfect." Cyrus leaned close, his soft lips grazing my ear. "And I'll make sure I hold on to this crop top for you, darling."

Thirty-Eight

CYRUS

TODAY WAS THE DAY. AFTER REECE KISSED ME AND AN-
nounced our relationship in front of everyone, I owed this to him.

I owed him the truth.

Today I was going to tell Reece that we were mates. Fallon was
going out after work, so we'd have the apartment to ourselves.

I waited for Reece to arrive, anxiously pacing the hallway, my
nerves too on edge to sit still.

How was he going to take this?

What if he pinned our entire relationship on the fact that we
were fated mates?

What if he didn't want this—want me—forever?

I was certain I'd die.

There was a knock at the door, and I shuffled down the hall,
uncaring if it seemed like I was waiting for him.

I opened the door and Reece greeted me with a smile. He was
dressed in a hoodie and gray sweatpants, his hair still wet from
showering. "Hey."

"H-hi," I stammered. "Come in."

Reece walked inside the apartment and up to me, his hand skating along my waist and over my backside as he brought me in for a kiss.

He pulled away and stared at me, a deep furrow etched between those perfect light red brows. "Everything okay, Cy?"

Shit.

I swallowed hard. "I think we should talk."

"If this is about what happened after the tri, I told you I was sorry," he blurted, hurt flashing across his face. "I know I should have checked to make sure you were okay with me—"

I cut him off before he could continue. "Gods no, darling. I told you that you had my consent to announce this however and whenever you wanted to. This is about something else. Something I've been meaning to discuss with you for a while now, but I wasn't sure how."

Reece grabbed my hand, twining our fingers together as much as my webbing would allow. "Please tell me."

My hearts raced and my tentacles clenched tight to my arms. As uncomfortable as the conversation was going to be, I had to do it.

But maybe I could show him exactly what it meant to be my mate.

Show Reece precisely what he meant to me.

"Come on, I want to show you something."

I held his hand tight as we walked down the hallway to the studio.

The rays of the fall sun seeped in through the windows, tinting the room a light orange.

It was fitting. It reminded me of Reece's hair.

We stood side by side in front of the windows, our hands still locked, quietly looking over Briar Glenn.

"Do you remember when we first met at the party?" I asked, my voice a hollow whisper.

"Of course I do. I'll never forget."

"Do you remember when my tentacle reached out and touched you?"

He huffed and shook his head. "Cy, I've told you time and time again I'm sorry for how—"

"No." I turned to face him. My tentacle coiled around his forearm, wrapping us together. "I know you're familiar with the concept of fated mates, but krakens have fated mates, too. When my mating tentacle touched you at the engagement party, it activated my mate response. I—I almost came, right there on the spot. In front of you, in front of everyone. It was completely unexpected." My voice wavered. "Reece Rollins, you are my mate."

He was silent, his mouth hanging open slightly as tears formed in the corners of my eyes.

I let go of his hand and moved toward the row of canvases lined up against the opposite wall. Paint-splattered drop cloths covered the finished pieces.

"After your reaction to my touch, I felt defeated. Hopeless over the fact that my mate found me repulsive. I was sure that a man as beautiful as you would never love someone like me. So I coped the best way I knew how. I came home after the party, and for the first time in months, I painted."

I pulled the drop cloth off the largest canvas, unveiling the painting of Reece and the merman. The very first painting I did of him.

Reece walked over until he stood directly in front of the painting. "That's me." He ran his fingers over the human's light red hair with gentle strokes.

"It's you. They're all you." Tears streamed down my face and my voice was a strained whisper as I shuffled along the row of canvases, uncovering all the paintings for Reece to see.

He stared at them, obviously shocked.

They were a tribute to him. A series of paintings of Reece wet after the pool, Reece petting a dog, the coffee shop we frequented, Reece emerging from the lake after a swim. In one way or another, they all focused on my mate.

My everything.

"Cyrus, they're beautiful." He was crying, too, his lips crinkled into a smile.

"You like them?" I asked, wiping my eyes.

"I *love* them. Come here."

I scuttled over as fast as I could and Reece wrapped me in a tight hug, his muscular arms pulling me as close to him as he could.

"And I'm in love with *you*, Cy," he said softly against my skin.

"Really?" I sniffed, glancing up at his handsome face. "You aren't freaked out about the mate bond?"

He shook his head. "Not one bit. What Atlas and Tegan have, what *we* have, I'd be crazy not to want this. It just means you won't be able to get rid of me."

I laughed and pressed my lips to his. "I love you, too. Very much." I gestured toward the paintings with a tentacle. "If you couldn't already tell."

Reece's hand darted out, his fingertips tracing over the merman in the painting. "Is—is this how you wish you looked?"

He knew me too well.

"Yes. I—I thought that if I was a handsome merman, I'd have a better chance with you. That it would be less of a shock you were mated to someone like me."

He took my face in his hands, slid them just underneath my fins, and pressed his nose to the flat plane of mine. "I happen to think you're handsome just how you are. I'm lucky to have a mate with a toe-curling British accent, who's a talented painter, a bossy swim coach, and is kind to everyone he meets." He lowered his voice. "Not to mention the tentacles."

It felt like an eternity had passed since I'd met Reece and done that first painting. Hearing how he felt about me and the way I looked through his eyes, it made me feel confident.

Reece rubbed his nose against mine. "Was that all you wanted to tell me?"

I nodded, then tilted my head to claim his mouth with a kiss.

After making out for a few moments, Reece pulled away with a chuckle. "As turned on as you make me, can we maybe just relax in bed today? I did race in a triathlon this morning."

"Yes, yes. Sorry. Where are my manners? Come on."

I grabbed his hand and pulled him across the hall to my bedroom.

Reece peeled back the covers before slipping into bed with a yawn.

"Do you want me to do the thing?" I asked as I climbed into bed next to him, tucking my tentacles beside me on the mattress.

"Not right now but, um, could you hold me for a bit? Just until I fall asleep?"

I loved this shy, sensitive side of him that he reserved just for me.

"Come on, then."

Reece shimmied closer and I wrapped my arm around him as he snuggled against my chest. My webbed fingers settled over his hip, rubbing soothing circles until his breathing began to slow.

This was everything I'd wanted.

Everything I'd spent the entirety of my long life hoping for.

"Cy," Reece mumbled.

"Yes, darling?"

"Are you going to have to bite me, like Atlas did with Tegan? Because with your teeth, I don't think that's a very good—"

Laughter rumbled out of me. I was glad that out of everything I'd just told him, *that* was his main concern. "No, kraken mate bonds are different. It's more of a mental thing."

"Huh, that would explain all the dreams I've had about you, then."

I'd never really thought about it until that moment, about how the mate bond between a kraken and a human would manifest itself, but it made sense.

"It very well could be. I wish I had more answers for you."

"S'okay. But, um, Cy, are you putting those paintings in a show?" he asked.

Shit.

With everything that happened today, that little detail had slipped my mind.

"Well, I had planned on it, but I completely understand if you don't want me to." My hand stilled, awaiting his response.

"No, I want you to. I want everyone to know. I'm proud of them. I'm proud to be your mate."

I leaned over and kissed the top of his head.

"I'm proud to be your mate, too."

WHEN LIGHT SNORES SLIPPED OUT OF REECE, I CAREFULLY got out of bed, doing my best not to wake him, and shuffled over to the studio.

He'd caught on to the painting of the merman and the human so easily, knowing how I felt about myself without me even saying a single word.

In truth, though, I didn't see myself that way anymore.

I mixed a palette, gazing at my stripes and patterns as I blended the perfect combination of colors.

There was no way that painting was going on exhibit looking like that.

For hours, while Reece slept, I painted.

I'd glance at myself in the mirror, then use my paintbrush to re-create my image on canvas.

When I was finished, I stepped back to take in the final piece.

While I'd left Reece unchanged, the merman had been replaced with a perfect rendition of myself. A beautiful blue-green kraken with a billowing parachute of tentacles below his waist, embracing his human mate underwater. They stared at each other lovingly, knowing that they'd make the journey back to the surface—together.

It was perfect.

I knew my mate would think so, too.

Epilogue

REECE

One Month Later

"I LOOK LIKE A FUCKING COLLEGE PROFESSOR," I HUFFED, checking my outfit in the mirror.

Tonight was Cyrus's art show, and I'd made the mistake of letting him dress me for the event.

He'd chosen a burnt orange sweater layered over a gingham button-down, dark wash jeans, and some sort of blazer-jacket hybrid.

It was out of my comfort zone, that was for sure.

Cyrus came up behind me in the mirror, rested his head on my shoulder, and wrapped his arms around my waist. "I think you look quite handsome. You can't wear gray sweatpants every-where." He turned his head, his soft lips grazing the shell of my ear as he whispered, "Even if your cock looks fab in them."

I curved my arm upward, rubbing my fingertips over the delicate fins along Cyrus's neck as I stared at the two of us in the mirror. "I love you so much, you know that?"

A wide smile spread over his face. "I love you, darling. But we'll see if you still feel that way when we're in a room full of people eyeballing a painting of your ass."

I let out a deep sigh as he pulled away, knowing exactly which painting he meant. The one he'd painted the day we met, the one of me and the merman.

I wasn't sighing because of my ass being on display, though. I was sighing because it killed me that Cy didn't see his beauty the way I did.

"Did you confirm your therapy appointment?" he called out from his bedroom.

"Yes," I yelled back as I straightened a few out-of-place hairs. "Confirmed for Thursday at five."

It was a long time coming, but I was finally committed to resolving the issues from my childhood with the help of a trained professional.

"Reece, we're going to be late."

"Are we still staying at my place tonight?" I asked as I followed Cyrus out into the hall.

Over the past month, we'd been spending most of our free time together, alternating between Cyrus's place and mine. I was hoping to change that soon.

"Yes, yes. Why do you keep asking that?" He tilted his head, raising the bumpy protrusions above his eyes that served as eyebrows. "Are you up to something?"

Motherfucker.

I was gods awful when it came to surprises.

"You're just gonna have to wait and see." I turned away from Cyrus to hide my smile and grabbed my keys from the console table. "Let's roll."

We held hands as we walked across the parking lot to my car. It was one of the perks of being open about our relationship. I could touch Cyrus anytime I wanted.

I slid into the driver's seat with Cyrus sitting beside me in the passenger seat. "You're going to have to navigate once we get to Rock Harbor because I have no idea how to get to the gallery."

Cyrus snorted. "Reece, you just helped me take paintings there the other day. You really don't remember how to get there?"

"Nope. You know I space out when I'm in the car."

"That's comforting, considering you drive around Briar Glenn for work. I'll navigate, but can you put some music on?" Cy asked, one of his tentacles tapping impatiently.

I connected my phone to Bluetooth and started the music. The sound of Robert Smith's voice filtered out of the speakers and filled the car.

"What's this?" Cyrus asked. He reached over the center console and grabbed my hand. "I thought you didn't like my sad boy shit."

I shrugged and pulled out of the parking lot. "Guess your taste in music is rubbing off on me."

The forty-minute drive to Rock Harbor passed quickly, with Cyrus telling me stories about his time in England and what it was like when he met Atlas and Fallon for the first time.

Compared to humans, he'd lived so many lifetimes. I tried not to think about what that meant for us in the grand scheme of things, but I needed to know what to expect.

"Cy," I said, pulling the car into a parking spot and shutting off the engine.

"Yes, darling?"

"I, uh, I wanted to ask you. Now that we're mated, what happens to you when I die? You know, because your lifespan is so long."

His grip on my hand tightened. "Well, I don't have a lot of information to go on, but I'd assume our life forces are tied together in some way. You'll live slightly longer, and I'll live a much shorter lifespan as your mate. But I don't think we'll ever have to experience life without each other. When you go, I go."

As sad as it was that Cyrus's lifespan would be drastically shorter because I was his mate, it also brought me comfort in a way. I'd never have to worry about how he'd cope without me.

I leaned over the center console and ran my hand along his jaw, then pulled him in for a kiss.

"I love you," I whispered against his lips.

"I love you, too. Now, let's hurry inside before Eduardo loses his shit."

As we walked through the gallery doors, Eduardo huffed, "About time."

The bright white space was filled to the brim with humans and monsters, all admiring Cyrus's artwork.

"Sorry we're late. There was traffic." Cyrus hugged Eduardo, then kissed both of his cheeks.

"Mm-hmm, I'm sure there was." Eduardo looked me up and down. "Well, don't you look handsome. He cleans up nicely, Cyrus."

I tugged at my collar awkwardly and Cyrus grabbed my arm to ease some of my discomfort. "He certainly does. Now, if you'll excuse us, I'd like to show Reece around. We'll catch up with you later."

With that, Cyrus put his hand on the small of my back and led me away from Eduardo.

"What is it with that guy?" I mumbled when we were far enough away.

"He's jealous of you. He tried to pursue me in the past, but I shot him down. It probably kills him that you're my mate."

"You never told me Eduardo was into you."

"I thought it was obvious, and you're my mate. It isn't like it matters. Come here, I want to show you something."

Cyrus led me through a sea of people, occasionally stopping to introduce me or to chitchat, until we arrived at an alcove in the back of the gallery.

"Come on." Cyrus unclipped the velvet rope partition securing the area and ushered me inside.

"What is this?" I asked as we walked down a bright hallway.

"Close your eyes," he whispered, and grabbed my hand.

I followed his instructions, walking blindly alongside him until he pulled me to a stop.

"I wanted you to be the first one to see this piece, so I had Eduardo set it up back here. Open your eyes."

My eyes fluttered open and took in the painting in front of me.

It was the one Cyrus had painted the first time we'd met. The one of me underwater, my bare ass on full display, but this time it was different.

Instead of a merman embracing me, it was Cyrus. Sunlight filtered through the water, catching on the delicate fins lining his neck and reflecting off his wide blue eyes. A soft smile tipped up his lips as he embraced me, the one I'd grown to love over the past few months.

He looked beautiful.

"It's you," I said quietly, my fingers tracing over his blue-green stripes and billowing tentacles.

"It is. I painted over it the night of the triathlon. Am I handsome enough for you?"

I turned to face him, wrapped my hands around his waist, and held him tight. "You'll always be handsome enough for me."

Epilogue, Continued

CYRUS

"GODS, I CAN'T WAIT TO GET OUT OF THESE CLOTHES," REECE said the moment we walked through the front door of his house.

We'd put a lot of finishing touches on his place over the last month. We had painted the kitchen, gotten some home decor items, and hung the photo of us as cowboys, as well as the sketch sheet of Reece, in the hall. It was quickly becoming my favorite place to spend time with him. Sure, I loved the apartment with its view and the terrace, but I loved the privacy of his house more.

"Mmm." I wrapped my arms around him, my mating tentacle uncoiling from my arm to lightly caress his throat. "I can't wait to get you out of those clothes."

"Always so horny." He snorted. "You're gonna have to wait, though. I want to show you something first."

"Well, this is just a night full of surprises. We are truly one of those sickeningly cute couples."

He rolled his bright green eyes and grabbed my hand. "Shut up. Come on."

Reece led me through the kitchen and over to the side door that led to the garage.

"If you got me one of those wagons you attach to the back of a bike, I'm going to throw a fit. I already told you I'm not riding—"

"Cyrus! Stop! Close your eyes."

I shut my eyes and Reece led me down the steps into the garage.

"Open," he instructed.

The whole garage had been emptied and covered with a fresh coat of white paint. Windows were installed along the exterior wall, allowing sunlight to fill the space during the day. Canvases lined the opposite wall, and there was a utility cart fully stocked with painting supplies.

"Do you like it?" He pulled me into the center of the room.

"You did this for me?"

He pursed his lips, his mustache curling down, and nodded. *My handsome grumpy walrus—who is much less grumpy these days.*

"I love it, Reece."

It was true. It was the most thoughtful thing anyone had ever done for me.

"Atlas helped me with the windows, but I did all the rest. I, uh, I was wondering if you wanted to move in with me." He gave me a hopeful look, his cheeks blushing bright red.

Gods, he was everything.

I lunged at him, wrapped my arms and tentacles, whatever I could, around him, and hugged him tightly. "I would love to move in with you."

We'd discussed getting married at some point, but we wanted to let Atlas and Tegan have their moment first. Moving in together was the next logical step, and I was thrilled that Reece had taken matters into his own hands.

"I love you, Cyrus," he whispered, his hands traveling down my back to where my tentacles began. "So fucking much."

"I love you, too. Now, why don't we get you undressed so I can fuck you in *our* house for the first time?"

We'd be happy here.

Together.

Me and my mate.

ACKNOWLEDGMENTS

I can't believe I'm writing the acknowledgments for my second traditionally published book. None of this would be possible without the continued support of my readers and their love for this series. While expanding and revising this book has been such a journey, I am so proud of the changes I've made to deepen the characters of both Reece and Cyrus. I hope it makes you love them even more.

As always, a huge thank-you to my husband. This wouldn't be possible without your love and support.

My editor, Kristine Swartz: Another one in the books! Thank you for your patience and detailed feedback, and for taking this series to a larger audience.

My agent, Jessica Watterson: Thank you for helping me navigate deadlines, the publication process, and everything in between!

Trinity: Thank you for all the love and care you put into sensitivity reading and trigger- and content-warning compilation for this series. Your feedback is invaluable, and I am so glad to have you on my team. *For sensitivity reading and trigger- and content-warning compilation, Trinity can be found on Instagram @ireadtoomuch._ or contacted via email at trinityreads10@gmail.com.*

Ahren: You have been my rock through each of these expansions. Thank you for reading everything I send you and for all your feedback on my stories. I couldn't do this without you. Love you, bestie!

Matt: Thank you for sensitivity reading and for all the feedback you've given me on this manuscript. I love and appreciate you.

And last but not least, my parents: It breaks my heart that you're not around to see this, but I know you would be so, so proud.

Keep reading for an excerpt from
the next book in the Leviathan Fitness series

MANTRAS & MINOTAURS

PAM

January 1

Look back at the past, marvel at how far you have come.

WINDING DOWN FOR THE EVENING, I SIPPED MY BOXED WINE, letting out a deep sigh as Harry kissed Sally in what was probably one of the most romantic cinematic kisses of all time. I mean, Billy Crystal definitely didn't do it for me, but Meg Ryan—that was a totally different story.

The holiday season had come and gone here in Briar Glenn, and I'd spent last night, New Year's Eve, alone at home watching romance movies with my cat.

Since the loss of my husband, Don, two years ago, a certain hairless gentleman had become my constant companion. My son, Reece, swore that Remi was some sort of alien, but the cat rescue assured me that he was a sphynx.

"You know, Remi," I said to him, lifting the blanket he was sleeping under so he would have to acknowledge me. "That right there is true love. When you meet someone and you just know."

My daughter, Tegan, and her fated mate came to mind. She'd called me raving about the buff wolven the same day he'd helped her scrape wedding cake off the pavement outside my bakery. *Well, it was her bakery now.*

When Don passed, he left me his life insurance policy and a sizable pension from the Parks Department. It was more than enough money for me to live comfortably, and I was happy to pass on my business to Tegan. She'd been helping out at the bakery since she was a little girl. Truth be told, she was probably glad I was out of her hair.

I'd been feeling like that a lot lately.

Both of my children had their own lives. They'd been drawn to their fated mates by the goddess. Atlas and Tegan were engaged to be married, and Reece and Cyrus were, well, they were new puppy parents.

Everyone else around me was thriving. Living. But it felt like I was stuck in the same place, watching as life passed me by.

Don't get me wrong, I had my hobbies: reading, knitting Remi and myself matching sweaters, and volunteering at the library two days a week.

But there was still a void.

Yes, Don was gone, but his passing hadn't affected me the way I expected it would.

Our relationship had been complicated since the very beginning. In high school, we were on again, off again, and when I got pregnant with Reece shortly after graduation, marriage seemed like the obvious step. There was no real honeymoon period because having a baby changes things. Suddenly you're responsible for this tiny helpless being, focusing all your time and energy on them. I always felt like Don resented me and Reece because of that. I got the sense that he felt like we'd ruined his life. By the time Tegan came along, Don had settled into fatherhood—but he always treated Reece differently.

There were some good moments, but they were outweighed by

disagreements and nights spent with the kids at my mother's house. When you have kids and a life that is so utterly inter-connected, especially in a small town, you're just sort of . . . *stuck*.

Seeing my children in such healthy, happy relationships elated me, but every once in a while, jealousy crept in.

This was one of those times.

I grabbed my phone, scrolling my social media feed absent-mindedly before pulling up my messages.

I typed out a quick text to Tegan, just like I did anytime I was bored.

> Pam: Hi, honey. I hope you and Atlas had a great New Year's. Are you up for a chat?

My phone rang a few moments later.

"Hey, Mom! What's up?" Tegan sounded awfully upbeat for it being New Year's Day, but then again she didn't really drink. Neither of my kids did. It made me proud but it also made me question if Don and I were the reason why.

Without thinking too hard about it, I took another sip of my wine before answering. "Just sitting at home with Remi. Did you and Atlas have a good New Year's?"

She let out a deep sigh. "It was okay, I guess. We went over to Javier's house. He and Fallon got drunk and wrestled in the front yard. Atlas had to break it up."

Javier was so sweet; I had a hard time believing it. "Are you serious? Is everyone okay?"

"Yeah. Atlas managed to calm both of them down, and every-one was fine by the time the ball dropped—but it was still a stupid display of masculinity."

"Were your brother and Cyrus there?" I was positive the

answer would be yes. Reece and Tegan had worked to repair their relationship over the past few months, and more often than not, they could be found hanging out together with their mates.

It helped that Atlas and Cyrus were best friends, too.

"Of course they were. They left before the fight happened, though. Reece said they had to go home to check on Beau. He is such a worrywart when it comes to that puppy," Tegan teased with a laugh.

"I still can't believe Cyrus surprised him like that. He is such a gem." I had all but given up on Reece finding a partner, but when he'd started training for the triathlon with Cyrus, it was obvious they had more than just a coach-trainee relationship. The two were mates, and for Christmas, Cyrus had surprised my son with something he'd always wanted but Don would never allow— a puppy.

"Yeah, he is. I'm still not sure Mr. Grumpy Pants deserves him, though."

I was mid-sip when she said that, my snort almost sending my wine out of my nose and all over my white knit blanket.

Her lighthearted giggle echoed through the phone. "What about you, Mom? Did you do anything fun last night?"

I answered as soon as the burning sensation in my sinuses subsided. "Well, I drank wine, watched romance movies on the couch with Remi, and worked on a new set of matching sweaters." Gods, it sounded so depressing when I rehashed it aloud like that.

"Mom . . ." Tegan's voice was heavy with concern, or maybe pity. "I really wish you'd get out more."

I did go out on occasion. Lunch with my friend Nancy, or dinner with Sue and Dale, Tegan's best friend's parents. But I knew that platonic relationships weren't what Tegan was referring to. *She meant dating.*

"I'd love to, but it's hard to meet new people when you live in a town like Briar Glenn."

"You know, there's this dating app Javier uses—"

I cut her off. "Don't you think I'm a little too old for a dating app?" I thought they were something used by young people to find hookups, not fifty-four-year-old women seeking companionship with the potential for romance.

Tegan snorted, which brought a smile to my face. She was definitely my daughter. "Mom, you're not old. I really think you should download it and make a profile. If you don't like it, you can just delete the app and it'll be like it never happened."

I did want to see who was out there . . .

"Fine. I'll check it out. What's it called?" I transferred her to speakerphone so I could search for it.

"It's called Mate Match. It only allows profiles to message you if you've already marked them as a match you'd be interested in."

Huh. Well, it sounded like there was a certain level of safety and anti-harassment built into the app. "All right, I'm downloading it now."

Tegan squealed and I jumped, almost spilling my wine.

"You have to tell me if you match with anyone. Promise me you'll tell me?" she pleaded.

"I promise, but I doubt I'm going to match with anyone."

"Mom. Seriously? You're a babe. Besides, some younger men are into older women."

I tsked. "Oh no, no, no. No younger men for me. They need to be my age or older—no exceptions."

"Make sure you set your age preferences on the app, then. Let me know if I need to come over tomorrow and help you with it, okay?"

I knew she was trying to be helpful, but I wasn't so old that I couldn't figure out how to set up my own profile on a dating app. How hard could it be?

"Will do, honey. Give Atlas my love."

"I will. And remember to text me if you match. I'm serious, Mom. I want to see pictures!"

"Pinky promise. Bye, sweetie."

I hung up the phone before she could get another word in.

Tegan seemed confident I'd find a match, but I wasn't so sure.

I peered down at my phone through my bifocals, the blue light reflecting off my lenses as I scrolled through my photo gallery, searching for a profile pic.

There were limited options. Me with Remi. Me with Reece and Tegan. Me with Atlas.

I didn't want to give the impression that I was already taken or that my kids were my entire personality. I mean, they were, but that wasn't the sort of information I wanted to advertise right out of the gate.

Eventually, I stumbled upon a picture Tegan had snapped of me last Christmas. I was wearing a rust-colored sweater I'd knit myself, a tight black skirt, and a pair of pumps that matched my sweater. My ruby red hair was streaked with gray and piled high on top of my head in a messy bun, my freshly cut bangs just barely touching the rim of my glasses. Even though the photo was a year old, it was recent enough that I still looked the same. And in the words of my daughter, *like a total babe*.

"Let's see here," I mumbled to myself as I uploaded my profile picture and scanned the categories.

Employment.

Well, I was retired, which was fairly uncommon at my age, but I supposed it was best not to lie about it.

Education.

That one stung. I'd always wanted to go to pastry school and get some formal training, but between Don and the kids, it wasn't in the cards for me. Let's just go with "some college." Surely the pottery class I took at the local community college counted as *something*.

Location.

Briar Glenn, of course. For the most part, I was well aware of who was available to date here. At my age, there were slim pickings, but with the recent town revitalization initiative and all the growth Briar Glenn had experienced, maybe I'd be pleasantly surprised. To cast a wider net, I selected a radius that would include the three neighboring towns.

About me.

Hmm.

Do you include that you're widowed in your profile? What kind of vibe does that give off? What if they think I'm some sort of black widow, meeting men on dating apps and murdering them once my name was listed as the beneficiary on their insurance policy?

Gods, I'd been listening to way too many true crime podcasts.

I tapped a manicured nail against the glass of my phone, pondering what else to say about myself. This was always so difficult.

Ultimately, I decided to go with:

Widowed. Knitter. Avid reader of romance books. Film buff. Former wedding cake baker and pastry shop owner. Mom to two amazing adult children (and one hairless cat). Looking for companionship with the potential for something more.

Sweet and concise.

Just like me.

Remi ambled back in from the kitchen and jumped onto my lap as I set the age range for acceptable matches.

"What do you think, Rem? Should I open it up to younger men? Is sixty too old? I mean forty is the new thirty, so fifty must be the new forty, making sixty the new fifty. I'm fifty-four, so it's only a six-year age difference."

The tiny wrinkled gremlin stared up at me, his wide eyes unblinking.

"All right, forty-five to sixty it is."

Was I really one of those people who stayed at home and asked their cat rhetorical questions?

The answer was yes, yes I was.

Once I'd set the parameters for appropriate matches, I watched eagerly as a loading bar flashed across the screen. This was the part I was most excited about. I'd heard about the swiping and I was anxious to experience it for myself.

The first profile suggested for me was a human man in his late forties. He was cute. His black hair was in a tight crew cut that fit his chiseled features, and the beginnings of crow's-feet formed in the corners of his deep brown eyes when he smiled. According to his bio, he was a mechanical engineer whose hobbies included reading and watching movies—but he was in an open relationship.

I admired folks who could do open relationships, but it wasn't my style. Even though I was looking for something casual, I wasn't too keen on sharing a partner. Apparently, all those years of monogamy had really done a number on me.

Photo after photo passed on the screen as I swiped left on pretty much every profile. A guy in his fifties who worked as a Rod Stewart impersonator. A gargoyle who owned a cranberry bog. A sixty-year-old naga who performed with a traveling Shakespeare group. They were certainly interesting individuals, but nothing about them really drew me in.

Until a candid shot of a curly-haired minotaur caught my attention.

His hair was a light cream color, full of cowlicks, which swirled in all different directions. A set of ridged, deep brown horns curled over the top of his head, running across his fluffy eyebrows and connecting above his snout. His dusty pink nose was adorned with a shiny gold ring, the type you'd commonly see on a bull. A buffalo plaid shirt stretched across his barrel chest, with a tuft of hair sprinkled with grays sticking out from beneath the unbuttoned collar.

Gods, he was handsome.

Another photo showed him standing next to an elevation marker on a rocky mountainside. A backpack was slung over his broad shoulders, and a wide grin was plastered to his face as he gave the camera an enthusiastic thumbs-up. It appeared he was quite the outdoorsman.

The third photo showed him sipping from a tiny espresso cup with his pinky out in a display of civility.

So he was a caffeine guy.

Now that I could get behind.

According to his profile, his name was Alistair.

Alistair.

How distinguished.

He was a fifty-five-year-old divorcé who worked in the agricultural industry. A suspicious maple-like leaf graced that portion of his profile . . . Did that mean he worked in the cannabis industry?

Although I'd embraced the whole grunge aesthetic in the '90s, I'd never smoked pot before . . . How would that even work?

I mean, not everyone who worked in that industry smoked pot, right? There was no way the investors with their tailored suits were toking doobies in their high-rises.

I was being ridiculous. Weed was legal. I was making a stink about nothing.

His location was listed as . . . right here in Briar Glenn?

He must have moved here recently. I would have noticed him around town; I was sure of it.

I scrolled to his "About Me."

I live in Colorado, but I'm visiting to help care for my daughter. I have a degree in agriculture and work in the cannabis industry. I enjoy the great outdoors, coffee, and good food with even better company. I'm looking for casual, no strings attached fun.

Well, it appeared I should edit my profile. His was much more professional.

My finger hovered over his photo.

He was visiting from another state, but I wasn't looking for anything serious. Maybe I was getting ahead of myself . . .

"Aw, what the hell," I said to Remi, and swiped right.

Now to wait and see if he'd respond.